Order your autographed copy ... 30% discount at **www.jihadwri**... post a review on <u>www.amazon.c</u>... his guestbook at <u>jihadwrites@bellsouth.net</u>

AUTOGRAPH PAGE

To be used exclusively to recognize that special King or Queen for their support.

Envisions

PUBLISHING COMPANY

Envisions Publishing, LLC
P.O. Box 83008
Conyers, GA 30013

PREACHERMAN BLUES II copyright © 2010 Jihad

ISBN: 978-0-9706102-5-6

First Printing July 2010
Printed in the United States of America

10 9 8 7 6 5 4 3 21

Submit Wholesale Orders to:
Envisions Publishing, LLC
Envisions07@sbcglobal.net
P.O. Box 83008
Attn: Shipping Department,
Conyers, GA. 30013

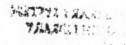

Envisions
PUBLISHING COMPANY

APPRECIATION PAGE

There are so many wonderful Kings and Queens that helped make Preacherman Blues II a reality, and I may miss a few but please family, chalk it up to my tired and exhausted mind.

First and foremost I wanna thank the creator, without your inspiration and your spirit I would've given up long ago.

I list book clubs first, because there is absolutely no way that I could have brought PREACHERMAN BLUES II out without your super support. I wanna thank all the wonderful fans and bookclub members that have continued to support me on my writing journey. Queen Monae Eddins, Queen Loray Calhoun and the Women of Distinction bookclub in Columbus, Ohio, thank you so much for pushing all of my work so hard. Queen Monique Smith and the Queens of Dialogue Divas bookclub Atlanta, Lisa Johnson and the Queens of Sisters on the Reading Edge bookclub Oakland, Queen Gloria Withers and Queen Janene Holland of Chapter 21 bookclub Philadelphia, Queen T.C. at R.A.W. Sistahs, Queen Kanika and K.O.M. bookclub Atlanta, Queen Lenda and Mo' betta views bookclub Atlanta, Queen Dr. Wright and the queens of Sisters in the Spirit 2 bookclub, Queen Tiffany and the Queens of Distinguished Ladies and Gents bookclub Memphis, Queen Wanda Fields, Queen Alethea Hardin and the Queens of Shared Thoughts bookclub New Jersey, Queen Ella Curry of EDC creations, Queen Ellen and the Queens of Reading is What We Do bookclub Newport News, The Queens and Kings of Sugar and Spice book club, NYC,

I know I've missed several Book clubs so please ad your name here. _____

My closest friends, thanks for putting up with me. Queen Victoria Christopher Murray, Queen Reshonda Tate Bilingsley, Queen Tiffany Colvin, Queen Jamise L. Dames, Queen Pamela Hunter. King Travis Hunter, King Rodney Daniel, King Hasaan Morrow, King Corey Mitchell, King Woody Jenkins, King Kevin Elliott, King Kwan, King Maurice Gant, King Wayne Hunter, and King Theodore Palmer.

Thanks to my family for their continued support, my son Prince Zion Uhuru, Mom, Queen Arthine Frazier, Brother King Andre Frazier, Brother King Michael Wharton and family, Sisters Queen Las-Shl Frazier, and Queen Karen Wharton, Nieces, Gu-Queitz, Luscious, Sadequa, Shami, Baby, Lameeka, and Ronni, Nephews, I-Keitz, D'Andre, and Billy.

SUPERFANS

Queen Ann Joiner of Norfolk thank you. Queen Kariymah of Philly thank you. Queen Tazzy Fletcher thank you. Queen Iliene Butler, New York thank you. Queen Martha and the queens of IPS transportation Indianapolis.

And I give a very special thanks to the Kings and Queens living behind America's prison walls. Without your letters and support, I would have quit long ago. And I may not respond to all letters, but just know that I read every one.

THEY SAY BLACK MEN DON'T READ. FOR ALL THE KINGS ON THE INSIDE AND OUTSIDE KEEP PROVING THAT MYTH WRONG. AND DON'T WORRY I WILL ALWAYS WRITE WITH YOU IN MY KING. I'LL ALWAYS REPRESENT.

PREACHERMAN BLUES II **IS FOR YOU, KING.** PREACHERMAN BLUES II **IS FOR YOU QUEEN**. By supporting my books, you help our young Brothers and sisters realize the kings and queens that they are.

And I'd like to give a very special thanks to President Barrack Obama. If a man with the name of Barrack Hussein Obama can get past the hate so can a man with the name Jihad Shaheed Uhuru.

Please log onto www.jihadwrites.com to find more about Jihad or to purchase any of his books 30% less than the store price, and if you purchase 3 books anytime on www.jihadwrites.com you get the 4th book absolutely FREE. Please tell others what you think by posting a review on www.amazon.com. Log on to www.jihadwrites.com to sign Jihad's guestbook.

Love and Life

Jihad

Also By Jihad

Fiction
STREET LIFE
BABY GIRL
RIDING RHYTHM
MVP
PREACHERMAN BLUES
WILD CHERRY
PREACHERMAN BLUES II

Self Help
THE SURVIVAL BIBLE: 16 Life Lessons for Young
Black Men

Anthology

Gigolos Get Lonely Too
The Soul of a Man

Please pick up any of Jihad's books at your local bookstore or you can save 30% and order Jihad's books from the secured site at www.jihadwrites.com. If you purchase 3 books the 4th is absolutely free. Please allow 3-5 days for shipping.

Special message from Jihad

One of the best kept secrets in the African-American literary industry is the independent author. We are told by you that our books are great and we should get them into all stores. The author can not do that. You, the reader, must ask the stores to carry our books. Most of us are not with the major publishers. Most of the African-American authors are independent publishers or self-published, and do not have the marketing dollars to get in all of the Barnes and Nobles and Borders bookstores. Not to mention, Walmart is virtually impossible for an independent publisher to get into. Now in Urban communities, myself and many independent authors are carried in the mainstream stores, however, many are not. It is you who can get us there by just making a phone call to the store manager requesting that our books are carried. There are several great writers you've never heard of because they are independent, and not enough of us are demanding that they be in stores.

Most important to anyone's success is support, and the best way to show support for any independent author is to help them maximize their sells so they can continue to write. Writing, good writing, is time consuming and very expensive. We love what we do, but we still have to pay bills like everyone else. So please help us continue to do what we love and what you love.

Thank you so much for reading and supporting family. www.jihadwrites.com

Love, Life, and Family

Jihad

PREACHERMAN BLUES II is dedicated to the three greatest women alive today.

ARTHINE FRAZIER: The Queen that gave me life. One day, I will write about you mom. For now, I am going to continue being selfish. I'm not quite ready to share your light, your story with the world. I love you mom.

ASSATA SHAKUR: The Queen that taught me who and what the Black woman is. And please every man and woman reading this page, go out and order, or buy the Autobiography entitled: Assata. After reading this Queens life journey, you will have a new overstanding of what it is to be Black, strong, and a woman. Any brother or sister will be hard pressed to address any black woman in animal terms after embarking on this cultural awakening reading journey. Assata, I love you Queen.

OPRAH WINFREY: The woman, not her show, not her awards, accolades or standing in the media. But her heart. Her essence. Agree or disagree with her tactics, but you can not deny that this one woman has impacted the world in a positive way that no black woman has ever done. She like the others above are activists that have fought for freedom their entire lives in one way or the other. Oprah, you have been a blessing and a motivating factor and teacher to me and I am sure to so many brothers from Americas ghetto's and barrios. I love you queen.

PREACHERMAN BLUES II

"When a person places the proper value on freedom, there is nothing under the sun that he will not do to acquire that freedom. Whenever you hear a man saying he wants freedom, but in the next breath he is going to tell you what he won't do to get it, or what he doesn't believe in doing in order to get it, he doesn't believe in freedom. A man who believes in freedom will do anything under the sun to acquire . . . or preserve his freedom."

Malcolm X

PROLOGUE

*T*he biggest trick a black man ever pulled was making white America forget that he was black. And Barack Hussein Obama had pulled the trick off flawlessly. Now, he was relishing his first twenty-four hours as the country's first black president.

For Shemika Money, witnessing this moment was a dream come true and honestly, was the only reason she hadn't killed her husband, TJ Money. Literally. After Shemika found out that TJ was responsible for the murder of Reverend Turner a few months ago, she was ready to take revenge then. But she had to wait on this day. And now that it had come, it was time to put her plan into action.

One. Two. Three. Shemika loaded the bullets into the 9mm. She took her time, counting slowly until all seventeen bullets were in the clip. She lay back on her king-sized bed and smiled. It was almost over.

She glanced over at the sleeping monster that she'd called her husband for the last three years. Bishop Terrell Joseph Money was the epitome of evil. He had raped her sister, made her life a living hell, and was even responsible for the death of her mother and sister almost twenty years ago.

Vengeance is mine, saith the Lord. Shemika chuckled as she thought of the sermon TJ had preached last Sunday. He had the nerve to say people should leave revenge up to the Lord. After everything he'd done? Oh, no. Shemika was sure the Lord had a special jail cell in hell for TJ and she wanted to speed up his path to getting his just due. She could feel the energy surging through her body as she imagined killing the man she had hated more than Satan himself. She was lost in her vengeful thoughts when the light behind the remote-controlled bedroom blinds cast a moving shadow on the wall. Shemika shot up in her bed as the figure took one step through the double French bedroom doors.

A mask of horror shrouded her face. Her screams came out as a blood-curdling gurgle. The first bullet to her neck did the job. The second one to the chest was insurance.

The killer took a couple steps toward the bed.

Bishop Money got up and walked into his bedroom closet and opened the safe, the killer on his tail. "Are you sure she's dead?" he asked, looking up at the killer from his kneeling position.

"Bishop, I'm a professional."

"That's not what I asked."

"I hit the carotid artery. Trust, she's dead as a brick," he said, holding a gym bag open as the Bishop put a couple handfuls of watches, rings, bracelets, and chains inside. "I don't see why you just can't give me cash."

"I can't insure cash. Besides, you're walking away with over eighty-thousand dollars worth of jewelry."

"Okay. You ready?" The killer put the night goggles back over his face and pointed the silenced .22 at the Bishop.

"You see the red mark on my thigh?"

"I told you, I'm a professional." The killer fired.

Chapter 1

*F*ired up! Those were the best words to describe the 2011 New Dimensions First Church of God Youth Choir.

"Please be patient with me," they sang their teenage hearts out. "God is not through, with me yet.

Ain't that the truth, Cheyenne thought as she clapped and sang along.

"When God gets through with me." She followed as the entire church stood up singing. "I shall come forth."

So caught up in the rapture, the Junior Senator's wife didn't notice that the older lady sitting next to her had disappeared. Cheyenne glanced down at the folded letter-sized manila envelope on top of her copy of the Marcus Garvey book the church had studied two months ago.

"I shall come forth as pure gold."

Reverend Solomon One-Free looked out at all the different cultures that filled the church. If it weren't for his close friends, Bill Clinton and President Obama explaining the importance of understanding all history, New Dimension churches all over the country would still be all-black. "In honor of his birth month, back in August, we studied the life of Marcus Mosiah Garvey."

Cheyenne half-listened as she picked up the envelope. Dr. Jamison-Hayes was neatly printed in red ink on the front. By the shape and weight, Cheyenne knew that there were pictures inside.

"Today, our topic is Moses and Marcus," the pastor continued. "I want everyone to open up their *Philosophy and Opinions of Marcus Garvey* to page 48."

Cheyenne loved New Dimensions and Pastor One-Free's method of comparing biblical figures and stories to great men and women of African descent. But as much as she loved his teachings, she couldn't put that envelope down. She eased it open as the pastor continued.

"In Genesis, chapter…"

Cheyenne gasped. Her hand shot up to her mouth. Her eyes became blurry with tears as she flipped through the five pictures. She was just as stunned as she read the letter nestled after the last picture.

2347 WINDSOR CROSSING, LITHONIA, GEORGIA, 30058 15 MINUTES. ALONE. NO PHONE CALLS. You're probably not a bomb expert, but you don't have to be to know what you are looking at. And you do see the date: September 12, 2010; 11:30 AM.

Cheyenne looked at her watch. 12:22 PM. Not even an hour ago, she thought as she got up and barreled her way down the aisle, stepping on toes and almost falling into someone's lap, before making it out of the second row. How? Why? Who? Those and more thoughts see-sawed through her mind as she knelt down to take off her heels. At least a thousand eyes were on her as she rose from the middle aisle of the 2,500 member church. And more eyes would have glanced in her direction if she hadn't taken off running like a stockinged-feet, dress-wearing Olympic sprinter with two black three-inch Dolce & Gabana heels in her hands.

Before closing the door on her white Lexus SC430 convertible, Cheyenne tried her husband's cell phone. It went straight to voicemail. She tried the house.

"Make another call to anyone, he'll be dead," a strange computer-like voice said, before the phone on the other end went dead.

With no traffic, Windsor Crossing was a ten, twelve minute drive from New Dimensions, but Cheyenne made it in five. Her heart fluttered like she'd drunk a twelve-pack of red bull. Everything was happening so fast that she hadn't had time to think, let alone be afraid of whoever was behind the front door of the older brick house she stood in front of.

Before she could knock, the door swung open. "Come in, Cheyenne, my name is—"

"TJ Money," she said enunciating every syllable.

"*Bishop* TJ Money, and please, come in. Your husband's life depends on it." He smiled.

If looks could kill, Bishop Money would be a statistic. Cheyenne stepped inside and closed the door. Standing face to face, she and Bishop Money were eye-level and she was only five-four. "I will castrate you and let you bleed to death if anything happens to my husband."

"So violent," he sarcastically shivered.

"Violent! You send me these," the pictures flew through the air before crashing on the laminate floor in front of the purple carpeted stairs, "while I'm at church."

"Please come in." He gestured toward the den. "Have a seat, I can explain everything." Bishop Money said as he walked into the den, with a slight limp.

She looked around the room. The house seemed very clean. Too clean. Every bright color in the crayon box seemed to be represented. The walls were painted blood red. The carpet was banana yellow. The couch was ocean blue. And the bed in the middle of the large open room had a Sunkist orange sheet spread across it. The room looked like something out of a fairy tale picture book. And the TV's. There was a flat screen TV hanging on every wall corner of the room. She took a seat on the opposite end of the couch.

"Cheyenne, it is okay that I call you by your first name?"

"My name is Dr. Jamison-Hayes."

"You're calm for someone who just received pictures of a bomb hidden under her husband's home office desk." Bishop Money sat on the edge of the bed, crossed his legs, and rested a palm on his knee.

"I was just thinking about a morbid DVD series I once saw called *Faces of Death*. It was about some of the most gruesome and painful deaths that people have suffered. I was just daydreaming about how many different ways I can cause you pain before I kill you."

Cheyenne was scared, but as a psychiatrist, and having dealt with so many psychopath-sickos in the past, she knew that her safest bet was to stay calm, and don't let on that she was afraid.

Bishop Money rose from the bed. "Cheyenne, I think you know why you're here."

"I hope my husband destroys you. I won't do anything to interfere with his special committee to expose crooked pastors." She shook her head from left to right. "You are that desperate. That scared."

"Scared of what?" The bishop asked.

"Of losing everything. Jordan knows all about you. Samuel Turner. He told Jordan everything. How you used church members tithes to buy property and finance other business ventures, how you lined city leaders pockets to get zoning permits for your precious mall. And," She smiled, "Samuel even told him how you where involved with his fathers murder, and how you were able to steal his church and his father's congregation."

Bishop money let out a loud high pitched laugh. "If I'm so evil, so wrong…" He smiled. "Why am I not in prison." He stuck a finger in the air, "I'll tell you why. A little five letter word. "Proof. Without it you have nothing but empty accusations that can get someone hurt or even killed."

"You don't scare me." She looked the bishop up and down. "Look at yourself. You look like a weasel. Act like a weasel. You're walking proof. It's over for you and now—

"I'm confused." He interrupted while taking off his pinstripe blue and peach Hugo Boss suit jacket. "Your husband is at home in his office with enough C-4 under his desk to bring that seven-thousand square foot house crashing down like the World Trade center and you're telling me how your drug addict, senator husband is going to brig me down." He pulled back the crisp peach colored sleeve and turned his wrist. "Babycakes, not only are you going to do every single thing I tell you, but you're going to enjoy it or at least act like it." He looked at his diamond bezel Jacob watch. "It's 12:57 PM, at 1:20 PM," he began unbuttoning his shirt, "the ever-popular, former crackhead, professional football player, husband of yours, Senator Jordan Hayes will be on that stairway to heaven, carrying your seven-year-old daughter with him."

"What do you want?" she shouted.

"Ahhh, the sweet sounds of fear and what was that word you used." He snapped his fingers, "Proof, that's right. He licked his lips and unbuttoned his pants. "Prove to me that you love your husband and child enough to do anything." He put his hand under her chin. "Anything in order to save their lives."

"I can't." she cried.

"You can and you will." He raised his wrist. "It is 1:00 PM you have twenty minutes to satisfy me or …"

"How do I know—?"

"You don't know." He shrugged his shoulders, smiled and let his pants fall to his knees. "Just have faith."

Chapter 2

"*F*aith," Bishop Wiley said into his cell phone. "Today, my sermon was about faith and putting your problems in God's hands." He paused. "I just wonder sometimes if I'm doing God's work."

"Faith is the key word. Have faith, Bishop. Sometimes you have to be God's hands," Bishop Money said. "Was it wrong for you to take the pictures I had sent you and transpose the image of a bomb and time and date on them? Yes, it was. Is it wrong for you to edit the video I just sent you of me and the Junior Senators wife? Yes, it is. But, if Jordan Hayes goes through with this stupid witch hunt, you and I and others will be ruined. All the lives that we affect. All the lost sheep that we shepherd. We are in a time where hope is the only thing that black folk have. No one is perfect, Bishop. Not even us, but we are men of God, and sometimes we have to do evil in order to preserve the greater good."

"You're right, Bishop. I just have a heavy heart sometimes. But you're right. We have to stop Jordan Hayes. When I get through doctoring the video and implementing sound effects, using the voice sample you sent over of his wife, we will have Hayes in our pocket."

After hanging up with his protégé, Bishop Money made another call. A moment later, he had the Orville Redenbacher of porno movies on the line. "Ron Fuego, Bishop Money here."

"Good evening, sir."

"Son, the church will accept the house."

"God is good," Ron shouted.

"Every day, all day," Bishop Money said. "You're right, Ronald. I think it will make a great transition house for recovering addicts. With hidden cameras in every room, the addict's activities can be monitored. But, I just have one question for you, Ron."

"The loud colors, right?"

"Yes, man. What kind of porno movies were you making?"

"I shot Alice in Wonderland part 1, 2, 3, and 4. They were my biggest porn movies, but those day are over thanks to you. Now that I'm saved, I want to do better and as you have taught me, I have to live better and be *in* the world but not *of* the world. Again, I just wanna reiterate, Bishop, that I have no problem paying whatever it costs to have the house readied for the transition center."

"I'm proud to know you, son. So many people talk the God talk, but you are truly walking the God walk. Ya know," he paused, "I spent most of the morning at that house praying. Looking for a sign."

"I thought you were in your car."

"I am, now. Son, I was looking in the wrong place. Now that I see what's in your heart. I see that your redemption is the sign. Your willingness to give back to so many that you have taken from. Together we will rebuild a house of ill repute into a safe haven and help center for the downtrodden."

"Thank you, Bishop. On another note, I still can't believe you were outside in this rain today. You have to take better care of yourself, so you can continue taking care of the thousands of people that look up to you. I just pray that you recover from the flu in Godspeed, so you can be back in the pulpit next week," Ron said.

"I thank you for your prayers and you heartfelt words, but my health is secondary. The congregation is my primary concern. And when my Father sends one of his lost angels to me, I have to do His bidding. You, son, remind me of the apostle Paul. Who, like him, the Father has made you clean, washed you of your sins, made you anew. God has put it on your heart to give back to your community. It's my job to make sure that God's work is followed out to the letter. If that means going out into this nasty weather with the flu, then who am I to interfere with the will of the creator? I'll be fine, son. Oops, I have another call, let's touch base sometime tomorrow afternoon." TJ lied to get off the phone. One of his favorite songs was on the radio.

"Drifting on a memory.... There's no place I'd rather be..... Than with you..." Bishop Money sang along with the Isley Brothers as he drove his Maybach through the sixteen-foot wrought iron double gates of the Money estate.

"Well... Well... Well... Loving you."

After pulling into one of the bays of his eight-car garage, he cut the engine, put it in park and pulled out his Blackberry.

SENATOR HAYES, I HOPE I DIDN'T DISTURB YOU THIS EVENING. I JUST WANT YOU TO KNOW THAT I WILL COOPERATE AND I HAVE NOTHING TO HIDE. AS PER YOUR REQUEST, I WILL BE AT YOUR OFFICE AT 9:30 TOMORROW MORNING. I JUST WANNA MAKE SURE THAT THIS PRELIMINARY MEETING IS STILL OFF THE RECORD.

After pressing Send, he got out of the car, went inside, and disarmed his state-of-the-art security system before turning on the kitchen lights.

"I doubt he returns your text."

"Sweet Jesus." Bishop Money placed a hand over his heart and looked at the two white men who had made themselves comfortable in his den.

"Not quite, but close. You can call me Franklin." The Tommy Lee Jones look alike said as he extended his arm toward a much younger man who was reclined all the way back in one of Bishop Money's twin massage chairs. "And this is my partner, Theodore," Franklin said.

Bishop Money turned and hit the silent alarm on the keypad by the garage door.

"It's been disarmed," Franklin said.

He opened the kitchen door that led to the garage. Bishop Money stared into the huge chest of a light-skinned, Blues brother-suit-wearing black man. The Mack-truck looking man had a coiled wire dangling from his ear. The man's mouth opened but TJ didn't give him a chance to get a syllable out before slamming the door. Immediately, he turned to the alarm pad, pressed the four digit code. The alarm pad slid to the left, revealing a hidden compartment.

Bishop Money grabbed the gun and turned toward the two men that w ere relaxing in the Bishops den. "I want some answers. Now!" Bishop Money waved the gun in both men's direction.

Ignoring the Bishops threats, Theodore exhaled long and slow, enjoying the mechanical hands as they made their way down his back.

"In time. We'll tell you what you need to know, but first, put the gun down," Franklin said with calm.

"Because I'm a man of God you don't think I'll blow your head off?"

"Like you did Drake Gardener?"

The bishop's mouth remained faithful but his eyes betrayed him.

"Oh, we're very well aware of what you're capable of, Mr. Money." Theodore spoke for the first time as he continued to

13

enjoy the massage chair. "What you are capable of and how far you are willing to go is why you were chosen. Now, if you would be so kind as to put the gun down ."

How did they know about Drake? I was the only one in the alley that day, and I was disguised. If they were cops then I'd be... No. "I'm going to ask you two one more time. Who are you and why the hell are you here?"

"I'm going to tell you one more time," Franklin said. "Put... the... gun... down..."

Bishop Money stepped down into the east wing den where the men were lounging, pointed the gun at Franklin's left foot and pulled the trigger.

"You might need these." Theodore threw a handful of bullets in Bishop Money's face.

Both men simultaneously came up from their reclined position.

Defeat crossed Bishop Money's face as he took a seat across from the men on the beige Corinthian leather love seat.

"For over twenty-five years, Professor Gardener worked for the same people we represent. As you know, he was much more than a white African-American studies professor at Morehouse College. And not just an ex-military, soldier of fortune hit man. He was a government agent. You are who you are because of *us*. All the mess you've been in, haven't you ever wondered why you haven't been exposed? Percival Turner, Jebediah Jones, your ex-wife, your son. I must say, you are the craftiest S.O.B. I have ever read about. Let's not even get into the people you've swindled out of their homes. Church members you've robbed. Women you've abused and taken advantage of. No one man in the history of America, has ever done so much dirt, over a twenty-year span and has remained so clean, and," Theodore pointed a finger in the air, "has managed to grow in epic proportions as a religious and community leader."

"At least not a black man," Franklin corrected.

"What do you want?" TJ asked.

"We want you to be the next president of the United States."

"Yeah, right. Me, president?" The bishop laughed. "When pigs fly."

Neither Theodore or Franklin cracked a smile.

TJ looked back and forth between the two of them. "You're serious?"

The men just stared.

"I don't know anything about politics."

"Ronald Reagan didn't either. And George Jr., he had to use his toes to count past ten. And look what we did for Obama. Do you honestly think he won the election because of a grass roots movement? Speaking out against Special interests, the money and power behind government? No. We allowed Obama to win."

"I'm a Christian Bishop. I don't have any experience in politics."

"Oh, yes you have. Way more experience than Obama. He was a first-term Junior Senator from Chicago. You are a tenured political leader. As you know, the church is as political as government."

"I can't believe we're having this conversation at 11:00 on a Sunday night," Bishop Money said.

"Believe it," Franklin said.

"It'll take a miracle for anyone to beat President Obama in next year's election," Bishop Money said.

"The miracle will begin tomorrow morning. We just need to know if you're our man?" Franklin asked.

"Why me?"

"Unlike Obama, we can control you," Franklin said. "Your answer?"

"Well—"

"Well is not a yes or a no. It doesn't matter if you doubt what we say we can do, but after nine-fifty-two tomorrow

15

morning, you will have no doubt. We just need to know if you are our man."

"What choice do I have?" Bishop Money shrugged his shoulders.

"You always have a choice," Franklin responded.

"I'm in," he said, not believing what they were saying, but not taking a chance if they were for serious.

Theodore pulled a metal briefcase from beside the chair he sat in, and opened the silver latches. "This is a much better video than the one Clarence Wiley was editing for you."

Okay, they know way too much.

"It's only two minutes, but that is all you'll need," he said, standing and handing over a blue folder to the bishop. "There will be no need to try and blackmail the Junior Senator. We have other plans as you will see after committing the script inside the folder to memory. As you read, you will see that everything is time sensitive. You do your job and we will make you rich and famous beyond your wildest dreams." Both men stood and headed toward the rear double doors.

"How will I get—"

"You won't. We'll get in touch with you. Tomorrow is key. Read those five pages and memorize every step. Several lives depend on you," Theodore said before he and Franklin stepped out on the deck, "including yours."

The bishop got up and went to the wall-sized picture window that overlooked the three- acre back yard. He watched as the men walked down the deck stairs and faded into the night.

He went and opened the garage door. The huge black man was gone. This was definitely some real-life spy mess, he thought as he went to the bar and poured and downed a shot of Grand Marnier, before heading into his home theatre room with the blue folder in hand.

Chapter 3

"*H*and in hand, Babycakes. It's all about me and you. Hold on," the bishop said, putting his Blackberry on mute. "Marcos?"

"Yes, Bee-shop," the driver said, not taking his eyes off the bumper-to-bumper Atlanta morning rush hour traffic.

"How many times do I have to tell you? This is America. You have to pronounce your words correctly. What if I addressed Mora as Whora?"

The driver turned his head. "Come on Bee-shop, that's my wife."

"And I," he put a hand over his chest, "am your savior. Yet, you call me Bee shop. I don't sell bees or honey. My name, my title is one of great importance." He held his hands in the air. "I am God's hand. Not His right or left. I am His hand. Doesn't God's hand deserve the utmost praise and respect?"

"Yes sir, Bee, Uh, Bi-shop," the overweight driver said, clinching his teeth, while gripping the steering wheel.

"I take care of you, right?"

"Yes, sir." Reluctant, the Hispanic driver bobbed his head up and down. "Very well, sir. Me and my family are very grateful."

Bishop Money took off his Gucci shades and leaned forward. "So why in hell," he unmuted his phone, "am I riding in my custom-made bullet-proof, seven-hundred fifty-seven thousand dollar Bentley stretch listening to a damn buzzing sound. I pay you thirty-six thousand a year for you to drive and keep my cars and my Falcon 900 private Jet cleaned, and maintenanced, right?"

Lord, just one time. Just a few seconds. Unite my hands with his neck. Marcos smiled, while turning the corner, entering the prestigious downtown Atlanta community of Buckhead.

"In the three years you've been with me, have I ever paid you late?"

"No, sir?"

"Have I ever come short or given you a bad check?"

"No, sir?" Marcos shook is head.

"Than why does the privacy window make that much noise closing and opening?"

"I-I don't know. I didn't pay any attention, I'm sorry, sir."

"Hell, Ray Charles is blind and dead, and he knows you didn't pay attention to my vehicle. Maybe I shouldn't pay you tomorrow. After all you don't pay attention to what I pay you to pay attention to. And, please refrain from telling me about your character flaws."

Marco decided not to bite on the sandwich his boss had just made, but his mouth took off before the message made it from his brain. "I no talk to you about no character flaws."

Bishop Money pointed to the back of the driver's clean-shaven head. "Now that's where you're wrong. You're always telling me how sorry you are. I know you sorry. Probably come from a long line of sorry folks, but I'm trying to raise you from amongst the dead as Jesus did Lazarus. But you refuse to let my wisdom seek in them holes on the side of your head." Bishop Money went back to his phone call. "Hello, Babycakes, hello."

"I'm here, Lil-daddy. Why you gotta be so mean to your employers?"

"I thought I placed my phone on mute."

"Still, you ain't have to be so mean to your employers."

"Employee, not employer," the bishop corrected.

"Huh?" she grunted.

He took a deep breath. "Babycakes, an employee is the worker. The employer is the boss."

"I ain't stupid."

Coulda fooled me and everyone else who knows you, he thought.

"You knew what I meanted. Jus' cause I ain't got no doctorial degree like your uppity ass, don't mean I'm dumb."

"Babycakes, I didn't mean anything by correcting you. I know you're not dumb. You're doing something with your life. How many twenty-three year olds with five kids are going back to school? I'm proud of you, Babycakes."

"You just sayin' that 'cause you want some more of this, meow, meow. You was just ready-culing me about school a few minutes ago."

"I was what?"

"Ready-culing me about me going to school to be a cashier."

"Don't you mean ridiculing?"

"See, what I'm sayin'. Yo' ass think cause you a bishop, you's God. You can't judge me. Er'body ain't gotta wanna be a brain surgeon. I wanna be a cashier at Publix. Not only will I get a twenty percent discount on groceries, but they close at ten. I can still hit the club before it gets crunk. And I get first crack at all the expired food for me and my babies. So now what you gotta say 'bout that, preacherman?"

Bishop Money was forty-eight, single, with no children. Tequila Mercedes Lewis was only twenty-three, had five kids and had graduated from ignorant, to stupid, to now, doorknob dumb, and since the bishop didn't hold conversations with doorknobs, instead of answering her, he pressed the End button disconnecting the call. He shook his head and pressed the privacy glass remote, thinking that he had to stop picking up women at the Bankhead welfare office bus stop.

"Yes sir, Bishop." Marcos made sure to say the word bishop slowly, before putting the car in park.

"Someone needs to tell black women that we treat them like toilets because more than half of what comes out of their mouths is crap."

Someone should tell him that maybe if he stops putting so much crap in their minds, then maybe so much wouldn't come out of their mouths.

"I think I'll do a sermon on it. I'll call it *From Trash to Treasure*. Yeah, I like that," the bishop said as Marcos opened the rear passenger door.

It was a sunny breezy Autumn Monday morning, but not nearly breezy enough for the peanut butter brown ankle length fur coat the bishop wore. Labor day had passed three weeks ago, but you couldn't tell the Bishop he wasn't making a fashion statement wearing a three-piece white tailored silk suit, white gators, white silk shirt, white silk tie, and white hat, with a long brown peacock feather dancing on top of his head. And there wasn't a rapper in the hip-hop industry that wore a Platinum cross bigger and with more diamonds embedded in it than the one the bishop sported around his neck. You would've thought he was auditioning for a role in an *I'm Gonna Get You Sucka'* remake.

Five minutes later, Bishop Money checked his watch. 9:26 AM. The hallway was empty, he noticed after getting off the elevator on the 32nd floor.

"Senator Hayes's office, please hold." The middle-aged motherly-looking receptionist said, adding the caller to the long list of blinking lights on the switchboard.

The bishop looked at the small receptionist-slash-waiting area. Only a small flat panel TV tuned in to CNN decorated the dull brown windowless walls.

Junior Senator Jordan Hayes's eyes were glued to the charity book signing invite he was reading as he burst through his office into the receptionist area. "Pam, please hold my calls, I have an important meeting," he looked at his watch, "in just a few…"

The Junior Senator didn't see Bishop Money. The Bishop placed a hand on the back of the Junior Senator's, white dress shirt. "Senator, how are you?"

Just as the Senator turned to him, Bishop Money grabbed his hand like they were old drinking buddies.

"Mr. Money."

"Bishop Money," the bishop corrected with the fakest, most insincere smile.

The Junior Senator casually but forcefully jerked his hand from the Bishop while turning back toward his receptionist. "Pam, after you take Mr. Money's coat, run out and pawn it. We could feed a third world nation with the proceeds."

The fake smile became clown-like. "I guess if selling political lies doesn't work, you could always embark on a career as an out-of-work comedian."

Moments later, the two men were in the Junior Senator's office. Bishop Money had only planned to use the edited and photoshopped video feed of him and the Senator's wife as leverage to get the Senator to stop his prominent pastor witchhunt. But, that plan had all changed last night when he was handed a script and another feed. Although the feed looked authentic, even the voices of the Senator's wife and niece were perfect matches, he still didn't believe the senator would do what TJ was supposed to tell him to do.

Chapter 4

*B*ishop Money looked around the small office before placing a large brown and yellow Louis Vuitton briefcase on the Senator's desk. "Good God, man. You have a million dollar address in a hundred million dollar building, and Uncle Sam gives you a broom closet for an office."

"Enough of the pleasantries." Senator Hayes took a seat behind his cluttered desk and reached for a file with Bishop Money's name on it. "If it's okay with you, I'd like to get down to business."

"Let's," Bishop Money said, opening his briefcase.

"Ho-hold on..." Senator Hayes put his hands in the air. "How did you get that past security?"

"If you don't mind, I'd like to ask the questions," Bishop Money said, one hand on the trigger and the other taking a Mac laptop out of his briefcase. "Just stay calm. This," he waved the gun in the air, "is just insurance. Once you see what I have on this," he pressed a key on the laptop, "you may want to do me harm."

The video began playing. The same video that wasn't needed. The same one that Franklin told him not to show the Senator. But this was the Bishop Money show and no one was going to tell him how to run it. Besides, the senator had to suffer for all the sleepless nights he'd caused TJ, worrying about what all the senator knew and how he was going to try and expose him. No. Jordan was going to suffer before the finale.

"What the…?" Jordan leaned forward, his knuckles began turning red from squeezing the wooden arms of his chair, "Good God."

"That's exactly what your wife said. Look at how she—

Jordan dove forward, sending papers and a three-tier, paper-cluttered credenza to the beige carpeted floor along with the bishop's laptop.

Bishop Money jumped up and barely avoided Jordan's grasp. "Now see, I figured something like this would happen." He pulled the stock back, loading a bullet in the small .380 caliber handgun, while standing over the Senator.

"Just tell me why?"

"Because I could. I felt like I was doing a community service. I mean, the way she begged." He placed a hand on his crotch. "Oh, did that Indian squaw wife of yours beg."

"You better use that gun." The senator nodded. "'Cause if you don't, I'm goin' to jail for murder."

"Promises, promises." Bishop Money looked at his watch. Nine-forty-six a.m. "There's more, and trust you want to see it. Unfortunately, you won't get the perverted satisfaction of watching me pound your wife in this next scene." The bishop said, holding the gun over the Senator as his body was still half on the desk and halfway on the floor. "Look ," the bishop said, pressing down on the F2 key before putting the laptop's seventeen-inch screen close enough where Jordan could see the next scene clearly, but not close enough for Jordan to grab hold of it or him.

His career, his life. The one he and Cheyenne pieced back together was falling back apart. His wife had killed his twin brother, whom had raped her for years while Jordan sat in prison for a crime his twin committed. But the woman on the video he was watching took the blame for his brother's murder.

"Cheryl Nutcase Sharell, or as authorities call her, Wild Cherry." Bishop Money shook his head from left to right. "Shame, Shame, Shame. What tangled webs we weave, when we practice to destroy and deceive Bishop TJ Money." Bishop Money took a knee.

Jordan had seen enough. Instantly he knew. That shady Bishop C. Wendell Wiley somehow must have... Nah, he couldn't have had anything to do with it. This had happened twelve years ago in a Motel 6. Jordan didn't even know there was a video, let alone why it hadn't surfaced before now? Jordan knew there was no way he could talk his way out of this one. A foursome with his wife's best friend, who sat at the top of the F.B.I.'s Most Wanted list. Not to mention the fact that the video caught a close-up of him smoking crack in a corner while watching two naked women mercilessly beating and stabbing Cherry, his wife's best friend. He squeezed his eyes shut, trying to drown out the images of that night.

Bishop Money looked at his watch. Nine-fifty a.m. "Get up!" Bishop Money shouted.

He walked over to the wall adjacent to the office window where a forty-two inch flat panel TV hung on the wall. "What channel is CNN?"

Jordan struggled to stand on his own wobbly two feet.

"Never mind," TJ said, thinking that news this big would be broadcast on every network in the country, the world. "I'm about to show you how far my hand reaches."

The Bishop looked at his watch again. Nine-fifty-two. So had happened between last night and this morning that lly forgot that he'd reset his watch fifteen minutes rder to be sure to be on time.

nior Senator just stood slumped over with a ession shrouding his face. If the Bishop didn't know any better, he would have thought the man was losing it.

"Jordan, I want you to listen very closely." The Bishop spoke slow and clear. "Your wife's life depends on these next few minutes."

At the sound of the words *his wife*, Jordan's melancholy look changed to one of intense worry. Jordan closed his eyes, and contemplated charging Bishop Money. No longer concerned about his life, he exhaled. "What else have you done to my wife?"

"Nothing." Bishop Money again pointed at the seventeen-inch laptop computer screen that was now perched on the corner of the Senator's cleared-off desk.

"You have cameras in my home. How in the..." Much louder, he repeated, "You have
cameras in my damn house." He grabbed the laptop. Held the screen inches from his face. "Oh... my... God..."

"And that is exactly who she will soon be reunited with if you don't do exactly as I say."

"What do you want from me?"

"Your life." Bishop Money pointed to the window behind the Senator's desk. "But before you open that window, I need you to type a letter, print it out and sign your name to it."

"You're serious?"

"As a suicide bomber."

Jordan shook his head. "I can't."

"Really," the Bishop said.

"You better shoot me now." Jordan dropped the laptop and stepped forward. Murder in his bloodshot, watery eyes. "I'll kill you."

Bishop Money took a couple steps back. "Only thing you are going to kill is your wife, and your dead brother's daughter, that your wife gave birth to." The bishop took another step back. Jordan took one forward. "You may get to

25

me before I shoot you, but can you get to me before I press Send on my phone." TJ pulled out his blackberry.

Jordan paused.

"Send, might as well be End, because it will be for your wife and your bastard seven-year-old niece. Oh, and if you think you can save them, you can't. Your wife's cell phone is scrambled and every landline on your block is down. So, this is how the next three minutes is going to play out. You will write instead of typing a short note that I will dictate. You will seal it in an envelope and give it to me. I will leave out of the office and chat with your receptionist for one minute. At that point you will have jumped to your death, or the two people you love the most in this life will be taken, just as abruptly as your twin, Jevon was."

A few minutes later, Bishop Money stood in the reception area talking to the Senator's receptionist, when they were interrupted by a loud beeping noise that came from the thirty-two- inch flat panel TV in the small waiting area.

"Breaking news. Twenty-two minutes ago, President Obama collapsed during a closed door meeting with Venezuelan President Hugo Chavez, and Cuban leader, Raul Castro." The reporter put something to her ear. "The President's helicopter has just arrived at Walter Ree... A stream of tears cascaded down her face.

The mask of seriousness she wore disintegrated before America and the world that was watching. Her breakdown lasted all of seven seconds, violating the unwritten code of non-emotional professional journalism etiquette. The world that was tuned in to CNN knew before Chin Li continued. "The 44th president of the United States of America, President Barack Hussein Obama born August 4, 1961 was pronounced dead on arrival at Walter Reed Hospital less than two minutes ago, as a result of a brain aneurysm.

Chapter 5

*"A*neurysm my a—"

"Samuel, you're in a place of worship," Reverend Solomon One-Free, reminded his young protégé.

He pointed to the TV in the church office. "Almost three years in office and they killed him. Just like they did Reginald Lewis, Ron Brown, and Johnny Cochran. You knew President Obama personally. The man didn't drink. He quit smoking a year ago. Worked out regularly. Perfect health. The whole country. The whole world cryin', sad and shit, holdin' candle prayer vigils. Bull—"

"Samuel!" The former Illinois governor, the Reverend One-Free shouted. "You know the masses are sheep, led by wolves, disguised as shepherds." He shook his head. "The people don't know. For the most part, they think the government is for the people." The reverend put a comforting hand on Samuel's shoulder. "It's been three days since our brother was called home. And, I assure you the matter is being investigated, but as you know it's hard investigating the invisible hand of government puppeteers."

"But, how can the world be so naïve? A decade has passed since we fabricated lies to start a war with a Middle Eastern country. We go and kill the sons of that country's president and plaster their gruesome death photos on the internet and the news, before we hunt that country's president down, and force that country's judicial system to kill their own president. For what? Huh, Rev? For what," the young man cried out. "Oil dominance. We ain't do shit then, and we ain't gon' do shit now."

Solomon sat next to the young man that he had grown so fond of since the young man's father, Bishop Percival Turner was shot down three years ago.

"That's where you're wrong, son." He put an arm around his dejected mentee. "We have close to forty-thousand Hispanic and Black Kings and Queens in the One-Free family, and thousands more that follow our truth-teachers around the country. For now we have to act with calm in the midst of the storm. We have to gather more intel, and strategize before we take any action, or make any accusatory public statements."

Samuel bobbed his head up and down. "I know, you right. I'm just mad. I mean, it's so clear. Black people were on the verge of finally getting something for the 400 years that our minds and bodies were raped and forced to work like domesticated animals for scraps of food from the white man's table."

"Closer to 450 years," Rev. One-Free said. "The difference then and now is that we don't realize that we are still slaves. Our minds are being raped every day that our children walk into public schools. Every time we turn on the news, every time our children turn their Xboxes or Playstations on."

"That's what I'm sayin', Rev. If Proposition 400 passed, we would have gotten free health insurance, free education and child care assistance for those who went to school and maintained at least a 2.5 GPA." He looked up at the man he'd come to love and respect as much as he had his own father. "Can you imagine?"

"No, I cannot." Reverend One-Free said. "History has shown us that the powers that be were going to do something to block this, but I didn't think they would do this. I guess I just didn't think. Although Biden, and Hillary are good people, they won't push this bill. They know what happened. They know why it happened."

Samuel's long dreadlocks looked like black helicopter propellers as he violently shook his head from side to side. His eyes were clenched shut. He didn't want to accept or deal with the reality of a reparations bill that would never pass.

"But they … We need more than just knowing." Reverend One-Free said, looking off at some spot on the church office wall that only he could see.

"You're right. I'm just so… You don't understand," Samuel cried.

You have no idea how much I do understand, Solomon thought. *The president and I had talked about this day often. The day the unseen hand behind the government and the economy figured out that the president was a man. A real black man.*

"I'm just so tired of ignorant cookie-cutter, milk-toast, toilet paper-soft black folk. In times of turmoil, we don't wanna fight. We wanna either riot in our own communities, or march. I mean explain the logic behind that. We get mad at the system and we set a match to our backyards. We go out and rob and loot our brothers and sisters, who have nothing to do with the system that angered us. It's like a teacher beats up a child for nothing and the parent brings the kid back to school and beats up his or her child in front of that same teacher, and then says to the teacher, 'I guess I showed you'."

Samuel was on a roll. "And marches. Come on. What are we marching for, besides the CSPAN and CNN cameras? They getting paid off of viewers watching thousands of blacks walk down a street and listen to a few good speeches by our media chosen black leaders. These same blacks aren't leading their thousands of marchers into the courthouses and jail cells and forcefully freeing our wronged and talented men and women. They just give speeches, sing and call for gas boycotts, when you know good and well, black folk will go to the gas stations after the one day boycott and buy twice as much gas as they would've bought the day of the boycott."

"Son, you preaching to the choir. You have to understand that we know better, but we don't understand better. And that's because we only read what we're told or trained to read." He extended his arm out. "Look at King Jihad. This brother is one of the best and deepest writers of our time. His eighth book, The Survival Bible: 16 Life Lessons for Young Black men hasn't sold 1,000 books in the three years it's been out, and he's everywhere trying to get the message out. Yet black violence among young black men dominates the headlines in this country. Our sisters have been crying out that there are no good black men. They are raising young boys in the hopes of them becoming positive black men, but a brother who has come from the same gutters that most young black men come from writes a passionate, moving and inspirational life-changing piece of work that will revolutionize the way we all look at things, and because his name is Jihad, and not Hill Harper or Steve Harvey, the black media, our own people, treat him and his work, like a leper."

"Goes back to your sermon last Sunday, Rev. *Jesus, The Grass Root, Barefoot Revolutionary*. Sort of like you said then, the masses didn't receive Jesus or his messages until decades, centuries after his earthly body had returned to the Father, and that was because he never had the backing of any part of the power structure. The message is clear, so why do the Tupacs, the Obama's, and most likely the Jihad's of this world have to die before their messages are received?"

"In the words of one of the greatest men I've ever had the pleasure of sharing oxygen with, President Obama once said, "Change we can believe in begins with a thought and then, not a *call* to action, but action we the American people can *call* our own." The reverend stood, and helped Samuel to his feet. He couldn't help but smile at the framed article that hung on the wall in front of him. No matter how hard last years, 2010 Forbes magazine 50 most influential men photo was photoshopped to make the reverend look like some dark, menacing demon, he still looked like a forty-year-old, six-foot-tall honorable black man, although he'd just turned sixty-two last month in October.

"Son," he handed Solomon a plane ticket, and looked at his watch, "I need you to be on the one o'clock flight out of Washington-Reagan, to Atlanta. Go to Queen Cheyenne, stay with her until Moses, Rhythm and I arrive tomorrow morning."

Solomon nodded. "I almost forgot about Senator Hayes's passing."

Chapter 6

$\mathcal{T}$he Atlanta autumn rain had been falling all morning and didn't seem to be letting up anytime soon. But that didn't stop or slow down the onslaught of traffic entering the massive wrought iron gates leading onto the forty-acre One World Faith Missionary Baptist church grounds.

CNN, FOX, and several other news agencies were busy filming the politicians, actors, hip-hop and R&B artists, Atlanta's movers and shakers. They all smiled and waved for the cameras as they walked down the well-lit and covered electronic moving sidewalk leading to the escalator that would take them in to the massive gothic-like church vestibule dome.

At exactly noon, Bishop Money's five-car motorcade and six motorcycle police escort pulled onto the church grounds.

"I thought President Obama passed away." One onlooker waiting to get in to the already packed church said.

"He did, but the king didn't," another replied.

"That nigga ain't no king. He just got king money, and a slick tongue," another said shivering, while leaning against his umbrella.

"So why you here standing outside in the cold rain waiting under the canopy like all of us to get in?" a young lady asked.

"Nigga put on a damn good show. He shadier than a four dolla' bill, but he sho' knows how to party preach."

"Party preach?"

"Yeah, it be like a club with live music and a big band, a light show, and all in the name of my Jesus. But I tell you this. I swear fo' God and all his prophets, that after I pay this twenty dollars to get in to the memorial service for the president and Senator Hayes, I ain't givin' that rich nigga no mo' of my money. How you gon' charge to get into a damn memor'al service," the man said.

"Why don't you take your evil behind somewhere else?" another lady said. "You're not going to stand here and speak ill of Bishop Money. He is the greatest thing to ever happen to the black community. And he charges to get into special church functions, because he know people like you are going to show up. This is his way of ensuring that the community gets fed, housed, clothed, and receives proper medical attention."

The man turned to the woman. "You act like he God."

"He's the closest thing."

Before he could reply, loud applause rang out. People began shouting, "Bishop Money, Bishop Money." Flashes from a thousand cameras lit up the dreary Wednesday early afternoon.

All of a sudden there was a pause as the Bishop got out of his stretch Bentley. Bishop TJ Money, looked like... like, a normal person. The crowd was taken aback. Gone, were the flamboyant suits, the jewelry. Even the hair. Bishop Money waved and smiled as he walked with a slight limp through the crowd with his entourage of bodyguards and fellow clergy. He wore a black suit. Still tailored, mind you. His shoes were made of black leather, not some exotic animal or reptile, like

33

he usually wore. His hair was no longer permed and hanging off his slender shoulders. It was cut very short and clean. His clothes looked comfortable on him, unlike before when he wore shirts that strangled his midsection and his arms.

An hour later, Bishop Money was on stage.

"On this, week before Thanksgiving, we stand before you Father on weak knees. Our hearts are bleeding. Our souls are crying. This is a trying time for us all, Father." He shook his head from side to side. "We're all grief stricken. But why, Father God? Why are we stricken with grief?" From behind the electronic podium, Bishop Money pointed a well-manicured ringless finger in the air. The Word says, "He giveth and…" He pointed out to the congregation.

"He taketh away," thousands of voices completed the proverb.

"But, did He take what was ours… or what was His? Just because we can't see our beloved president or the senator, doesn't mean they're gone. Can we see Jesus? Is he gone?"

The standing room only, twelve-thousand plus people inside the newly remodeled convention center-like church were in awe of the Bishop's words. Even the cameramen seemed to be mesmerized.

"Last month, I flew out to Jackson, Mississippi to comfort a brother, John Higgins and his adopted family. If you don't know who John Higgins is, he is the man; white man, that had a one-night stand with a sister. The sister ended up pregnant. And because she was on crack, John offered to raise the baby. Well," the Bishop loudly exhaled. "She told John she'd sell him the unborn baby for five grand."

"That's a shame. A dog gone shame," someone voiced from the front row.

"John Higgins's lack of education tied him to the warehouse job he'd had since dropping out of the tenth grade ten years prior to sleeping with this woman. No wife. No kids. Brother Higgins made twelve dollars an hour. Of course, he didn't have five-thousand dollars, but he did own a five-year-old Ford pickup truck. Without a thought, he gave his only form of transportation to the woman for his little black baby. Because of what he had done, whom he had done it with, and the color of that precious baby's skin, his own mother and father had disowned him. He'd lost his job because he couldn't get to and from work. Thanks to the Jenkins, an elderly couple next door helping with the adorable little girl, he was able to work at a Burger World and at a Smoothie Paradise eighty, to sometimes one hundred hours a week to support him and his special needs, bubbly baby girl."

The Bishop swallowed hard as if he were composing himself before he continued. "Six years had gone by, no word from the little girl's mother, and out of nowhere one Saturday morning, with red eyes, a runny nose, and a thick head of hair that looked like it was the home for several different insects, she showed up at the front door of the small house John rented. Of course, John refused to let her see the little girl. He advised the woman to get an attorney and go through the courts. Of course, what he had told her was too much like right.

A couple days later the woman came back, cleaned up, hair half combed. John was working this late summer Monday afternoon. The little girl was playing in her little sandbox inside the Jenkins' yard. The woman unlatched the metal gate and walked up to the porch. After confirming that the child was hers, before the couple could act, the woman lifted the child up and ran with the scared baby screaming in her arms." Bishop Money paused for effect. "Two days later, the police arrested the mother in a flea bag Motel 6. No child. Come to find out the mother had resold her little girl for crack." Bishop Money took out a handkerchief and wiped his invisible tears. "Days later the little girls remains were found behind a dumpster near the drug infested area where she was sold..."

"Take your time, Bishop," someone shouted.

"John Higgins was stricken with grief. He asked me…" Bishop Money closed his eyes before repeating. "John Earl Higgins asked me how could I believe in the goodness of a God that let something like that happen to an innocent little girl."

The church was deathly quiet.

"I smiled and asked him, how could I not believe? After all, isn't death what we live for? Aren't we trying to live in His light so when we are called home, we are accepted into His kingdom? Don't we believe that the greatest place to be is with God? So, yes that little girl suffered briefly in this life to live forever in His light. I told him and I'm telling," he waved his arm in a half circular motion, "you all, that God's goodness was in calling that child home so she could be with her Father. So she wouldn't have to see a tomorrow where murder runs rampant in America's urban communities like running water. A tomorrow where men and women of color lovingly degrade each other with words, like nigga, dog, cat, fox, bitch and they don't see anything wrong with that. A world where the mother and father have become dinosaurs, replaced by Playstations, cell phones, and TVs. So," he paused and held a finger in the air, "I say to you as I said to John Higgins on that day. Honor the memories, and pray that you will follow in her footsteps one day. Honor the memories and the messages of President Obama, and Senator Hayes."

A reporter standing at the back of the church nudged her cameraman. "Did I miss something?"

The cameraman shrugged his shoulders.

"What does that story have to do with President Obama and Senator Hayes?" she whispered.

"Nothing, but it sure sounded reader worthy."

The cameras caught thousands that had been moved to tears by the Bishop's speech. Rick Warren, the author of *The Purpose Driven Life* stood up from behind Bishop Money and began the applause, followed by Bishop Jakes, Bishop Long, and Joel Olsteen, before the entire church was on its' feet.

The bishop, put his hands up and slowly brought them down, gesturing to the church that he wasn't finished.

Minutes later he continued. "They say the good die young. I guess this is their reward from God for being good. They are able to come home sooner than most. But if I can borrow a slogan from our departed President. Change we can believe in begins with the head. As I am the head of the One World family," he stepped away from the podium and held out his arms so all could see, "Gone is the flamboyant dress, gone is the hair, and the jewelry. I only dressed as I had for the past two and a half decades, because I wanted to show our young people that God is cool. God is Hip-Hop. God is anything and everything associated with righteousness and his work and his workers come in all colors," he waved an arm behind him, "shapes, sizes, and monotheistic religions. Yes, I said it. Monotheistic religions. Belief in the one God. Call him what you choose, in your native tongue, but call Him and only Him, because He is, was, and will always be the only salvation for this world and any world. And in honor of our dearly departed Senator, I am opening up all my books to the IRS, because that is what Senator Hayes wanted. And that is what I want. I want to show you and the world, that I have nothing to hide. This I do in Senator Hayes's honor. And in honor of the proposed reparations bill and the Health Care reform bill that President Obama fought for so hard, over the next year I am not going to try, I give you my word that I *will* raise a half billion dollars so everyone, black, white, yellow and brown will not have affordable health care, but have free health care."

The cameras flashed like mad, as photographers took pictures of the Bishop.

"You might be thinking that a half billion dollars won't go far with over 310 million Americans. It's not meant to. That money represents your voices. It will be the catalyst for change. The late President John F. Kennedy said, *'Ask not what your country can do for you, but what you can do for your country.'* I can show you better than I can tell you and I will bring change that you can believe in, change you can see and feel."

Everyone was so engrossed in the Bishop's new look and his words, that not many noticed or paid attention to the woman in the brown suit, with the brown hat covering her face moving to get out of the N section and into the middle aisle.

Bishop Money pulled out a check and began to write on it from the podium. He walked back into the middle of the stage and waved the check in the air. "I am donating most of my savings to this cause. Now we are six million dollars closer to our goal."

Applause rang out.

The lady was in the aisle walking forward. An usher was quickly approaching her.

"Not only am I giving this. I am putting my ten million dollar estate home, my multi-million dollar exotic car collection, and one of my two private jets up for sale. Every single dollar will go to our half a billion dollar goal."

She took off her hat and pulled a gun from her purse.

Bishop Money shouted, "Noooo!"

Bang! Bang! Bang! Bang! Bang! Bang!

The sound of gunshots echoed though the church. It was pandemonium, People were screaming and running for the exits. Others were hugging the floor. Every one was doing something except for the woman holding the smoking gun and Bishop Money. She and Bishop Money's eyes met as his bullet-riddled body collapsed onto the stage.

Chapter 7

"*O*h my, God!" Rhythm gasped. Her eyes welled up with tears of rage. "Who did this to you?" she asked, looking at one of her closest friend's swollen and bruised face as the two female guards took off the handcuffs.

"Is he dead?" Dr. Jamison-Hayes asked a little above a whisper before wincing in pain while holding her side and gently sitting in the metal folding chair behind the stainless steel table.

Through clenched teeth Rhythm addressed the guards, "My client needs medical attention."

"Is he dead? Please tell me he's dead." Cheyenne asked again.

A tall, stocky, female deputy stepped forward. She stood inches from the much smaller caramel-colored attorney. "I 'on't care who you are. I 'on't care 'bout this job." The huge woman looked down at Rhythm. "Psst." She bobbed her neck. "And I r'ally don't care 'bout you balling and unballing your fists. All I gotta say is, you just better pray real hard that Bishop Money lives."

Rhythm wanted to snatch every red and glitter gold braid out of the woman's head. But instead, she asked, "Is that all?"

"If the bishop dies, it ain't."

39

Rhythm smiled, showing a perfect set of white teeth. Slow and clear, enunciating every word she said, "You have fifteen minutes to get my client medical attention."

The guard crossed her arms. "Bit—, heifer, shit, you 'bout to make me curse. *Who* you think you are?"

Rhythm looked down at her Movado. "It's ten-twenty-five a.m. You have until ten-forty a.m.to get her a paramedic or a doctor. If my request isn't met I'll show you *who* I am."

The deputy laughed, before walking to the steel door of the attorney-client visitation room, the other guard behind her. Upon grabbing the doors handle, she said, "You lucky I'm on the job." She licked her big brown lips. "Let me get outta here 'fore I find better use for them pretty lawyer lips of yours." She turned her head to Cheyenne. "And as for you, killa', I get off in twenty minutes, but I'll see yo' trigger-happy behind tonight." The guards locked the two women in the room.

"So, he's still breathing?" Cheyenne asked. Disappointment resonated in her voice.

"Barely. He's in the critical care unit at Dekalb Medical. That's as much as I know." Rhythm pulled her chair around the table. She grabbed her friend's hand and looked into her swollen discolored eyes. "Did that guard do this to you?"

She dropped her head, breaking eye contact with Rhythm. Her silence told a better story than her words could have.

"It was my understanding that you were being held in protective custody."

"I am. But, who's going to protect me from those who put me there?"

I can. And I will, Rhythm thought. Rhythm One-Free was in her early-fifties, but like her husband, Moses she didn't look a day over forty, which was surprising considering all the hell she'd gone through in her past. On more than one occasion, she had stared death in the face. And on more than one occasion she sent death to hell. "Sweetie, I'm going to get you out of here."

Cheyenne lifted her head. "Rhythm, you been a great friend and I love you. My life's over. I died with Jordan. I don't care what they do to me. I just want Samuel to raise Ariel. I haven't spoken to him. But I know he loves her and she loves him. I know it's selfish, but I've been going crazy since TJ killed my husband. The police, my friends, no one believes me. That man is evil. I had to do it. I had to."

"Listen to me, Cheyenne." Rhythm grabbed her friend by the shoulders. "I know Jordan didn't commit suicide. Just like I know you'll raise your daughter. I'm going to talk to the A.D.A. handling the case at five this afternoon. I know Tiffany Cole, she's tough, but she's fair." Rhythm patted the back of Cheyenne's palm. "We'll get you a bond. Worst case, we'll plead temporary insanity."

"Rhythm, you're not listening to me. My life ain't shit. Don't waste your time. I tried to murder that bastard, and if I get out I swear I'll finish the job if God doesn't beat me to it," she said doubling over, wincing in pain.

"Cheyenne?" Rhythm said, squeezing her friend's hand.

Cheyenne made a grunting sound before losing consciousness and falling to the shiny concrete Dekalb County jail floor.

Chapter 8

$\mathcal{F}$or the past hour, Rhythm had threatened to sue every department and every person that worked in the Dekalb County Jail. She couldn't believe Cheyenne was taken to the jail infirmary instead of an outside hospital. Now she was sitting behind the wheel of her Range Rover, fuming.

She was startled out of her thoughts by the vibration from her cell phone.

"Bazz, I know you haven't gotten that address for me already," Rhythm asked while turning on her windshield wipers.

"Come on, Queen. This Shabazz. Lifetime MVP in the hustlers hall of fame, although that don't begin to define my game or my name." He paused. "You got a pen?"

"Let me see." She fumbled through her purse as she tried to pull out of the Dekalb County jail complex. "I can't find one. Can you—"

"Come on, Queen. How you gon' win, without a pen, especially when you planning to use my G to sin."

Shabazz was an old school con man, surrogate father, former heroin addict, white-skinned, black man in his early forties. He was now part of the vast One-Free family. He was the man that could get anything on the low. One day he'd be in the hood, shootin' craps with the dope boys, preachin' to them about how they needed to get out the game, and the next day, he'd be advising a senator or congressman over dinner. If he didn't have anything else, Shabazz had game.

"Text me the address, please." She turned the volume up on her hands free phone. "Have you spoken to my niece?"

"Everyday. That American history class is kickin' her tail."

"I don't know why she just didn't stay at home and go to Spelman," Rhythm said.

"You know good and well, why. You graduated from Howard," Shabazz said. "I just got off the line with Babygirl. She's excited about coming home in a couple weeks for winter break. I just hate she's not going back until next Fall. But then again, maybe that's best. Because she at a HBCU learning U.S. Mystery, 'cause I'm explaining way too much history. Had to break down the Navigation Act of 1761 and the real reason the American Revolution begun."

"Bazz, you should go back to school. Get your degree and teach."

"Queen, I teach every day, every way, high and low, 'till they brains is tired and can't think no mo'. Didn't cost me a dime, but it damn sho' wasn't free. Got my Bullshit, my more of the same, and my piled higher and deeper degree from Penitentiary State, and Sidewalk University. Ain't no better ledge to know than the beat of the streets, and the feats of our peeps put down in books, stolen by history crooks to keep us as they coat hooks. So, as you see, I'm gon' stay free and keep doin' me and everybody else who wanna be free. But without further adieu, I'm gon' send that text to you. Gotta go, gotta date with Destiny and I can't be late, that big-bootie cutie just might not wait."

*****

43

She'd been patiently waiting in the parking lot of the apartment complex for about two hours, listening to Dr. Mark Naison's new book, *The Boogie Down*. The late November rain was picking up, but not bad enough for Rhythm not to see anyone coming out of the townhouse. She looked at the clock on the dash. Two-thirty. She prayed that the woman left the townhouse before Rhythm had to leave for her five o'clock at the D.A,'s office. She was starting to wonder if the woman had another car, besides the black Honda Accord parked in front of her door.

Her cell phone vibrated.

Rhythm pushed the Talk button."Greetings."

There was a lot of phone static in the background.

"Hello," Rhythm said.

"I got your message. What can we do?"

Message. Message. Oh yeah, she thought, just now remembering that she had asked her husband, Moses to get Cherry the news of Jordan's death. That was quick, considering Cherry had been on the outskirts of Havana, Cuba ever since she was featured on America's Most Wanted a year ago. "Tamika?"

"Yes," Cherry answered, responding to the code name, her, Cheyenne, and Rhythm set up after Cherry took the blame for killing Cheyenne's husband's twin brother a couple of years ago.

"What do you mean, what can *we* do?"

The woman that Rhythm was waiting for came out of the townhome with a big red umbrella over her head.

"Me and my mom."

Rhythm opened the driver's door of her Range Rover.

"Girl, you still there?" Cherry asked.

"Tamika, if you can, call me tonight. Gotta go." She threw the phone onto the cream colored leather passenger seat and jumped out the car and half walked, half jogged toward the woman standing at her black Honda.

Officer Eadie Calhoun was only a few feet from her car when she spotted Rhythm quickly closing the distance.

"I'm a Christian woman. Don't make me act ugly in this rain."

"Act ugly? If you aren't getting royalties off the use of the word, than you need to sue somebody," Rhythm said.

"You sure you want this," the huge woman asked, as she put the umbrella down next to her ten-year-old car.

"All I want is for you to leave my client alone, and make sure the others do the same."

"Oh, that's all you want?"

Rhythm nodded her head. "That's all."

"How 'bout we get out this rain, and go inside. There, we can talk about what I want, "the ox-like woman winked, "cutie pie."

A minute later, Officer Calhoun closed her front door and turned to face Rhythm.

Pop!

Officer Calhoun grabbed her nose. "Bitch, you broke my nose." She pulled out a foot-long, black metal flashlight. "I'mmo' break your damn face."

At least David had a slingshot and some room to work before slaying Goliath. The five foot six , hundred and thirty-five pound middle aged attorney was in close quarters and she had nothing but her fists and feet. Officer Calhoun was six-foot-forever and might as well have weighed a ton.

"You try and hit me with that flashlight, I'll fracture your ribs on the left side, and break your right index finger," Rhythm calmly explained.

Officer Calhoun charged forward in what seemed like slow motion.

Rhythm sidestepped the behemoth and kicked her in the knee. As she was falling, Rhythm grabbed her right index finger and bent it back until the bone popped.

45

"Ahhhhhh!" Officer Calhoun hollered. She dropped the flashlight and reached around and grabbed a handful of air, barely missing a handful of reddish brown dreadlocks.

Rhythm dropped to the burgundy carpeted floor, grabbed the flashlight, rolled to her right, bumped into the couch, and hit Officer Calhoun in the shin with the butt end of the flashlight. On her way to the ground, Rhythm timed her swing and cracked Officer Calhoun's ribs.

Seconds later, Rhythm stood over the fallen giant, who was visibly in agonizing pain. "Now that I have shown you who I am, let me introduce myself." She dropped one of her business cards on Officer Calhoun's leg. "My name is Rhythm One-Free, Esquire, and attorney at law. I apologize for cracking the right rib. I told you the left. I guess I'm getting' rusty, but my trigger finger is good and oiled up, and if my client is touched by anyone I'll be back with a body bag."

"I can't go to work like this. I can barely breathe." The huge woman cried from her prone position on the floor.

"Unlike you did my client, I won't deny you medical attention. I never said you had to go to work."

"But, how can I protect her if I'm not at work?"

"I have no idea," Rhythm said, walking to the front door. "Oh, and I want my client in an outside hospital. Don't worry, if she's not transferred tonight, I'll let you continue sharing my air, but I will break a bone in your body every day until she is."

"I don't have any control over who's sent to an outside hospital," the officer whimpered.

"Sounds like a personal problem to me."

Chapter 9

"*G*ood, God."

The female security officer that had just searched Rhythm looked over at LJ, the mouth almighty, tongue dummy, head of the security detail at the downtown Atlanta State building. "Negro, whachu' Good Goddin' about?"

"Lawd, lawd, lawd." The old man took out a monogrammed handkerchief and wiped his brow. "Looka here, looka here, looka here!" The sixty-seven year old security guard paused. "Whewwwww. Boy, looka here. She can get it. I mean every last cent of it." He shook his head. "Umph, umph, umph. You ain't gotta do nothin' to that. She 'on't need no hot sauce, no salt, pepper, nothing. She seasoned just right. I ain't takin' nothing from that Beyonce, or Rhi-anna, but they ain't ripe yet. They ain't seasoned, but 'dat dere." He nodded in the direction of where Rhythm stood. "I'll give that fine mamma-jamma my paycheck, my wife's paycheck, and if that ain't enough, I'll hit one of them dope boys over the head and give her that nigga's money, too," LJ said as Rhythm stood at the elevator wearing a fitted, but professional beige Donna Karan pantsuit.

"LJ, yo' old behind can't do nothin' with that," Yaris, the twenty-something year old officer said, looking at Rhythm disappear inside of the elevator. "You be done OD'ed on Viagara tryin' to keep up with her. Now, a young bull like me. I'd—"

"Dogs. All ya'll." Ella looked at the other three security officers who were lusting after the movie star-gorgeous fifty-two-year-old attorney.

"Look!" Ella pointed to one of the forty-two inch TVs that hung from the gray and black speckled granite lobby walls.

"We interrupt your regularly scheduled program to bring you this special report."

A second later, the broadcast went to the outside of Dekalb Medical, where a sea of people holding candles and praying flooded the hospital grounds in the forty degree clear November Atlanta weather.

"This is Sadequa Frazier reporting live from Dekalb Medical Center where Bishop Terrell Joseph Money, the charismatic leader of One World Faith ministries has succumbed to injuries resulting from four gunshot wounds. I repeat, Bishop Terrell Joseph Money has died as a result of injuries sustained from several gunshot wounds."

*****

"No deals."Tiffany Cole stood behind the desk in her small eighteenth-floor office. "Your client will be the first woman to die in a Georgia electric chair."

"Excuse me?" Rhythm said, as she closed the A.D.A.'s office door. She couldn't help but notice all the papers, books, and pens. Even the state's flat panel computer monitor was on the floor. It looked like someone had just swept everything off of the A.D.A.'s desk.

Tiffany made a feeble attempt to straighten her clothes and compose herself. The silver iPhone was about the only electronic device that wasn't on the floor. *Bishop Money is dead.* She read the headlines as they flashed across the two-inch screen that the red-eyed district attorney held out in front of Rhythm's face.

"I'm so sorry," Rhythm said, truly meaning it. Not sorry for TJ. If anyone deserved to be dead, he did. She was sorry for Cheyenne. Her friend had been through pure hell over the last few years. And in Georgia, there was no way she'd get a fair trial. Hell, she wouldn't get a fair trial anywhere in the south, and even if she did, the game had changed since TJ was now dead.

*****

A few states away, in Quantico, Virginia, at CIA headquarters, five of the most powerful men in America and, quite possibly the world, including a former US President and a current Senator were in a closed door meeting surrounded by fifty inch computer monitors.

"Genius! Rupert you are an absolute genius." George Bush Senior pointed up at the monitors. "Just look. NBC, CBS, ABC, CNN, your network, and even the BBC followed your lead."

"Senator, how you got your medical team assembled and into Dekalb Medical so fast is nothing short of a miracle," Bush said.

"It's time," Prince Nathan, England's next King interrupted, looking at the flashing red light on the wall near the heavily guarded six-inch steel door.

"For years, we've used fear tactics to scare the American people into furthering our goal to establish a One World Order," Bush said, picking up the red phone that sat in the middle of the rectangular table facing the twelve monitors that hung from the ceiling in the underground strategy room.

"Taking care of Obama was child's play compared to what we're about to do gentlemen."

"Not really," Rupert Murdoch, the media mogul that owned the FOX network, interrupted from his seat at the end of the table. "Hope follows fear. The people think we are at war against who? Jihadists? Muslims? This is still a Christian country. For the most part, Americans believe in God. Hell, we got that idiot son of yours elected the last time on a Christian platform, GB."

Phone still in had, Bush interrupted, "What does that have to with what we're doing?"

"Everything," Rupert said. "Osama Bin Laden is a Muslim and the devil in the eyes of the public. The bible prophesizes about a Messiah coming back to save the people."

GB smiled before imprinting his thumbprint over the phone's scanner before passing the phone down the line. Every man did the same, before the phone finally reached Rupert. "Do it," were the only words spoken into the receiver once the computerized voice came onto the line.

*****

Glorious Withers had just read a line from Brandon Massey's latest sci-fi horror mystery before the elevator noise down the hall scared her into action. She jumped up from the mop bucket and put the book inside the pocket of her hospital coat, grabbed the mop, and wrung it out in the clean, cold mop water.

She looked up just in time to see that the elevator had stopped on the basement level where she was supposed to be working. A young brother with earphones in his ears sang the lyrics of the latest Bo Jack Jones hit, *Smoke til' ya Choke,* while wheeling a dead body toward the hospital's morgue.

"Ah, it's only you, Man-Man." Glorious rolled her eyes before pulling the book back out of her pocket. "I thought you was somebody."

"I is somebody, shawty. Bet if you knew who I was takin' down to da cold room until the county show up, you'd respect my gangsta shawty," the young orderly said as he pulled his hospital scrubs up on his behind and wheeled the gurney toward Glorious.

"Why I care who you got under that sheet? Hell, they dead, can't do nothin' for me," she said.

Man-Man stopped in the hall next to Glorious. "Bet you ain't never been this close to royalty."

"Psst." She put a hand on one of her twenty-two-year-old hourglass hips. "Negro, you ain't royalty."

"I ain't say I was, but I got Bishop Money under here," Man-Man said.

Her droopy, red eyes lit up. "Swear to God?"

"On er'thing I love, shawty. Let a nigga lay hands on you." His eyes feasted on Glorious's rap video body. "I'll let you touch him."

"Let me touch him?" She looked the tall, skinny, clumsy-looking orderly from toe to head, and from head to toe. "Negro, you must be on crack."

"Nah, but there's a crack I'd like to be up in," he said.

She touched his cheek with one hand and grabbed a piece of the sheet covering Bishop Money with the other. "Playa, I'm like a buffet, all you can eat, but please believe, you can't eat for free," she said pulling the cover from Bishop Money's head.

Both Glorious and Man-Man looked at Bishop Money's face, just before his eyes popped open.

"How much is a plate?" Bishop Money asked.

Man-Man hollered like a ten-year-old girl and ran into the wall behind him, before taking off toward the stairs. Glorious wasn't far behind. "Swear to God, I ain't smokin' no more

Cush. I'm gon' stick to regular weed," she said dropping her book as she ran.

Chapter 10

*P*OPULAR AFRICAN-AMERICAN BISHOP DIES IN HOSPITAL AND COMES BACK TO LIFE AN HOUR LATER. MIRACLE, MESSIAH OR MEDICAL MISHAP?

Newspaper presses all over the world printed the front page story. Television networks scrambled for any new details. It was a media blitz, as big, if not bigger than the one created a week ago after President Obama had passed away.

Less than seventy-two hours after he'd literally came back to life, Bishop Money was granting "60 Minutes" an interview from his private hospital room.

"Bishop Money, you were shot multiple times while memorializing the late President and the late Junior Senator from Georgia. You were pronounced dead less than four days ago, on November 26, 2011. Ironically, you died on Black Friday and rose on Black Friday."

Although he'd just risen from the dead a few days ago, you'd never know it. He sat cross- legged on the beige loveseat, an arm draped over the top of the mini-couch, wearing Perry Cuomo two-tone brown leather and suede loafers, coffee-colored pinstripe slacks, matching vest, and as ordered by Franklin, he wore no jewelry. He'd had his barber, massage therapist, nail technician, and even a stripper disguised as a nurse cater to his every whim over the last twenty-four hours.

"What was going through your mind as you lay on the stage waiting for the paramedics?" Andre' Maurice asked.

"Never have I owed so much to so many."

Andre' Maurice wore a perplexed look on his face.

"While on that stage. I made a promise to America and to the world. I promised that I would rebuild the integrity of this nation one brick at a time. I made a promise that I would fulfill Dr. King's dream. The late great president, John Fitzgerald Kennedy once said," he held a ringless dark finger in the air, "'there are risks and costs to a program of action. But they are far less than the long-range risks and costs of comfortable inaction'. America votes and expects one man," he waved the finger he held in the air, "one man, to implement change when it takes a village to raise a child. We are all but Children of God. And it will take a village to raise this nation." He finger jabbed himself in the chest. "I'm the big brother that's going to help build up the village."

Andre' Maurice leaned forward in his chair. "Bishop Money, many are calling your fastidious recovery a miracle."

"The miracle is not in one man's awakening, the miracle will be in the reawakening of the spirit for which this great nation was founded on. A nation where the people are governed by a system that caters to and fully represents the poor, just as it does the rich. That will be the miracle," the bishop reiterated.

"Three years ago, you and your wife were shot, victims of a home invasion. You lived. She died. Five days ago, you were shot four times. You spent fourteen hours in surgery. Less than twelve hours after surgery, your heart stopped. You were pronounced dead. An hour later, for lack of a better phrase, you rose from the dead."

Bishop Money nodded his affirmation.

"People are coming from all over the world to see you. I'm going to give you three words. Tell us which best describes you."

Again, Bishop Money nodded.

"Messiah…. Prophet….Miracle…."

"None of the above." The bishop smiled. "Andre'," the bishop closed his eyes. A couple seconds passed before he reopened them. "You see, I'm a man. Simply, a man of God. My resurrection is proof that God not only exists but He is active. The best word that describes me is the word *tool*. That's what I am. That's who I am. A *tool*. Now that God has repaired His *tool*, it's up to His *tool* to repair the hearts, minds, and souls of men, so we can repair this nation and then the world. And as I said at the beginning of our interview, I made a promise. And while I lay bleeding on that stage, I prayed for God to let me live to make good on that promise. That promise is why I say, never have I owed so much to so many."

*****

"If I ever get my hands on you, I'll take mine out ya ass." Shabazz said to the TV that everyone's eyes were glued to. "Y'all know I hate the word nigga, but," Shabazz sat on the edge of the couch, "that's exactly what he is. Enough shit come out that nigga mouth to fertilize the Sahara desert."

"The worst part is, people not only believe him, they believe in him," Reverend Solomon One-Free said, standing next to the 55-inch flat panel TV, eating a chicken wing.

"He doin' too much." Shabazz shook his head. "Way too much. Ol' shade-tree jackleg, Jesse Jackson wanna-be, mini-me, tooty-fruity loose booty. Nigga make George Bush look like Ghandi."

"Samuel, baby, you okay?" Rhythm asked looking at the tears running down his face.

Samuel shook his head from left to right. "I just don't understand. My dad, my mom, my auntie, and so many have died because of him. How many have to die before he does. I just can't believe he lived. Sometimes…I don't know, I just," he paused like he was trying to find the right words. "Sometimes, I just feel like a coward."

"Samuel, you are not even close to being a coward," Solomon said. "You're a hero to so many inner city kids at Boy's and Girl's clubs all over the city. And that little girl. Sister Cheyenne's daughter, adores you."

"Rev., all that sounds good, but Dr. Jamison-Hayes is in jail for something I should have done long ago."

The reverend took a sip from his glass. "Romans 12:19, you know the part about Vengeance is mine, saith the lord. Well, in laymen's terms what God is saying is," the reverend turned and looked Samuel in his eyes, "that it is not our place to judge and exact revenge on others in return for wrongs they've committed against us. We are to trust that God will bring about His justice in the end; that's His job and—"

They smile in your face and all the time they wanna take your place; backstabbers. A verse from The O'jays seventies classic hit filled the room.

Shabazz jumped up from the couch. "That's my new doorbell ringtone."

Solomon was about to finish, when Moses, Solomon's younger brother and Rhythm's husband, cut in. "That's so true, but if memory serves me right, I think it's in Exodus where God said, if a man schemes and kills another man deliberately, take him away from My altar and put him to death."

Shabazz opened the door. For maybe the first time in his life, Shabazz was speechless.

"Damn, white boy. I know cat ain't got your tongue. I still got my clothes on," Cherry said, stepping forward and giving Shabazz a big hug.

Everyone was just as speechless as Shabazz had been. They stared in awe at the two women who stepped inside the small condo.

Tears welled up in Shabazz's eyes. He broke the embrace and grabbed the other woman's hand. "Before I went to prison, and read your story, I didn't realize that I had no respect for women. Bitch and whore were just words that I used in casual conversation when referring to sistas I either didn't care for, or ones I wanted to go up in. Your story made me dissect the black male mindset, and in retrospect I went on a cultural reading journey, only to discover the cause and effect of my mindset, and today, years after I read *Assata*, I drop Master G on brothas and sistas who casually disrespect the black queen with their negative dialect. It was your story, Queen, that hipped me to the scene, that Whitey used to keep us all green and with low self-esteem. So," he got on one knee, "it is my honor to kneel to you, my sista, my queen."

"If you don't get up off yo' damn knees, boy." Cherry playfully popped him upside his head.

"I've heard so much about you, Shabazz," the sixty-four-year-old reddish brown and gray speckled dreadheaded woman said, before looking up at the others, who were frozen where they sat and stood. "And all of you, it's like I already know you, and I am proud to be here. I never thought I'd see this country again, and quite honestly, I didn't care if I ever did, but you need my help."

Rhythm got up from the butter-beige chaise. "Ms. Shakur, I think I speak for all of us." Her mind went blank as she became an emotional rollercoaster. Tears streamed down her face.

Samuel didn't take his eyes off of the living legend as he silently walked over and stood in front of her. Assata Shakur took the young man in her arms. A minute later, Moses, Solomon, and Rhythm embraced the distinguished-looking woman.

"Can someone please help me up?" Shabazz asked aloud, still on his knees.

A half hour later, the four men in the apartment left to do some grocery shopping. It was decided that the men would shop and cook for the women.

Rhythm, Assata, and Cherry sat at Shabazz's small, round glass dinner table.

"Cherry, I didn't get word to you. I mean, I didn't send the message of Jordan's death for you to come back and risk your freedom and your life."

"I know you didn't. Cheyenne's my girl. I want to be there for her, and when I found out about her arrest, I knew I had to come."

"But—"

"But nothing." Cherry took Rhythm's hand in hers. "I'm not the same Cherry I was a year ago." She smiled and turned to Assata. "Thanks to Assata, I understand my purpose for being. You see," she turned back to Rhythm, "I am who I am because of my experiences and everyone that has crossed my path. Cheyenne was the only person who cared. I mean really cared for me back when I was her patient in the last nutsville mental institution that I was in. I'd never known the meaning of unconditional love before her. And the senator would've been dead long before now for what he let happen to me back in his crackhead days if Cheyenne hadn't taught me how to forgive."

Cherry turned back to Assata. "And this woman," she took Assata's hand in her free hand, "she made me fall in love with being a woman. A black woman."

"That's beautiful," Rhythm said. "But this is your freedom we're talking about. And yours, Ms. Shakur."

"Freedom, my child can only be truly achieved when the dome," she held a finger to her forehead, "is free." Assata smiled. "And that can't exist when the minds and souls of the masses of our people are blinded by the machinations of a system that has them subconsciously worshipping the dollar instead of God, and the God in them that they don't even know exists."

"But, what can you two do?" Rhythm asked. "You're risking your life just being here."

"Life," Assata began, "Rhythm, we are all living on borrowed time. I don't know when my time will be up, but as long as the clock continues to tick, I will continue fighting. And I may get killed in battle, but I would rather die with the dignity as the free black queen that I am, than die of old age not knowing that I lived my life as a slave to a system designed for me to push out as many dogs as my body will allow, than to give birth to black kings."

"Bottom line is," Cherry squeezed Rhythm's hand, "we here to get Cheyenne." Cherry said. "No way we gon' let her have that baby in jail."

"Baby?" Rhythm's eyes became golf balls. Images of that big bull woman and other guards beating Cheyenne played through Rhythm's mind like a 3D action movie.

"She didn't tell you she was pregnant?" Cherry remarked.

The words, *she's pregnant* paused the mental movie.

"I wasn't the biggest fan of Jordan's, but he was a good man, and she deserves, at the least to raise his child," Cherry said.

Rhythm was hurt. She couldn't believe Cheyenne hadn't told her. She had no doubt that Cherry was being truthful. "I'm going back to the A.D.A.'s office in the morning." She thought back to how the A.D.A.'s office looked. She thought back to the emotion in Tiffany Cole's voice. "I'll talk to the judge. I should be able to get Cheyenne a bond now that Terrell is alive."

Cherry and Assata just stared at Rhythm.

"What?"

"You don't really believe what you're sayin', girl." Cherry said. "That little booty-bandit monster, might as well be Jesus Christ. You know good and damn well, after all this publicity, them Flintstones ain't 'bout to give our girl no bond. And if they did, how long would it take?" Cherry shook her head from left to right. "Nah, girl. I know Cheyenne like I know myself, and after all she been through, she gotta be ten seconds from crazy, and one minute from suicide."

Rhythm thought back to the other day when she went to visit Cheyenne. Her friend was so out of it, she couldn't even begin to discuss the case. All she cared about was TJ being dead. Now that he was alive, she didn't want to think about what was going through Cheyenne's fragile mind." Rhythm shrugged her shoulders. "Cherry, I don't know what else to do."

"That's why we're here." Assata's brown eyes lit up like headlights in the middle of midnight nowhere.

Chapter 11

"*N*owhere and yet we're everywhere," the Tommy Lee Jones look alike said.

It was two in the morning. The man known simply as Franklin wore what seemed to be his signature uniform, a plain black suit and tie. He sat in Bishop Money's library, behind the Bishop's antique Louis XV hand carved wooden desk, with his legs crossed and one hand resting on his knee as he explained the facts to Bishop Money and Sinclair Charmaine.

"Sinclair," Franklin said, looking in the direction of the fifty-something ex-body builder and government operative, "from this day forward, she will be advising you on all matters."

Bishop Money looked over at the woman and back at Franklin. "What do you mean all matters?"

For the first time since they arrived at the Money estate, the woman got up from the barstool she sat on and made her presence felt. "Money," she said, taking a few steps until she stood in front of the bishop, "I will make sure you do nothing to jeopardize our plan at bringing you into power. In the past, you have," she paused trying to phrase her next statement as diplomatic as possible, "been involved with illegal and illicit activities that could undermine everything we are doing for you. We have to make sure that you don't—"

"Ho! Ho! Hold on." Bishop Money looked at Franklin's smug demeanor. "I'm a grown ass man. I don't need a guard dog. What I need is security. Y'all know so much about me, but you let that, that crazy woman attack me. I could've died."

"But you didn't," Franklin said. "That *crazy* woman shooting you is the best thing that ever happened to you. Look at what we were able to do. Your God had nothing to do with the miracle we created. And that miracle will help catapult you into the White House."

"First thing you need to do is provide me with round-the-clock security. Next, stop coming to my home without calling. And third," he pointed to Sinclair, "you can keep your guard dog and send me a real advisor."

The woman didn't move from in front of the Bishop.

He attempted to rise from his seat but the five-foot-seven inch black woman pushed him back into the brown leather office chair. She pointed a finger in his face. "You don't have to like me. But you will respect me. And you will do as I say. From this moment forward, you will not stick your little thing," she looked at the crotch area of the terrycloth robe he wore, "or your foul tongue in any woman. Provided you use a prophylactic, I might let you satisfy yourself inside me."

"Sinclair, right?" Bishop Money interrupted.

She nodded. "Yes."

He smiled. "If you, me and an HIV-infected rabid German shepherd where the last living creatures on God's green earth, and I was ordered by God himself to make a choice, copulate with you or the animal, I'd try my best to get that German shepherd pregnant."

"Suit yourself or shoot yourself. But until you do the latter or force my hand to do it for you, you will act like we are a couple, and before we win the democratic nomination next May, we will be married."

"Over my dead body."

"That can be arranged," she said.

"Sinclair, Terrell," Franklin interrupted. "Enough. Terrell, the men who I represent are willing to pay you an annual salary of five million and forgive your past indiscretions, along with making you the most powerful man in America. But you have to play the game by their rules."

Suddenly, Sinclair didn't seem all that bad. He studied her face and then her body. She wasn't ugly or fat, but she had to be the plainest looking black woman in America. Not that looks mattered to the Bishop, but the woman had to be around his age, which was twenty years too old. And worst of all, she was built like a wall.

"Do we understand each other?" Franklin asked, leaning forward, looking the Bishop in the eye.

"I think so," Bishop Money said, thinking of ways he could start using his new power and resources to help him get rid of the witch that shot him, Samuel Turner, and them damn One-Frees. "I just have one request at the moment."

"That is?" Franklin said.

"The late senator's wife. The woman who tried to take my life. She knows too much. So much, that she could destroy and undermine all of your, our efforts," he said.

"If Dr. Jamison-Hayes has an unfortunate fatal accident say, in the next twenty-four hours, you will follow Ms. Charmaine's instructions to the letter?"

"To the letter," the bishop replied, before extending his hand to Sinclair.

Sinclair gave Bishop Money a look that said it all. Having spent her life recognizing and cleaning up bullshit, she could identify it in all its forms. Without a doubt, Terrell Joseph Money was king of the beef eaters. Exactly who she'd spent her life fighting.

Sinclair Charmaine had come from a long line of patriotic black men who served America in every war from the Civil

War to the Iraq War. From as early as she could remember, she'd been in love with the red, white, and blue. Like a nun was married to the church, her only husband had been the military and the special op units she'd been assigned to over the last three and a half decades. And her children were the seeds of democracy that she had dedicated her life to fight for. And death, she would be more than honored to lay down her life for her country, just as she had done in the past. Even if it meant laying down with the enemy, or extinguishing out the life of the enemy, she had done whatever and would continue to do whoever she was asked to do in order to protect and further the interests of America.

She took the bishop's outstretched hand and squeezed. Ignoring the pain on his face, she kept the pressure on. "We can do this the impossible way, or my way. One way or the other we *will* do this." She smiled, relinquishing the deathhold she had on his hand. "You may wear the pants, Money, but I have the balls."

Chapter 12

"The balls of my feet are killing me," Babygirl said into the button-sized wireless microphone that was transmitting hers and the voices of Rhythm, Assata, and Cherry's over the walkie-talie airwaves. She hurried in her four-inch heels and skin tight gold lace mini skirt around to the hood of the black Chevy Suburban SUV.

"The target is two cars ahead of me. He's getting onto the I-285 interstate at Memorial Drive. You got about five minutes," Cherry said, as she followed the brown and yellow Dekalb County sheriff's car.

"I can't believe I'm out here at four in the morning, standing on the side of the road. Girl, It's freezing out here."

"Babygirl, it's supposed to be freezing. It's December. Besides, none of us can stop traffic like you can, girl."

"Pa-lease! Cherry, you got a butt you can balance a glass of water on. And Auntie, I see how men look at you when we together."

"I can't argue with facts," Rhythm joked into the mini-microphone attached to the hospital lab coat she wore while walking into a hospital linen closet. "But none of us can work it like you can, girl. Besides, your butter-gold smooth skin, shoulder length black hair, combined with that hourglass figure, is irresistible to men and you know it," Rhythm said.

Flashing blue lights broke up the women's conversation. The sheriff's patrol car pulled over to the side of the road. A minute later, Deputy Rodney Danielson tried to pull his pants up onto his waist, which would have been magic, because the man hadn't seen his waist in at least twenty years. "Hello there," the heavy set, forty-three-year-old deputy said, in his best Barry White voice.

Babygirl's head was under the hood. The mini she wore had ridden up to the indentation where her legs ended and her butt began. "Officer," she said, in a little girl's voice, "my engine won't start."

"Woman, you gon' catch pneumonia out here." The officer molested the young women with his eyes as he approached the front of the full sized SUV. "What seems to be the problem?"

"I don't know. It just cut off. I left Stroker's. I was angry. Nigga's was tippin simp money instead of pimp money. They wasn't even makin' it drizzle. I got two kids. I'm behind on my rent, and I'm about to be evicted if I don't come up with twenty more dollars by nine a.m., and now this." She poked her bottom lip out.

"Sooo, you dance?"

Nah, I'm an astronaut and this is the space shuttle, she wanted to say, but instead she smiled and said, "Yes, but I only do it to give my babies a better life than I had."

"Bubble gum drop, I'm not a mechanic, but," he rubbed her arm with his calloused beefy hands, "I can fix your biggest problem." He pulled out his wallet, took a twenty out, waved it in the cold air and smiled. "Maybe we can help each other out."

"I'm not that kinda girl, but you are a big cutie." She played with the badge on his chest, "And I do need the money, and we are on the side of a dark road, and I have all this room in back of my suburban."

He looked at his watch. He had fifteen minutes to relieve Johnson at the hospital. Common sense told him to call Johnson, have him cover for him for a few minutes, but the Johnson fighting to get free in his pants overruled common sense.

Babygirl opened the rear doors and got in first. "Uh-uh," she said.

"Don't worry. I always keep a Trojan on me," he said about to climb in.

"No, I meant your belt. I'm terrified of guns. Can you not bring your belt inside? Better yet, take off your pants and put them beside the rear wheel."

"I-I don't know."

She seductively crawled forward from the back of the vehicle. Now her mini had ridden all the way up her behind.

He'd never seen any woman as fine as the one that licked her strawberry lips in front of him. "I wanna ride your Trojan, daddy," she whispered.

For the second time in two minutes, common sense was thrown out the window, or better yet it was left beside the rear right wheel of the stolen black Chevrolet suburban.

As he was climbing into the rear of the SUV he felt a sting. "Ouch," he put a hand on his behind.

"Now, you honestly think my girl gon' let your big old, ugly, hairy black behind go up in her?" Cherry said.

"Big boy's already in la-la land," Babygirl said to Cherry while climbing over the seat. "I just knew we were busted when you pulled over. I can't believe he didn't here your tires crunching on the pavement.

"Girl," Cherry looked at the flabby fat officer sprawled out in back of the suburban, "Sleeping ugly's heartbeat was too loud for him to hear anything. He only had one thing on his mind," Cherry said, moving and bending his legs to fit all the way inside the suburban.

After they tied him up with duct tape, Babygirl and Cherry shut the rear hatch inside of the stolen SUV.

"Bagged and tagged," Cherry said into the microphone so Assata and Rhythm would know that everything was going as planned.

A minute later, Cherry jumped inside the sheriffs' vehicle. "Follow me," she said, leading Babygirl to a foreclosed house off the next exit that had a garage they could stash the patrol car and leave the SUV in.

Fourteen minutes, later. Babygirl and Cherry had walked back to the expressway and had gotten into the stolen Dodge Magnum that she had left parked on the side of the highway.

"Three-fifty-eight," Babygirl said.

*****

"Four-oh-four and thirty-one seconds." He studied the time while screwing the brushed nickel silencer onto the .22 magnum. He'd wait a few more minutes. He wanted to give the shift change time to take place. Baron Livingstone was the best of the best. He'd gotten his orders twelve hours ago, and already he'd studied every possible scenario. He even studied the hospital blueprints, planning as many alternate escape routes as possible. He'd been a special contractor for the US government for twenty years. His record was unheralded. Twenty-nine targets, fifty-three kills. The twenty-four untargeted kills, he and the government had chalked up to collateral damage. The hundred and fifty pound bookish-looking killer didn't care. A human life was no more valuable than any other creature that walked, slithered, or crawled the earth. He took out the picture of Dr. Cheyenne Jamison-Hayes one last time before dropping it in the bottle of acid in the passenger's seat of his unmarked Lincoln Navigator. Baron was a stickler for exactness. His whole life revolved around the ever-moving seconds hand. Again he looked at his watch.

*****

Assata looked at her watch. Everything had to be perfectly timed for this to work. Assata knew that better than anyone else as she got onto the elevator dressed as a decorated police officer. She went through her mental checklist. Deputy Danielson, taken care of. Check. Sign in at the jail. Check. Deputy Johnson, the officer standing guard over Cheyenne. Check. She had thought about wearing a disguise, but time was of the essence. Besides, no one had seen her in over thirty-years. The only pictures of her were on her website, and her facebook page that famous rappers Mos Def, and Talib Kweli had set up to garner support and teach the hip-hop community who she was and why she needed to be exonerated.

*****

I hope he ain't out in the car on that Facebook mess trying to trick somebody with them fake pictures of himself. I gotta trick for that fat, twinkie-eatin' bastard. Wait 'till I come in thirty minutes late tonight. Fat Krispy Kreme donut-eatin' walrus, trynna be slick and not answer his radio. I oughta report his—

Assata interrupted the deputy's thoughts. "Roland Johnson?" Assata said, standing in front of the chair the deputy sat in.

"Yeah?" he said with his head still down. Tired was an understatement. This was his third double in a week. He had four little girls and a wife that he had to buy presents for. Christmas was two weeks away and he was broke. His wife sill didn't know he'd lost their savings to a real estate con

69

man. The con man was floating in some sewer but that still didn't help him get his money back.

"Johnson?" she said much louder.

He looked up, for the first time seeing that he was in the presence of a superior officer. One he'd never seen or heard of. Instinctively, he jumped up from the metal folding chair next to the prisoner's hospital room door.

"What the hell are you doing? Or shall I say not doing?"

"Lieutenant, uhm." He blinked, bringing the name tag into focus. "Rickshaw. What are you...? What precinct...?

"Step inside," she said, leading him inside Cheyenne's hospital room, not even thinking about looking back at the elevator. The same elevator that Baron Livingstone was waiting for on the lobby level.

Before the elevator door closed, Deputy Johnson had inhaled the chemicals on the rag that Assata held over his mouth and nose. No struggle. The drugged rag worked instantly. It took Assata twenty-three seconds to drag the unconscious man into the hospital room bathroom.

Chapter 13

*P*op-tart opened up his fur coat, revealing the butt of the .45 he had in his pocket. "Nigga, what you *need* to do," he pointed at Shabazz, "is pop ya' collar, let the foot off the clutch, and hit the gas."

It was four in the morning, breath-freezing cold and Shabazz was outside wearing Timberland boots, and pajamas. He looked at the small cannon the king pen of Drummond Street had in his pocket. "Only thing I *need* to do is stay black and die. And why I gotta be a nigga?"

"What?" Pop-tart asked.

"You addressed me as nigga. Why I can't be a black man, a king, a brotha?"

Pop-tart turned and gave his boys a *what this nigga smoking look*. They shrugged indifference from the porch of the crack house a few doors down from Samuel's place.

"You done been called nigga so much, that's what you think you are. Now you out here actin' like a certified card carryin' nigga, killin your people faster than the slavemaster killed his slaves." He pointed a finger toward the young drug dealer. "Now I suggest you take your money, invest in some real estate, buy that crack house and rent it out. Do something with your life other than trying to break into the penitentiary and the graveyard."

Pop-tart put his hand on the gun. "If you don't get up outta here and take your white ass back home."

"You gon' what?" Shabazz patted his chest. "You gon' put a bullet in me? I'm s'possed to be scared? I'm supposed to cry? King, I was born to die. Look at me! My skin. Told my whole life by black and white, that it was my sin. White skin. Wit a soul black as coal. But yet I was invisible when I made them laugh and grin, All my life, like you, I thought I was playing to win, never thought I'd spend seven years in the pen. But that's when I learned what it was to be amongst real men. Nothin' to lose, everything to gain, they showed me love by putting me up on game. So pull out ya gat and bust a cap, cause I'm gon' die a free to be me, man, a black man that stood up and took a stand. Danced to my own beat, so kill me now or get off my street."

The seconds hand, the sands running down the center of the hourglass had never moved so slow as manchild and man locked eyes and saw through to each others souls. Only a sixty second infinite eternity passed before manchild conceded to man, breaking the stare.

Shabazz turned, leaving Pop tart and his crew mesmerized by the passion, bravery, and love that he conveyed through his words and his stance.

Shabazz had agreed to stay over at Samuel's while the girls executed their plan. He hated lying to the brothas, but he promised Rhythm. The only reason he was made privy to the plan was they needed him to get the stolen vehicles. Rhythm had convinced him that Rev and Moses would have fought against the timing of the plan. And Shabazz owed Rhythm. She almost single handedly took down Frank Lester, Stevie Brown and the St. Louis Black Mafia, saving his and Babygirl's life six years ago.

"Uncle Bazz?"

He jumped outta the kitchen chair and ran smack dab into a wall before falling on his -face. "Girl, you trynna' kill me?" He looked up at the pretty little heart-faced girl wearing her Princess and the Frog pajamas.

The moonlight coming in from the window over the kitchen sink cast an angelic-like glow in the room. The tears on Ariel's seven-year-old face looked like crystal raindrops in the moonlight glow.

"What's wrong, Princess?" he asked as he dropped to his knees.

She ran and hugged him. "Uncle Bazz, a long, long, long time ago, I wasn't listening on purpose, for real I wasn't, but I heard mommy on the phone. She said you could get anything for the low. Can you get anything for the high?" she asked.

He broke their embrace. "The high?"

She nodded.

"Help me up off my knees, princess and we'll see," he said crawling to a chair. After a minute of pushing and pulling, he was sitting in a kitchen chair, still in the dark. Samuel must be in a coma, he thought, thinking of the noise he'd made crashing into the wall and cold tile floor.

"Princess, what do you need?" he said, patting his lap.

She took her cue and put out her chubby little dark chocolate arms so Shabazz could put her on his lap. "I wanna go to the sky."

"The sky?"

She nodded. "On top of Stone Mountain. That is the highest place I know, and from there I can touch the sky."

"Why do you wanna touch the sky, Sweetie?"

She snuggled up on his knee. "Well, God's house is heaven, and heaven is in the sky. So, if I talk loud, than God will hear me. I'm only seven, and He can't ever hear me when I talk to him now 'cause grown-ups are taller, and they always askin' for stuff."

"God hears everything, Sweetie."

She shook her head. "Unh-unh, he didn't hear me when I asked him to send Uncle Jordan back. So, I got up and stood on my bed and asked him again, he still didn't hear me. So one night, when mommy was asleep, I climbed up on the countertop on the island in the kitchen and looked up to the ceiling and asked him to make mommy happy again. He didn't hear me then neither, so I know He'll hear me if you take me to the sky. Then I can make Him a deal."

"What kind of deal?"

"I'm going to see if He will trade me for my mommy, but he has to make her happy again." She shook her head. "Mommy has been so sad since Uncle Jordan moved to Heaven."

Chapter 14

*H*eaven or hell. He didn't believe either existed. If either did, he would soon send his target to one or the other. For the briefest of moments, the government's MVP of contract killers, eavesdropped. Listening for sounds and movements behind the hospital room door.

Assata shook Cheyenne. "Huh? What?" Cheyenne said groggily.

"This police get-up I have on is part of a plan to get you out of here."

Chyenne blinked Assata into focus. "Who. Who are—

"A friend." Assata looked at the door. "Can you walk?"

"Yes." She nodded.

Assata looked at her watch. "Come on, we have to move quietly and quickly."

"Huh?"

"Come on, child," Assata said half pulling Cheyenne out of the bed.

"Wait," Cheyenne said, pulling out the two IV's that were in her wrist and arm. "Okay."

Rhythm stood outside in the corridor, hoping Assata would be able to get Cheyenne out. That's when she noticed the deputy. Where had he come from? And why did he have his ear to Cheyenne's hospital room door? Something didn't feel right. Rhythm had seen enough. She took the gun out of her pants pocket and slipped it under a sheet as she wheeled the cart toward the room.

The doorknob slowly turned. After stepping one foot into the room, Baron Livingstone felt the needle but not the liquid being plunged into his neck. Assata quickly moved to grab the gun but the man collapsed before she could get her hands on it.

Rhythm came through the door with the laundry cart in front of her. She almost ran over the gun. "I knew something wasn't right," she said looking at the silencer attached to the hitman's gun.

"Time?" Assata whispered as she dragged the hitman into the bathroom with the real deputy.

"Not enough," Rhythm said. "Four-eighteen."

"TJ tried to have me killed," Cheyenne remarked.

"Get in, Girl," Rhythm said after tipping the laundry cart over. "I'll explain later."

Cheyenne opened her mouth to protest.

Assata pushed her into the cart. "We have less than two minutes before the P.A. comes in to take your vitals."

Dr. Cheyenne Jamison-Hayes laid in a ball at the bottom of the laundry cart, covered with clean bed sheets while being wheeled to freedom. She almost strained her jaw muscles smiling at the thought of having another chance. This time, not even a miracle would save him. If she had to go along for the ride, this time she'd make sure Bishop Money made an uninterrupted trip to hell.

*****

"Hell, if I will. This is my show." Bishop Money said. "I'll be damned to hell wearing gasoline draws before I forget about that bottom feeding bit—"

Sinclair held her index finger in the air. "I have to take this." She depressed a button on her ear piece. "Sinclair Charmaine." She smiled before opening the library double doors and stepping into the hallway.

It was five-thirty, Thursday morning. Bishop Money was tired, sleepy, and still sore from being shot a couple weeks earlier. He'd had less than three hours sleep, and his phone had been ringing more than a 911 operator's the forty-eight hours he'd been home from the hospital. He paced the hardwood library floor of his home, looking up from time to time at the wall-to-wall books encased inside the two-story walls. He'd played it ice cube-cool for the cameras and everyone that he came into contact with since the shooting, but he was more nervous than a cat in a room full of rocking chairs. Every out-of-place noise made his nerves scream.

"Money?" Sinclair said, walking back into the library.

"What?"

"Relax. Everything's under control," she said.

"Control? Is that what you call it? You come over to my house, waking me up at five something in the morning to tell me that- that- that psycho-psychiatrist heifer escaped." He threw his hands up. "I knew it. I knew it."

"You knew what?"

"If it can be muffed up, no one does it better than the U.S. government," the bishop replied.

"I told you that none of what we are doing is sanctioned by the U.S. government. We are a private—"

He extended his hand, palm up in a stopping gesture. "Save the lies for the cameras. All I know is that if you want something done right, do it your damn self."

"Just calm down, Money. We'll get her. I assure—"

"Assure. The ass-u-r, that's what I think about you, and the clowns that botched this up. You were supposed to off the woman, not let her walk out the damn hospital."

"We are doing everything we can—"

77

"Everything my ass." He stood in Sinclair's face. "We are doing everything we can," he mimicked. "You geniuses can't even find a bearded old man wearing a dress in the Afghan desert with a kidney machine strapped to his back."

"Now you listen here, Money," Sinclair began.

"No, you listen, woman. First, you will address me as Bishop Money, or TJ. Second, I understand the game, Babycakes." He nodded. "Trust me, I do." He smiled, trying to think of where he wanted to go with this. "You're working for some powerful people. I get that. They've spent a lot of money making the world believe I'd died and came back to life. They killed the president. I know if I don't play ball. I'm dead, but I also know that they need me. For whatever reason, they need Bishop TJ Money. Now if I am to fall into line and be their puppet, you," he rubbed a hand across the side of her face, "will be mine. God forbid they find out that you are incompetent and can't keep me under control."

She grabbed his wrist. "And what do you think will happen to you if I can't control you?"

"Listening is not a strong point of yours I see." He pulled a small gun out of his pocket and put it to her neck. Did you not here me just say that I knew if I didn't play ball. I'm dead? Considering all the money they've already spent to make me the most popular person on the planet, I'd say our fates would be similar if you failed."

She released his wrist.

He put the gun down to his side as he backed away. "Now, I am about to sit at my desk and map out a plan of action." He walked the few feet to his desk, unbuttoned his gray slacks, let them and his boxers drop to his knees. He extended a hand out. "Before you."

"Excuse me?"

"You're a slender women. In great shape. Strong grip. Let's see how strong your jaw muscles are," he said, gently rubbing the head of his penis.

She came forward. Her fists in a ball. "I don't like you. You don't like me. Fine, but you will not—"

"Leave out of this room with a frown on my face." He said before raising his arm. The cold steel barrel touched the middle of her forehead. He stuck his tongue out and licked her lips. "If I pull this trigger, you die. I call Frank, he comes, raises hell. I apologize. I assure him that it was an accident. He sends in a clean-up crew and somehow he sends me another Sinclair, hopefully, younger, good looking, with a body this time. But I am not going to pull this trigger. Do you know why?"

She didn't say a word.

He pulled the hammer back.

Still no comment.

"Okay, I'll tell you, before you do something stupid like trying to disarm me. I'm not going to pull this trigger because you are going to get on your knees like the obedient dog you are. Crawl your flat behind under my desk and service me and you will not stop until my cannon explodes."

She'd been in three wars. Helped topple three governments, but the wars, the espionage training, three decades in the military, nothing prepared her for this man. He was a new kind of evil. She could snap his neck almost as easy as breaking bread, but she was married to her country and if she had to degrade herself to this level, then that's a small price to pay for the overall good of America.

A half hour later, TJ pulled up everything on the web that he could find on Cheyenne's attorney. He pushed his chair back and grabbed Sinclair's head. "Babycakes, I think this just might work. You've found your calling, now start with my baby toe and use that mouth on the others," he said before letting her head go.

Sinclair's only relief was that Bishop Money couldn't see her tears.

For the next hour, he studied torcher techniques used throughout history to make people talk. As long as he was discreet and let Franklin know before anyone else discovered the bodies, he could torture and kill this Rhythm One-Free and anyone else that blocked him from getting to that witch doctor client of hers.

"Child," he shouted, pushing back from the desk. "Sinclair, I can't believe I forgot. The good doctor has a child."

Sinclair crawled out from up under the desk. "No." She shook her head. "I will have nothing to do with—"

"I didn't ask you." He smiled, before getting out of his chair and pulling his pants up. "Exodus 20:5. I, the LORD, your God, am a jealous God, punishing the children for the sin of the fathers to the third and fourth generation."

"You can't interpret that to mean—"

"I am the Lord's shepherd." Bishop Money threw a fist in the air. "Shepherding His sheep. And if I see a wolf threatening me, I will strike down that wolf and her offspring, for she will grow up to be a threat to His sheep and His shepherds."

"Dr. Jamison-Hayes' daughter is not an animal." Flustered, Sinclair said, "She's a child."

Chapter 15

" *My* child. I wanna see her." Cheyenne said as the four women sat in the den of Dr. Naison's summer home in the North Georgia Mountains.

Rhythm grabbed Cheyenne's left hand. "Ariel's fine, Sweetie. She's with Shabazz and Samuel." She pointed to where the master bedroom was. "You should get some rest."

"How can I?" She began to cry.

"Its gon' be okay, Girl," Cherry said, hugging Cheyenne.

"It won't be okay until TJ's six feet under." Cheyenne pulled back from Cherry's embrace. "He killed my husband." She stood up, "No, I have to..." She broke down crying. "Jordan is dead. Why? Why did you leave me Jordan? Why did you let him? What did he say to make you jump?"

Assata got up and went to Cheyenne. "Come on, baby." She put an arm around the crying woman. "Come on, baby," she said, leading the broken woman back into the master bedroom of the white, Fordham University, African-American studies professor's summer home.

Minutes later, Assata had Cheyenne undressed and into the queen-sized bed. She sat on the edge holding the troubled woman's hand. "I lost almost everything when I escaped from prison and fled to Cuba almost thirty-five years ago. At times

I didn't know if it was worth it. I wondered if I should have just given up. But I didn't. I knew that if I gave up, then the enemy would win. I never did what the government said I had. My only crime was intelligently fighting for the liberation of my people. The intelligence aspect is what made me the most dangerous woman in America in the mid seventies. And that same aspect is what divided the victims from the victors. But before our fight can even begin, we have to have an ideology and philosophy. No revolution has ever been successful without these."

"This isn't a revolution. I'm simply going to kill one man," Cheyenne said matter-of-factly.

Assata squeezed her hand. "Sweetie, when a man has killed, pillaged the minds of thousands, and committed other atrocities against a people, his people, and has not only gotten away with these monstrous acts, but has flourished in the community and has gained power over the people, he is not working alone. No man is an island. Maybe an active volcano," she smiled, "but not an island. What's been done with him at the helm is revolutionary. That is why we have to be revolutionary in formulating our ideology and philosophy as a preface, a foundation for the strategy we put together. You are too close to the problem. You have to know when to step forward and when to take a step back." She paused to let Cheyenne ponder her words. "That beautiful little girl of yours needs you now more than ever. So, you have to decide, is you killing this man worth sacrificing yours and your daughters future? Is it?"

"Yes, it is. How many mothers, daughters, sons, fathers, has he destroyed? Worst, how many more will he destroy?" Cheyenne asked.

"That's why I'm here. That's why Rhythm, Cherry, and Babygirl are here. I'm not risking my life just to free you." She held a hand to her chest. "The souls of hundreds, thousands of black folks that have died for freedom speak to

82

me through my actions. The blood of the slave today and yesterday runs through my veins. The American media labels me a terrorist, but the people who know me and have read my story call me a freedom fighter. And that I am. I'm here to emancipate the people who have been duped by Bishop Money. So give us a chance." She got up from the bed. "Now you get you some rest, let us plan." Assata left the room and closed the door.

"How is she?" Cherry asked as Assata sat down at the kitchen table with Rhythm, Cherry and Babygirl.

"She's angry, she's scared, somewhat despondent."

"I'd be in a nuthouse." Rhythm looked at Cherry. "I'm sorry, I didn't mean—"

"Yes, you did. And I was in one for six years, and I'd be back, too if I went through what she has over the last few weeks. That nigga think he God."

"Especially after his recovery," Rhythm chimed in.

"God doesn't bleed." Assata looked at the others before scooting her chair back. "We have a long road ahead of us ladies. And after yesterday's and this morning's events, we all need to rest. There is no telling the next time we will get to sleep." Assata looked at her watch. "It's nine-twenty a.m. At five, we'll put together an ideology.and begin piecing together a plan."

Chapter 16

The planning proved to be the easy part. The act of carrying it out seemed impossible. Bishop Money sat in the dressing room behind the set, talking with his closest friend Bishop Clarence Wendell Wiley.

"I'm confused," Bishop Money said. "It took me what, three days to plan and trick a U.S. senator into taking his own life. It took two days to plan and help get rid of your ex. It's been three weeks. We're in a whole other year."

"TJ, it's not that simple. It took me a week to find out where the girl was."

"Why didn't you tell me?"

"Tell you what?" Bishop Wiley asked.

"Where Osama Bin Laden is." Bishop Money just stared at the man he put into power leading the newest and second largest One World Faith church.

"Osama?"

"The girl, idiot. The damn child of the witch that shot me. Why didn't you tell me you knew where she was?"

Knock! Knock! "I'll be back to get you in fifteen minutes Bishop Money," the voice outside the dressing room door, said.

"I'll be ready." Bishop Money turned his attention back to C. Wendell.

"You said you didn't want to hear from me until I had the girl in my possession."

"I don't care what I said. You know me. You know how I work. And you know how much pressure I'm under. I've done every news show but Oprah over the last thirty days. I've got armed babysitters I can't even see, watching my every move. And that's not including Sinclair."

The chubby, forty-year-old Bishop Wiley rubbed his goatee while studying his friend and mentor. "TJ, we've been close for seven years. And we've been friends twice as long. I've followed you through clean and murky waters, and you know I will do whatever you ask—"

"C. Wendell, are you going somewhere with this? If so, spit it out. I have to go on the set in a few."

"Something's up. I can feel it. The security, your overnight super stardom."

Knock! Knock! "Bishop Money?" The voice called out.

"One second," Bishop Money answered. "C. Wendell, something is up. And it's big. Watch the show. It will all be revealed, and you just continue being loyal and you will be rewarded beyond your wildest dreams. If it weren't for what I am about to do, I would handle the witch doctor and her bastard child myself." Bishop Money and Bishop Wiley walked to the dressing room door. "Where is the little girl anyway?"

"On the Westside, with Samuel Turner."

"Sam Turner?" Bishop Money shouted before punching the wall. "This is the last time, you hear me C. Wendell?"

Bishop Wiley nodded his head up and down, not knowing why.

"The last time that boy is going to get in my way."

"Should I hire—"

"Get the girl, CW. And I mean get her yesterday. I took care of Sam's daddy, I'll take care of the son."

*****

"Son, what it do?" Pop Tart stood in the dark, outside the corner store, givin' dap to Samuel.

"You tell me, Soldier."

He gestured Samuel to follow him through an alley behind the variety corner store in the hood. "Peep game," the young hustler said pulling out a handful of five-by-seven color photos. "Know any of these L sevens?"

Samuel looked through the group of pictures. He shook his head. "Never seen 'em."

"They damn sho' seen you. They been eye jackin' and ear hustling you and that crazy white boy." Pop Tart paused. Looked around.

"What's up?" Samuel asked.

"Thought I heard movement. I can't be caught slippin'. Since I done took a break from the dope game, it seems every Jack and Jill wanna test my gangsta." He opened his coat, revealing the handle of a glock in each pocket. "Playa, it's the wild, wild west out here, and I'm the black Jesse James. Nah, I better rephrase that, your man is Jesse James. I still can't believe the way he stepped to me and mines last month. That was some real cowboy courageous shit. Say, Playa, what's white boy's story anyway?" Pop Tart asked.

"Shabazz's mother was white but black blood flowed through her veins. Don't ask me why but she hated her blackness so much that she lived as a white woman until her husband, Shabazz's father, a white Klan leader discovered that she was black. Then, he tortured and killed her in front of Shabazz, who would have been next, but he escaped and ended up on the black side of Jackson Mississippi and was raised by a black woman and her militant drug addicted, drug-dealing son in the seventies, early eighties."

"Real talk," Pop Tart interrupted.

"Real talk." Samuel put the photos back in the manila envelope and slipped them inside his North face bomber jacket. "Only reason I'm telling you this is because Shabazz thinks you have promise."

"What do you think?" Pop Tart asked.

"I wouldn't be here in this alley if I didn't agree." Samuel smiled.

Moments later, the two parted and Samuel walked the two blocks to his house.

He kicked the snow off before taking off his boots and leaving them at the door. "Your man came through," Samuel said, holding up the manila envelope.

"Didn't I tell you he would? I knew that king was somethin' special the night I flipped the script on him." Shabazz didn't look up as he integrated the bug with the module hooked up to the laptop next to him.

Shabazz and Samuel had been pre-recording conversations and playing them back for whoever was bugging Samuel's home and his car since Pop Tart discovered the surveillance.

"You think you were being watched?" Moses turned his head toward Samuel.

"No question, but at ten o'clock at night with heavy snowfall in a dark alley, there's no way they could see much," Samuel replied while walking into the den and dropping the pictures and the license plate numbers on the coffee table.

"Now we can find out exactly who's had you under surveillance. I wanna meet this Pop Tart," Moses said. "If it weren't for him, we might still not know you were being watched." Moses leaned forward and picked up the picture closest to where he sat on the couch.

"We know it's either the Man or TJ," Shabazz said.

"Speak of the devil," Moses said, pointing the remote at the TV.

*****

"Bishop Money, this past November we lost President Obama. Many Americans feel that we have lost our way. Some even feel that President Obama didn't die of an aneurysm but was murdered."

"David, I am a black man."

"Noooo." Letterman leaned forward.

"I'm afraid it's true." The studio audience broke out in laughter. "Seriously," Bishop Money crossed his legs, "America has its flaws. That I can't deny. African Americans in this country have been persecuted since the first slave ship landed in the Americas. But to insinuate that in 2012, there's some type of conspiracy, that anyone could mastermind a cover-up assassination of a U.S. president, is absurd. President Obama was a great man, loved by white, yellow, and brown people from all walks of life, on all parts of the globe. But he was a man. No one knows why anyone that dies of natural causes at such a young age is called home to glory. But called they are. It's up to us, the living, to keep the dream of change alive, as President Biden is doing."

"What about the reparations bill. Do you want it to pass?" David asked.

"If the people want it, then I want it. I think it's a very important piece of legislation, but my immediate concern is for the fourteen U.N. dignitary families that have been kidnapped."

"And if we are to believe the video that has gone viral all over the web, than Al Qaeda has killed The former U.N. Secretary-General's son." David Letterman looked out at the teleprompter.

"I don't deny the reports, but I can't believe that these people cut the head off of Kojo Annan."

"Why don—"

"That's why I'm flying out tomorrow morning with the blessing of President Biden to the Afghan desert, where I will be picked up and taken to where the hostages are."

First shock, then the studio audience gave Bishop Money a standing ovation. A minute passed before the studio audience took their seats.

"I applaud you as the rest of our viewing audience is probably doing, but don't you think you're over your head? Aren't you afraid for your life?"

"I'm definitely over my head. I don't know the first thing about hostage negotiating. But, I do know God. And nothing is above Him or below Him. I can't say what Al Qaeda believes, but I do know what they believe in." He held a finger out to the audience. "One God. They believe that they are killing and being killed in their God's service. I will gladly die in the service of God. So, that alone gives us some common ground."

"You really think you can reason with terrorists?"

"We'll soon find out."

Chapter 17

"Find out what?" Cheyenne stood up from the table. "I really appreciate everything you've done, but that midget-madman is becoming more popular by the minute. We know who's been spying on Samuel. We get to C. Wendell and we get to TJ."

"Cheyenne, we don't know who's behind TJ," Cherry said.

"I don't care if President Biden is behind that devil."

"You need to care," Rhythm chimed in. "TJ's not smart enough, and doesn't have the power to rise on the world stage like he's done without a lot of money and political influence behind him. Solomon and the Clintons are good friends. Solomon's spending a lot of time with Bill in DC in hopes that he'll learn something useful. Shabazz and Samuel have their street soldiers watching the watchers. And Moses is in Haiti helping with the One-Free Heritage school building projects, but when he gets back in the states next week he'll be able to help."

"That's wonderful, but I still don't see why we can't act on what we know now. I hate TJ and everything and everyone involved with him," Cheyenne said.

Assata reached over and patted Cheyenne's hand. "Hate is a cancer that corrodes rational thought and eats away at the soul of man or woman. Hate can't drive out evil." She smiled, "Only love can, and child, you have to learn to love again, before that hate eats you alive."

"But—"

"I don't hate the cops that beat and abused me," Assata explained. "I don't hate the system that caged me. I don't hate the government that placed a million dollar bounty on my head. I don't even hate the mercenaries that came to Cuba in hopes of collecting that bounty. When they were dealt with, I made sure their bodies were sent back to their families. I fight out of love." She paused in hopes that her words would get through to Cheyenne. "I'm a hopeless romantic, in love with people working as one unit for the common good of mankind. I'm in love with the freedom of being. I'm in love with the culture of my ancestors. That's what I fight for. I have never fought in anger or killed a man out of anger."

"Dr. Naison just sent me a text," Rhythm said. "He wants us to go onto his computer and log in to Fordham University's secure intranet server.

"How does he know about *us*?" Cherry asked.

"I told him last week when I flew up to New York. Don't trip, if we couldn't trust him we'd all be in jail," Rhythm said. "After all, we've been at his cabin for almost a month."

"You know how much luck I haven't had trusting men. And I never met a white man that I didn't want to castrate," Cherry said.

"Mark Naison is the whitest black man you will ever meet. The man has dedicated his life to raising awareness of self in the African-American community. He gets it. He knows more about black folk than most scholars in academia. He's taught African-American studies for over forty years. As socio-politically intelligent as he is, and with his nationalist and revolutionary efforts, the man would have been dead long ago if he had dark skin. Now, come on." Rhythm led the way to the walk-in closet-turned-office in the master bedroom of the mountain cabin.

"You all go on. I have to pee," Cheyenne said. "I'll be in in a few.

After logging in as instructed, a middle-aged white man with salt and pepper hair and a salt and pepper goatee appeared on the screen. "Rhythm?"

"Yes, Mark I'm here."

"Were you able to bring the lawn chairs in?" he asked.

"Lawn chairs?" Cherry said.

Rhythm hit the mute key on the computer. "That's our code for everyone being here. He can't see us."

Cherry nodded as she stared back at the concerned looking man sitting in a cluttered office.

"It wasn't easy." She looked at Cherry. "But I brought them in."

Cherry playfully pinched Rhythm.

"I hope you're sitting down for this." Dr. Naison exhaled. "Less than three hour ago, Bishop Money walked out of an undisclosed location in the Afghani mountains safely, with all fourteen of the hostages."

"Fourteen? I thought Kojo Annan was beheaded," Assata said.

"You and everyone else," Dr. Naison shot back. "News networks from Arkansas to Australia were showing live broadcasts of Bishop TJ Money holding Kojo Annan's hand in the air along with the other hostages."

"Wow. Wow," Assata said.

Dr. Naison nodded, waited for everything he'd just said to register in the minds of the ladies that he was addressing.

"TJ's comment on Letterman." Rhythm nodded.

"Yes. Less than two weeks ago on 'The David Letterman Show' Bishop Money said that he didn't believe that the video footage of Kofi Annan's son being decapitated was authentic. And his comment stating that he didn't believe a monotheistic people would chop the head off of the son of the Nobel Peace prize winning former UN Secretary-General was used by journalists all over America to discredit the Bishop," Dr. Naison said.

"And now. He's about to be the most popular man in America," Rhythm said.

"The planet," Assata said.

"You got to be kidding me?" Babygirl spoke for the first time.

"I wish I was." Assata turned to her.

"How did he… What were the terms… I mean, I'm happy for the hostages and their families, but this is just too much. I just knew him going over there... I didn't believe he was really going… The mans a coward…" Cherry said.

"I'm afraid it's only the beginning. I didn't say this, but there's speculation that the kidnappings, the hostage crisis, and the release were all staged." Dr. Naison said.

"By who?" Rhythm asked.

Cherry and Assata shared a look. A moment of clarity.

"That, I don't know." Dr. Naison said. "Remember, Rhythm, this is all speculation."

"Now, things are beginning to make sense," Assata whispered.

"Thanks, Mark, for everything."

"Please." He waved her thanks away. "You know how I get down. As some of my younger urban African-American students say. 'I just look like this'."

The women sat in the small office in stunned silence after logging off.

Babygirl was the first to speak. "What did you mean by things are beginning to make sense?" she asked Assata.

"The first Black president, arguably the healthiest president we've had, dies of natural causes on the same day Cheyenne's husband, a Junior Senator, allegedly jumps out of a nineteen story office window. Days later, TJ's shot. An hour after he's pronounced dead, he wakes up. Less than seventy two hours after that, he's doing *60 Minutes* from his hospital room, and within six weeks, he's the most popular person on the planet. And now, he single handedly, armed with nothing but a red letter chain reference bible, gets dropped off in the Afghani desert and rescues fourteen hostages. Only one thing comes to mind." Assata took a deep breath. "Cointelpro, the Counter Intelligence Protection Agency."

"That was dismantled forty years ago," Cherry said.

"Yep, but trust, there'll always be paramilitary intelligence agencies funded by government and private corporations to keep government moving in the direction that the dollarcrats want it to go in. America has never been a democracy. Read the ambiguous language used in the preamble to the constitution. America has always been for the rich, slave holders. Or better stated, mind holders. White, yellow, and brown. This Bishop Money thing is much bigger than I ever suspected. What I don't understand is, why him?" Assata looked around the small office. "Where's Cheyenne?"

"Last thing I remember is her saying that she had to use the restroom," Rhythm said.

Cherry got up, left the room and looked at the open master bathroom door, before calling out. "Chey?"

The ladies looked in every room.

Rhythm pulled the blinds back and peeped out the bedroom window facing the covered parking pad. "Shit! My truck is gone."

Chapter 18

*W*anda Wiley hadn't been loved since her grandmother had stabbed her only son, Wendell to death when she was eleven, in 1938, Gafney, South Carolina. Wanda had never known her mother or father, having been abandoned the day after she was born naked on the dirt floor of her grandmother's shack. Despite being taken in, loved and raised by her always-working, sharecropping grandmother, Wanda never forgave the woman, never visited her in prison, and even lied to the authorities, denying the sexual relationship her and her grandmother's son had been having since as long as her then-eleven-year-old mind could recall.

After her grandmother went to prison, an older couple, friends of her grandmother, had taken Wanda in their home. Leroy and Calcutta Templeton were everyday Christians. In church, every day there was something going on. Wanda didn't like Leroy, because he not only turned the pre-teen away when she made advances toward him, but he tried to beat the whorishness out of her.

By the age of seventeen, Wanda had dropped out of school and was living with any man of any age that let her in their homes and most importantly, into their pants.

Over the years, in and around the small town of Gaffney, she became known as good-time Wanda. She gave the local prostitutes a bad name, always giving it up for nothing more than a little conversation. All she wanted was to be loved. She'd always thought that love was synonymous with sex. Although she'd been treated for every STD and infection known to man, she'd never been pregnant, until she was forty-two in 1971. She had no idea who the father was and could care less. She'd never known a man intimately again, after her Clarence Wendell Wiley was born.

They were so poor, they couldn't afford dirt. If it weren't for welfare, there is no telling how they would have survived in the seventies and early eighties. Wanda was a healthy woman and had been a hard-working city employee until she had become pregnant. She quit her good city job to raise her son.

C. Wendell was barely a year old when Wanda heard him singing along with the cast of *The Flip Wilson Show*. At three, he could read the paper. Around other kids, he was quite stand-offish. The kids teased him at school, calling him fat-fat, dirt-dob, and goody-good. Fat-fat because he was a chubby kid, dirt-dob because he always looked dirty, and goody good, because all his clothes were either hand me downs, or from the Goodwill.

C. Wendell's childhood was far from normal. He became infatuated with having money at an early age. Whenever he had candy money, kids liked him. At ten, he began working as a farm hand after school. He'd do anything, work any job to get money so the kids at school and in the neighborhood would like him.

It was Easter Sunday, April 8, 1981. That was the day eleven-year-old C. Wendell laid eyes on his destiny. The man got out of a diamond white Cadillac that seemed to stretch a city block. White boots, white pants, white bell bottom slacks, white belt, with a chrome belt buckle with the letters C C engraved in diamonds, white shirt, white tie, knee-length, white three and a quarter suit jacket, white ankle length fur coat, and a white Stetson, with a long white quill that covered his shoulder-length fried and dyed midnight-black straight hair. The man was so dark, he made night seem like day.

The man's teeth were as white as his clothes glistening in the Easter Sunday sun. The Reverend Clipper Calhoun had come all the way from Atlanta to preach this particular Easter Sunday morning. For two hours, the man screamed, hollered and did the James Brown up and down the pulpit. You would have thought God's last name was Humph, because every other sentence began or ended with the words, God Humph. The eleven-year-old child studied the man's movements and gestures. He couldn't study the words, because the man talked so fast and so incoherent, no one knew what he was saying, except for the God Humph parts of his sermon.

Preachers rode around in Cadillacs, made lots of money, and everyone loved them. That's everything young C. Wendell wanted. So, for the next thirty years, he transformed himself into the image of that visiting pastor he'd seen only one time. C. Wendell didn't care about anything but becoming that superman he'd seen on that pulpit when he was a child. And now, at the age of forty-one, he was that man, thanks to his closest and only friend and mentor, Bishop TJ Money.

It was Saturday, January 15. TJ's plane wasn't due to touch down for another five hours, at a quarter after one. The television showed satellite views of the Air Force One jet that TJ was on as it streamed through the sky over the Atlantic.

Other pictures showed the crowd that had already begun to gather at Dobbins Air Force Base, in anticipation of his arrival. News stations were still broadcasting the tearful family reunions between the hostages and their U.N. dignitary families.

Bishop Wiley had mixed emotions about seeing TJ. On one hand, he wanted to share the Bishop's spotlight, knowing that if he stayed in the good graces of TJ, he could ride the man's coat tail into the stratosphere, and on the other hand, he hadn't gotten Dr. Jamison-Hayes's little girl yet. And he'd rather suffer the wrath of God than face the wrath of Bishop Money.

Bishop Wiley just needed a few more days. He laid in bed naked, holding his new mail order teenage blow-up doll, while contemplating exactly what to say to Bishop Money when the front gate bell rang.

He reached over to his nightstand, grabbed the TV's remote and changed it to Channel 3. A nervous looking white kid popped up on the screen carrying a bunch of balloons, some flowers, and a rectangular watch-sized box with a red bow on it.

"Delivery for Clarence Wiley," the young delivery boy said.

"Use the balloon string to tie the stem of the…" The large wrought iron double gates opened inward. "Better yet come on up. I'll be down in a minute," Bishop Wiley said, shutting off the TV, before getting out of the California king-sized canopy bed and slipping into his wool slippers and grabbing his robe on the back of the bedroom door. He turned his head back toward the bed. "I'll be back in a few, sweetie. Now, don't go getting jealous, my darling," he said to the wide-eyed life-sized doll, before blowing a kiss its way.

Moments later, he was down the stainless steel spiral stairs. He could see the delivery boy's silhouette through the oval stained glass of the huge Oakwood front door. After pushing a few keys on the alarm pad, and unbolting all six bolts on the huge two hundred-pound door, Bishop Wiley turned the knob.

While the door opened, the young boy dropped everything, jumped off the slate stairs, and hurdled the Koi fish pond before doing an academy Award-winning Ussain Bolt Olympic dash.

Cheyenne wore a death smile on her face as she entered.

The first thing the bishop noticed was that she had no gun, no knife, no weapons in sight.

Chapter 19

" *J*nsight asshole." The man hit Pop Tart in the knees with the rusty tow chain. "That's all we want."

Pop Tart dropped to the ground, where his little brother laid, staring back at him with lifeless eyes. Pop Tart spit a glob of blood in the direction of his captors. "I ain't tellin' you shit, you Uncle Tom suit-wearin' faggot."

"What are you waiting for? Shoot the drug dealing punk, Seymour," the other man said, while his partner beat the young man. "It stinks in here. This old house gives me the willies."

"Jason," The ape-sized man looked to his partner. "man up soldier."

"Man up?" Jason rolled his eyes, put one hand on his hip and waved the silenced semi automatic at Seymour. "That's your job."

"Well, let me do my job."

Pop Tart coughed. "I can't believe I'm gon' die at the hands of two down low, low down homo thugs."

Seymour undid the belt on his black slacks. "How long have your guys been watching us?" He unbuttoned and unzipped his pants. "What all do you know?" His pants dropped to his knees.

Too angry to be scared, and in too much pain too care. Pop Tart laughed, while trying to break the gray duct tape that had his hands concealed behind his back. Pop Tart was sweating bricks, despite being bare chested in the freezing abandoned house in the middle of nowhere. "Punk ass nigga, you bet' not even think about it."

"Seymour?" Jason shouted. "What are you doing?"

Seymour turned to Jason. "If this punk don't open his pie hole, I'll open up another hole."

Pop Tart looked down again at his younger brother. He hadn't prayed in what seemed like forever, but prayer was all he had now. So he prayed for his brother's soul and for God to send Shabazz and his soldiers before it was too late.

*****

"It's too late." The man-child shook his head. "Too much time done already passed."

"Ho-hold up king, slow ya roll, and give it to me slow," Shabazz said standing in front of the hooded young soldier that barged into his church office.

"Peep game." Extra tapped Shabazz on the shoulder. "A little shawty from around the way put D'bo, one of Pop Tarts ex-communicated soldiers up on some treachery. First, we thought playa was on some fifty-four fake out, brownie point re-instatement move. But we called PT eight times, and his joint kept going straight to voice mail. So we went and snatched up the shawty that put D'bo up on game. We put the full court press down on both of 'em, and they both stood the test of crime."

Shabazz was afraid to ask what the test of crime consisted of. "Hit me in the head, king, 'cause I still ain't graspin' the game you trynna put me up on."

"A couple bulls in suits, ridin' low and slow in a meat van snatched PT and his little bruh, Anwar."

"Why didn't you call me?" Shabazz asked, walking to his cluttered desk.

"Playa, the whole click been blowin' up your phone for the last three hours."

"My phone didn't," he just remembered, "my bad, my phone don't get no reception back here. And I been here all mornin'," he said, putting on his coat.

"And ya man, Sam Turner, he MIA, too."

"Sam is spendin' the weekend down at the crypt with some hard heads from the One-Free Boys and Girls clubs," Shabazz explained.

"Parents let him take they kids down to the crypt? Extra asked. "Them some hard core young juvey killas locked up down there."

"Sam is trying to save them and the young heads he took down there. They using *The Survival Bible* to teach them the tricks and traps they fell or, are falling victim, to."

Extra nodded. "Yo that's pimpin'. I hope them young heads 'preciate Sam's gangsta." They walked out of the church. Extra tapped Shabazz on the shoulder. "You talkin' bout The *Survival Bible,* the book by that OG, what's his name?"

"Jihad."

"Yeah, OG wrote that joint, *MVP*. That's the first book I ever read. That joint was certified."

"True 'dat," Shabazz said pulling out his iPhone. "I'm gon' send out an APB to the local One-Free fam. We gon' find Pop Tart."

"No disrespect, Bazz, but what are church folk gon' do? I mean for real, for real. We need soldiers."

Shabazz finished sending a mass text. The two stood out in the sunny cold weather, coated, gloved and booted. "The best soldiers, the most loyal and gangsta are soldiers in God's army. When it's time to pray, we pray. When it's time to fight, we fight."

"That don't sound like no church folk I know," Extra said.

"The One-Free nation is a family that sticks together. Truth binds us. In our churches, we forge African and African-American culture with religion. We study and teach history, the bible, Quran, the ancient African texts, and men and women from Imhotep, Malcolm X, Dr. King, to Geronimo Pratt. We don't have preachers, we have truth teachers, and our truth teachers tie everything back to God and His purpose for us."

"That's sea deep, twenty-thousand leagues below my comprehension," the young man said. "I ain't never been one for sittin' up in a building talkin' bout we shall overcome, and then go home to the same ol', same ol'. Preacher blingin' harder than Lil' Wayne, pimpin' stronger than Sir Charles, and Bishop Don Juan ever did."

"I can dig it," Bazz said. "Where you parked?"

"Where I stand. I'm on Tom and Jerry," Extra said, pointing to his black polo boots.

"Come on, I'm over there," he said, pointing to the church parking lot at his six-year-old money green Denali, sittin' on twenty-twos.

"So, what's the plan?" Extra asked, getting into the SUV.

"You get on the horn, have your soldiers scour the city and keep their ears open." He held his iPhone out in front of Extra's face. "How many texts you see right now?"

"Damn. Twenty-six, seven, eight."

"This is how the One-Free family gets down."

"You just sent out the text."

"Our response time is quicker than the Po-Po at an Al-Qaeda rally in front of the White House." Shabazz looked at Extra. "I sent out Pop Tart's picture and where he was last spotted. My fam will holla back if they need any more info. Other than that, they won't get at me until something pops up. Right now, we gon' go see the head of the snake."

Chapter 20

" *H*ead of the snake." She looked the big belly, ashy-legged man up and down. "Maybe the underbelly, but you too damn dumb to be the head," Dr. Jamison-Hayes said, walking through the door and past Bishop Wiley.

"You really must be some kind of crazy, barging into my home," he said, pressing the silent panic button on the alarm pad, while admiring her pretty little butt and big legs in the black tights she wore. He'd often drooled over the video he doctored to make it look as if she where having sex with TJ. The same one TJ showed her late senator husband before he jumped to his death. "You know this is trespassing. By law, I have every right to shoot you."

She turned around, unbuttoned the men's black petticoat she had taken from Dr. Naison's closet. "What's wrong with your trigger finger? You got arthritis?"

"Get out!" He pointed to the door.

"Put me out, fat boy."

He pointed a finger at her. "I'm warning you."

"Like you warned Monica before you killed her?" she said, speaking of his ex-wife and her old friend.

"Her death was ruled a suicide." He smiled.

"So was my husband's." She took a step toward the five-foot-seven chubby man. "But we both know they were murdered." Seeing that he had no weapons, she let her coat drop to the black marble floor next to the stainless steel spiral staircase.

"If I wasn't a man of God…"

"You'd what? What would you do, Porky?" She took another step, closing the distance between them. "I'll tell you what you'd do. Nothing. Your only power is in your lips."

He stepped to the door and opened it wider. "This the last time I'm going to tell you to leave my house and get off of my property."

She took another step. "How many last times are you going to give me?" She watched his chest swell as his breathing became more erratic. "There are two ways I will leave. One is, you tell me how TJ got my husband to jump out that window."

"And why would I do that?"

She pointed. "So he did have something to do with my husband's death?"

"You're insane."

"No, I'm pressed for time. You gon' tell me what I need to know or am I gon' have to beat it out of you?"

He opened his robe and grabbed his semi-hard erection. "Beat this, bit—"

She lurched forward. Her movements were so sudden, he didn't have time to act. He screamed as a hundred fingernails dug into his face. He tried to grab her arms but she was too fast. Too erratic. And when he did get an arm, she did a Mike Tyson, biting off part of his ear.

Bishop Wiley's screams sounded like a high-pitched siren. He rolled himself into a ball. She still didn't let up, pulling clumps of hair out of his head, between elbows to the head.

A round in boxing lasted three minutes. It had only taken two minutes for Dr. Jamison-Hayes to knock the man that lay before her out. She got up and looked down at the bloody heap. Her hands trembled. She couldn't believe that she was capable of such brutality. A beeping noise brought her out of her daze. She turned her head toward the source of the noise. The alarm pads blinking red emergency light was flashing. She looked out the door and down at the street. No police. An SUV was pulling in front of Rhythm's Range Rover. It looked like Shabazz's. She couldn't be sure. The light snow fall and the distance impaired her vision.

*****

Shabazz's brow furrowed with worry. *What was Rhythm doing here?* he wondered, as he threw the gear shift in park, right in front of Rhythm's platinum Range Rover. "Let's roll, King," Shabazz said, jumping out of his SUV and running in the snow up to where the huge monogrammed gates came together. Shabazz squeezed his tall slim frame through the opening, Extra was right behind him.

"Damn," Extra said, admiring the hilly landscape while running up the hill. "Ol' boy pimpin' the God game hard."

"You don't know the half," Shabazz said, climbing the cobblestone stairs of the huge modernized nineteenth century Victorian home.

"Somebody already beat us to the punch," Extra said, looking at Bishop Wiley's lifeless body through the open door.

"You ain't got nothing on you, do you?" Shabazz asked as the silent roar of distant sirens became louder.

"Nah, I'm good."

"No warrants?" Shabazz asked.

The young man shrugged his shoulders. "Not that I know of."

"I damn sure hope he ain't dead. I bet my life this fool know who took Pop Tart," Shabazz said, kneeling down to check for a pulse.

"Police, don't move!"

Out of instinct, Extra put his hands up, right as one of the officers landed a blow to his head. Extra collapsed to the ground.

Shabazz stood up. "Hillbilly racist honky." He looked at the other cop that had his gun drawn. "And you boot-lickin' Uncle Tom house negro. He's only sixt—"

Shabazz blacked out from the first blow to his head.

Chapter 21

"*G*et it through your head, we run the show," the man's voiced boomed over the satellite phone.

Bishop Money got up from his seat and walked to the back of the plane, away from Sinclair and the two speech writers. He'd complained and balked about reading the prepared document since being handed the speech upon setting foot on the presidential Air Force One jet back in Afghanistan.

"You may be an expert on the intricacies of government, but I know how to capture the heart and minds of *my* people, and this speech is too long, too scripted, and it's just not me," the Bishop said into the big black military satellite phone.

"It's just not me." The man on the other end mimicked the bishop. "*Your* people. I could give a rat's ass about *your* people. *Your* people are lazy, trifling and easily manipulated. They blow whichever way *we* stir the wind. Idiots been chasin' their tales, running in circles ever since we brought their asses over here. *Your* people are weak! Weak! Weak! Weak!" the man shouted. "Buffoons, clowns. Their only use is to entertain and follow orders. Like animals. No, animals have a better sense of themselves than *your* people do."

TJ took the phone away from his ear and stared at it. He couldn't believe that he was being talked to in this manner. He put the phone back to his ear. "I don't know who you are, but I'm a black man, and you have no right—"

"I have every right. *We* create the right and the wrong. And you only have the rights that *we* allow you to have. You can get angry at my words and my delivery, but you cannot deny the truths that I speak. I'm trying to get you to see that *we* know what *we* are doing. Obama wanted to change the mindset of America and the way that government does business. A noble idea for the poor, but an impossible task because the poor and middle class only have the voice that *we* give them. And in the blink of an eye."

Bishop money heard a finger snap in the background.

"*We* can and *will* silence the mouth of that voice. James, JFK, X, King, Diop, Lewis, Brown, Cochran, Obama, I could go on, but neither of us have the time." In a calmer tone the man continued. "Now, we've made allowances, making an unscheduled stop at Andrews Air Force Base to put the speech writers on the plane to quell your doubts. Obviously, they have been unsuccessful but I don't give a damn. You will get off that plane hand-in-hand with Sinclair, and you will hold the press conference at Dobbins Air Force Base. There, you will read word for word the speech that has been prepared. Do *we* understand each other?"

TJ had never felt so powerful and yet so powerless. At least he hadn't felt so powerless since he was a small child growing up on the Westside of Atlanta in the Perry Homes housing projects. Born a runt, premature and heroine addicted, Terrell Joseph spent his first three years in and out of the hospital, and his next eight in a foster home with seven other foster kids. Fannie Mae Money, one of several heroine dealers in Perry Homes watched as kids, girls and boys, ridiculed, belittled, and used the severely undersized Terrell as a punching bag. One day, Fannie Mae got fed up and went to

Terrell's foster mother and complained about the way he was being abused. An argument broke out between the two women, which resulted in Fannie Mae taking Terrell and later on adopting him. But by then, an irreparable amount of psychological damage had been done to Terrell's psyche. Once Fannie Mae Money started showing the then, eleven year old boy love and attention, he craved attention worst than her customer's craved the heroine that she sold. By the age of fourteen Terrell had learned from watching and helping Fannie Mae with her heroine business that everyone was hooked on something, find out what that something was, supply it and they'd love you for life. He took it one step further. He began selling dreams and getting people hooked on the words that came out of his mouth. Since then he'd been developing his craft and before he got out of high school he was Mr. Popular, Mr. Everything, and he did whatever he wanted and to whom he wanted to do it to, just like now.

As bad as he wanted to tell the faceless voice to stick that speech where the sun don't shine and follow it there, he couldn't. He was still a little shaken after Sinclair had told him that the ten-man crew of the U.S.-trained Al-Qaeda imitators hired to kidnap the hostages were killed in a manufactured suicide bombing before the plane had left Afghan air space.

"Do we understand each other, Terrell Joseph Money?" the man repeated.

This faceless man, these faceless men, were the closest thing to a God that he himself didn't truly believe existed. "Yes, we do," TJ replied.

"Yes we do, what?"

"Yes, we understand each other," TJ said before hanging up the phone and slamming it against the wall of the plane.

"Is there a problem?" TJ shouted at Sinclair, the speechwriters, and the Four-Star General that had turned their heads in his direction. *I'll play their game, but I'll force them to play mine,* he thought while going through a mental checklist of those that had to die. It had been a long time since he mentally planned the death of so many. But like his seven foster brothers and sisters that he killed over a twenty-year period, he would do the same to the One-Frees. The difference then and now was that he was a seasoned killer, with money, power, and unlimited resources. And now, that witch's attorney made the starting line-up of those that were on his growing to-kill-list.

*****

"What the?" Rhythm saw flashing lights in her rear view mirror. "Get down. I'm being pulled over."

"Girl, you better hit the gas. You forgot, we ridin' in a stolen van," Cherry said. She had a bad feeling about stealing the minivan only a mile away from the cabin.

"Thank, God." Rhythm unconsciously put a hand over her chest before exhaling as the squad car went around her. It was followed by several others."

"They just turned onto Bishop Wiley's street," Rhythm said, leaning forward and looking through the windshield.

"What are you doing?" Assata asked, thinking that Rhythm was going to turn around any second.

"I'm going to ride past the estate."

A minute of silence passed before Rhythm blurted out. "Oh, my God."

Cherry peeked out the rear window. More than a couple Dekalb County police were driving through the open sixteen-foot monogrammed black gates.

"My Rover," Rhythm said, pointing to her four-year-old Range Rover. "Heavenly Father, please cover Cheyenne with Your protective hands."

Assata and Cherry said a similar prayer in silence.

Rhythm pulled to the curb behind the SUV. "I got a spare key in my bag," Rhythm said, rummaging through her Dolce & Gabana cream colored handbag. First, she pulled out the key and then a hundred dollar bill.

"Drive the van. I'm taking the Rover." Cherry climbed over the seat as Rhythm got out on the driver's side. "You know how to get to the Dunwoody train station?"

"Yeah." Cherry nodded. "It's about ten, fifteen minutes from here.

"Right. Take this." Rhythm handed the hundred dollar bill to Cherry. "Dump the van at the train station park and ride. Across the street, there's a Mickey Dee's and a Quik Trip gas station. Buy a minute phone, put some time on it and call me. I'm going up there to see about our girl."

Before she got into her truck, she spotted Shabazz's Denali in front of her Rover. *No need to alarm Assata and Cherry, neither of them knows what he drives,* she thought as she watched them drive by in the black minivan.

It took Rhythm five minutes to circle back around. As she drove up the hill of the estate, she counted seven squad cars and an ambulance. As she got out of the SUV, she saw Shabazz and another young man being escorted out of the house in handcuffs.

"What's going on?" Rhythm asked the closest officer.

"Do you live here, ma'am?"

"No, but" she pointed to Shabazz, "he's a client of mine."

"I'm sorry, ma'am," the officer put a hand on her upper back. "I have to ask you to leave. This is a crime scene."

"What happened?"

"I can't say. Now, please leave."

"What about my client?" she asked.

The officer thought a minute. "How did you know your client was here? Better yet, wait right here." The officer began walking toward the front door. "I think Detective Roberts will want to speak with you."

Rhythm made eye contact with Shabazz right before he got into the back of a squad car. He twitched his cheeks toward the front gate several times. She went back to her Rover, and backed down the one-block hilly driveway so no one could get her tag. Who was the ambulance for? She prayed it was there for Bishop Wiley. Then again, it could've been there for Shabazz and the young man that he was being arrested with. Both had turban-like bandages around their heads. But where was Cheyenne?

Rhythm didn't know what to think. She knew she had to wait a few hours until Shabazz was booked to find out what was going on. She just prayed that it wasn't as bad as it looked. She passed three news vans as she turned off Bishop Wiley's street.

Her mind was full of what ifs, what fors, and what to do's as she rode in silence to the McDonald's restaurant where the girls waited. Her mind was so heavy that she hadn't given it any thought as to why they hadn't called.

Fifteen minutes later, she got out of her Rover and went inside the fast food restaurant. Now she saw why they hadn't called.

Chapter 22

" *I*n the words of the man we celebrate on what would be his eighty-third birthday today." Bishop Money stood behind the podium outside in the sunny, unusually cold Atlanta winter afternoon addressing the world and the thousands of people that came out to greet and hear him speak of how he walked into a hostile terrorist den and was able to get Al-Qaeda to release the sons and daughters of several UN officials.

Bishop Money raised his bible in the air and stepped away from the podium. Reporters and photographers began pressing their cameras into action. "I've been to the mountaintop and I've seen the Promised Land. This soil," he pointed a black leather-gloved finger at the frozen ground, "enriched with the blood, sweat and tears of our ancestors. This soil we all stand on is the promised land. America is the greatest country on God's green," he bent down picked up some snow, "and white earth."

People laughed and applauded.

"But seriously. This land. Our land. The land of our mothers, fathers, mother's mothers and father's fathers. Our ancestors." He made a sweeping arc with his arm. "All of them bled, and made sacrifices for us today. Mistakes were made. Mistakes are a part of human development and growth. Are we perfect? No. Will we continue making mistakes? Yes. Some say America has lost her way. I say. America has never found her way. And as Dr. King once said, I repeat, 'I've been to the mountaintop and I've seen the promised land. I may not get there with you. But I will see you there.' I'm already here. We're already here. We just have to til the dirt, get rid of the old. Make this once-fertile ground fertile again. It's going to take hard work. It's going to take all of us. But we can do it." He gestured for Sinclair to join him at the podium. He took her hand and raised it to the sky. "Together, we can change America. Together, we can call for our troops to come home. Rebuild the infrastructure of our great country. Give tax credits to corporations to entice them to stay home and come back home so Americans can work and make an honest living."

"We love you, Bishop Money."

He let go of Sinclair's hand and extended his arms in front of him. "I love all of you," he said. "And my love for God, my fellow man, and my country is why I am running for President of the United States of America on the 2012 Democratic ticket."

The crowd was stunned into momentary silence, then sudden overwhelming applause. It took three minutes for the crowd to quiet.

"We are less than a year away from the election. You may ask what does a Christian Bishop know about politics? About running a country." He gripped the brown wood podium with his gloved hands, looking out at the sea of attentive faces.

"Absolutely nothing. But," he raised a finger, "I know God. I know what's in the hearts of men. I know how the clock ticks in the minds of men. Remember, I been to the mountaintop, I've seen yesterday, today and tomorrow. And the yesterdays of the Bush era scares me. Because of a lot of promises and lack of action, if I don't run, then we may be handing over the reins to another Bush. It's about time we got out of the bushes and came into the light. Don't you think it's about time that a man, a person untrained in the trickonometry of politics takes the reins? A man that will be honest and upfront. A man that knows he doesn't know and asks what you, the American people think about the issues that our country faces ahead. No one man should ever have the power over you. No senate and no house can ever fully represent your thoughts, feelings, and ideals. Let's make this government a corporation where all three-hundred and ten million Americans sit on the board of directors."

*****

It was a good thing it was winter. Because if it were summer, a fly was sure to fly in at least one of the mouths of the three women standing in front of the sixty-five inch McDonald's flat panel TV.

*****

TJ turned to Sinclair. "Sinclair Kennedy Charmaine." Bishop Money pulled the microphone from the podium and led Sinclair away from the podium so all could see. He got down on one knee. "I cannot imagine taking another step without you at my side. I do not want to breathe another breath without you exhaling beside me. I'll be doing a disservice to God, and our country if I didn't ask you to take this leap with me. I will not do it without you." He shook his head from left to right. "You are my everyday. You're my light whenever I lose my way. Right now, in front of millions, I dedicate my love to you. I love you now, tomorrow, and forever. Will you bless me by becoming Mrs. Terrell Joseph Money?"

The cameras zoomed in, catching the tear drops that fell from her eyes and onto the thin veil of snow that carpeted the wintery ground.

She nodded. "Yes." Louder, she said, "Yes, I will."

Chapter 23

"*W*ill, this is Rhythm." Rhythm had just dropped Assata and Cherry off at her and Moses's home in the Atlanta suburb of Conyers. And now she was about to get onto the I-20 interstate.

William Dodson used to be a vice squad cop. And a damn good one, until he came out of the closet and his superiors put him into another closet. He worked down in the basement of the Dekalb County prison complex in the property room. He enjoyed it. No one bothered him. He watched TV and surfed the web between checking evidence in and out.

"You heard, I take it?" He looked around the property room in the basement as if there were others around to listen to his conversation. "Can you believe it?"

"Nope, I'm still in shock. The sad thing is, that if I didn't know the devil, then I'd probably vote for him," Rhythm said. "But I'm calling to ask a favor."

"Sorry, I'm all out of those," he said.

"Please. Pretty please," she begged.

He exhaled. "The things that I do for my friends." He shrugged his shoulders and shook his head. "What, Girl? Make it fast. You know I got to watch Ms. Oprah."

"I didn't know she brought the show back?"

"She didn't. It's a rerun. One I haven't seen. I got my Kleenex ready. You know how sensitive I am."

It was her turn to cut him off. "I need to know what Shabazz One-Free and the young man he was brought in with a couple hours ago were charged with, and most importantly, what evidence you have on them."

"I ain't got nothin' on nobody. I'm just the man that work for the Man, but please believe, I ain't the Man. Now that I've made myself clear. What's the other gentlemen's name?"

"I don't know. He was about five-ten, five-eleven. Muscular build. Smooth copper brown skin. Very young looking"

"How young?"

"William Dodson, the man is straight," Rhythm lied, not even knowing who the brotha with Shabazz was.

"They all are, until I make them bend." Will said, doing a little dance behind his cage.

"Will!"

"Okay. Okay. Give me a minute. I'll call you back."

"No, wait. Also, can you see if a Cheyenne Jamison-Hayes was brought in?"

"That wonderful woman that shot the right reverend Bishop Sho-nuff Shady. They shoulda' gave her a medal instead of a jail cell."

"You're so stupid. What am I going to do with you?" She laughed before hanging up.

Twenty minutes later, she was pulling into the Dekalb County Jail complex.

Her phone rang. "It's about time," Rhythm said.

"I had to wait for the commercial." He sniffed. "Your girl is still MIA. Hold on." It sounded like he was blowing his nose. "Sorry. Shabazz One-Free and Hasaan Moore where charged with one charge of trespassing, one charge of breaking and entering, one charge of kidnapping, one charge of attempted murder, and one charge of resisting arrest. It seems that they did a number on Bishop Butterball. I made a couple calls, they say his face looks like a striped tiger."

"A tiger?"

"Look, Girl, I'm just the messenger. All I know is that Bishop Smiley Wiley is over at Hillandale being treated. You ain't heard it from me, everything so hush, hush around here, but he was admitted under the name, Maurice Gant."

"Why? And who is Maurice Gant?"

"Girl, you know if I knew, you'd know. I ain't never heard of him. But who cares, Smiley Wiley's in room 416, for what I understand are non life-threatening injuries. Oops gotta run, Oprah's back on. Got some more good cryin' to do." He hung up, leaving Rhythm wondering what happened in that house, and where was Cherry?

She dialed the number to the minute phone that Cherry had picked up. She answered on the second ring.

"Domino's Pizza," Cherry joked.

"Girl, you got a pen?" Rhythm asked.

"One second," she said, rummaging through her small black Poach purse. "Okay."

"First, our girl is still missing. Second, Shabazz and another brotha where charged with attempted murder plus some. The story is a little fishy but I'll have more after I go in and see him."

"Okaaay. Why did you have me go through my bag for a pen?" Cherry asked.

"Oh, yeah. FYI. C. Wendell is at Hillandale hospital. Room 416. I don't know the level of his injuries."

"What, you want us to pay him a visit?" Cherry asked.

"No." She thought a second. "Not yet. Besides, there's probably a round-the-clock entourage of church folks at his bedside." She doubted if anyone was by his side. How could they be when C. Wendell was in the hospital under an alias. Someone for some reason didn't want anyone to know about the beating. But why? The why was the reason she'd lied to

Cherry. She wouldn't be able to forgive herself if they went up to the hospital and got arrested. She felt bad enough that Cherry and Assata were in the country.

"So, why did I write down the hospital info?"

"I don't know. So much is happening, I can't think straight. And now Shabazz, jumping on C. Wendell? It just doesn't add up."

"What do you mean?" Cherry asked.

"It's just the way C. Wendell's injuries were described to me." She paused, trying to piece her thoughts together. "I can't see Shabazz beating the man half to death in the man's home. And it doesn't make sense that he was even over there, unless Cheyenne called him. But why would she call him? He didn't pick up when we tried to reach him. And I know I called him ten times at least. Girl, I'm overthinking. Let me get in here and see what's going on. I'll call you as soon as I leave the jail."

Chapter 24

"*C*racka, you must wanna leave up out the county jail in a body bag," the short stocky young man said, standing in front of where Shabazz sat. "I *said* you was in my seat."

Shabazz's head was still stinging from the blows he took from the cops. Trouble was the last thing he wanted, but trouble seemed to always be first in line in his life. He lifted his tall, lanky six-two frame up from the concrete bench. "My bad brotha'," He pointed to the slab of concrete he just got up from. "It's all yours." Shabazz moved to another part on the long concrete bench that took up two walls of the pissy-smelling, crowded six-by-ten foot holding cell. He felt bad about Extra, but he wasn't too worried because Extra was being held in protective custody until he could be moved to the juvenile detention center.

The cocky, braid wearin', butter-yellow young thug, waddled over to Shabazz. "Dat my seat too, Dog."

Shabazz was cool as the wind. He had similar mannerisms and sort of looked like a white version of Snoop Dog. He even wore his stringy brown hair in a ponytail. He looked up, his droopy tree bark brown eyes made contact with the young thug's marble black orbs. "Please, relax your mind. I promise," he shook his head and patted his chest, "you don't want this, li'l bruh."

The young man stepped a little closer. "Li'l bruh. Nigga, I look like Harry Potter to you? Huh?" He took a step closer. "Is my face bleach pink? Is my hair stringy brown?" His leg grazed Shabazz's knee. "Answer me, fool."

Shabazz put a hand over his forehead and began massaging his temples. "I'm asking you nicely, King, please, please ease up off me."

The young bully turned his head. His eyes briefly rested on the faces of the seven other young and older black men in the cell. "King." He nodded up and down. "I like that." He turned back to Shabazz. "Yeah, Whitey, get off my bench and bow to the king."

"I'm 'bout to bow these size thirteens up that ass."

The young man swung. Shabazz ducked and swerved to his left.

"Owwwww." The young man screamed out in pain. "You made me bust my hand on the wall," the boy said, holding his throbbing hand.

Shabazz was off the bench and standing in the middle of the cell. "Only thing I'm gon' make you do is wear this ass whippin," he said, takin' off his belt. "Act like a slave, I'm gon' beat you like one."

The young man looked at the others, silently hoping that they'd help him jump Shabazz. When no one moved, he said, "Bump this." He pulled his pants-on-the-ground jeans up over his butt before he charged forward.

Shabazz dropped his belt and hit the young man with a three-piece. A shot to the jaw, the chin, and one to the gut. The last shot doubled the boy over. He dropped to his knee and fought to catch his breath while Shabazz picked his belt up off the nasty discolored coppery stained concrete ground. He struck the boy with his belt.

"Ahhhhh. Stop," the boy shouted while arching his back.

"You come in here showin' your ass. You need to be pulling up them damn pants and puttin' some knowledge in that hat rack on toppa yo' neck insteada' trynna' make a name off me." Shabazz whipped the young man some more.

"Somebody make him stop. Po-lice, po-lice, guard," he shouted.

"Now you wanna call Harry Potter? A minute ago you were spittin' on his name. Don't call the white man to help you now. That's what's wrong with you fake-paper-weight-keepin'-it-real-young fools. Don't know how to do nothin' but hate yourself," Shabazz started putting his belt back through the loops of his RocAWear acid washed black jeans. "Pull up your damn pants, put on a belt, and pick up a book, fool. Ain't no self-respecting man, black, white, red, yellow, brown, ever gon' treat you with respect when you don't walk or dress respectfully. Only person wanna see yo' ass in here and on the streets is a tinkerbell. I don't see why you saggin' and baggin'-pants-on-the-ground young fools can't see that shit."

"Shabazz One-Free, attorney visit," the guard said before turning the key and opening the orange steel door.

Rhythm had a file on the metal table and was taking notes when the key turned in the attorney-client visitation room door. Shabazz had been like a little brother to Rhythm since she saved his and her niece Babygirl's life from the black mobster and head of the St. Louis Black Mafia, Frank Lester, five years ago.

"What did they do to you?" Rhythm asked, hugging Shabazz not caring that the deputy hadn't left the room. "I'm tired of this mess." She pushed Shabazz to the side. She pointed a finger at the deputy. "There's more police brutality in this city than in any Klanville, U.S. town." She extended a hand back at Shabazz, while keeping her eyes on the black man wearing a badge. "Have you no compassion? Sense of self? This is your brotha, born from a different mother, but still, a black mother. How could you?"

"Ay... Ay..." The deputy held a hand out. "Sis, I didn't have anything to do with the bandages on the brotha's head. I'm not the problem. I'm just trynna do my eight-hours, five days a week so I can support me and mines. I can't speak for none of the other officers. But, I believe in treatin' a man like a man as long as he acts like a man."

Shabazz nodded. "I can respect that, King."

The deputy smiled before turning his back and leaving the room.

"You know how one-time get down, when a brotha don't bow down to they Gestapo ass. I got some scars, a little bruising. It looks worse than it really is." He shrugged his shoulders before taking a seat in the prison cell-sized box-like room. "Queen, I'm good."

"Good? How can you say that? You're never good when those who are being paid to uphold the law, break the law over your head, Shabazz."

Shabazz stood back up and went over to Rhythm and hugged her. He whispered in her ear. *"If you can keep your head when all about you are losing theirs and blaming it on you. If you can trust yourself when all men doubt you, but make allowance for their doubting, too."*

She smiled, remembering reciting the Rudyard Kipling poem to him years ago when he was about to get himself killed trying to take on the St. Louis Black mafia by himself.

"Hell, nah, I ain't good for real-for real. Cartoon cops go upside mine and my guy's head for no reason. Either one of us could've been killed or had brain damage, but it wasn't in the cards. Now I'm up in this piece, charged with some trumped-up charges, can't even see a judge about a bond 'til Tuesday, 'cause of the MLK long weekend."

She broke their embrace. They both took a seat opposite each other behind the metal table.

"What happened?" she asked.

"Hell if I know. You know the young king I told you about. The one we put on the payroll to watch the suits watching Samuel?"

She nodded.

"This morning, around nine, two suits snatched him and his li'l brother up. The young king you saw me with at CW's crib, is the brotha who pulled my coat to the kidnap caper. Long story short, the streets was lookin' for me and Sam to give 'em some game and guidance, but you know Sam had dropped Ariel off for the weekend at Cheyenne's mother's spot before going to the crypt for the weekend, and you know they don't allow cell phones in the youth prison. And I can't get any service at the church. I was there, dissecting the info you gave me, the info Solomon and I had gathered, and I was on the phone with Constant Contact, finding out how much it would cost and if they could even handle a twelve-million e-mail list."

"No wonder your phone was going straight to voicemail when I called," Rhythm said. "You need to get rid of that Metro PCS and go over to Verizon."

"I ain't got no Verizon money. Besides, you know can't nobody get no service in here. Only service that'll pick up in the church is God PCS." He paused, trying to remember where he'd left off before Rhythm interrupted. "Where was I?"

She looked down at her notes. "The e-mail list."

"Okay, yeah. So, I don't know how Extra, that's what the young king calls hisself. I don't know how he found me, but he came bargin' into my office in a panic, putting me up on G. First thing comes to mind when he described the slaves that snatched the young kings up, was CW."

"I don't understand?"

"Remember a few days ago, I told you that the suits watchin' Samuel and the house were seen with CW twice."

"You also told me that Pop Tart was a gang leader and had been into some of everything. And that he thought others were going to try him since he quit selling drugs. So what makes you so sure that C. Wendell was or is behind the kidnapping?"

"I'm not sure, but it's all I had. And I had to run with any crumb I could scrape up. If anything happens to that young King..." Shabazz shook his head before continuing. "So, anyways, I grabs Extra and we jump in the green machine about one-thirty, and heads up to CW's. We get there, one of the front double doors is wide open and CW's beat up body was sprawled out on the foyer floor. Only hand I laid on his scratched and scarred up ass, is the one I used to check for a pulse. Next thing I know, a black metal flashlight is coming at me."

"You didn't hear them coming?"

"Yeah, I heard sirens. I even heard them pull up. My dumb ass, trynna help the clown that got my dude under the scope, and probably had somethin' to do with Pop Tart's kidnapping."

"Wasn't anything dumb about trying to save another man's life," Rhythm said.

"A man's life, not a snake's. I just needed CW to be alive so he could tell me where Pop Tart is and maybe even get the 411 on why he was paying a blackwater mercenary outfit to keep tabs on our man."

"You say C. Wendell was scarred and scratched up?" Rhythm asked.

"Yeah, Queen. Dude's face looked like he'd been attacked by some wild animal with major claws. And his wig. Somebody had pulled clumps of hair out of his head. Oh, yeah, part of his ear was on the marble floor next to where he was laid out. Something or somebody did a number on him."

"Cheyenne," she mouthed, not saying her name aloud.

"What?"

Rhythm just looked at Shabazz until he got the hint.

"You bullshittin'?"

"I'm dead serious."

He thought a minute, remembering seeing Rhythm's Rover near CW's house. He was glad he hadn't mentioned that, just in case the cops were listening. They weren't supposed to be. It was illegal to listen in on attorney-client conversations, but so was beating innocent unarmed men with metal flashlights.

The two were interrupted by a key turning in the door. A second later, a white female wearing a black pantsuit followed by two uniformed officers entered. "Rhythm One-Free?"

"Yes?"

"You are under arrest for obstruction of justice and aiding and abetting."

She stood up. "What?"

"Cuff her," the woman said, waving a CD in the air. "You're an attorney. Let me restate that." The women smiled. "*Were* an attorney. I can't believe you didn't know that prison hospital rooms were under twenty-four hour surveillance?"

Chapter 25

*A*ssata came down the stairs wearing some Nike Air running shoes, a dark ECKO jump suit and a black winter coat.

"Where'd you get a hat big enough to hide all that hair?" Cherry asked.

"Same place I got everything else. Rhythm's bedroom closet."

"I guess what I should be asking you, is where're you goin'?"

"*We* are going," Assata waved a set of keys in the air, "to take Moses's truck and go get some answers."

Cherry was kicked back, sitting in one of two of the his and her cream colored recliners in the den, sucking up the heat from the blazing fireplace that crackled in front of her. She put the book down on the chair's leather ledge. "You don't think we should wait for Rhythm?"

"It's going on eleven. She hasn't called and her phone is still going straight to voicemail."

"Eleven!" Cherry jumped up. "I can't believe it's that late." She looked at the book that she had just put down. "That damn, Jihad, he got me all caught up in his book, *MVP*."

"Didn't I tell you? His books are like crack. All of them'll have you hooked," Assata said.

"You were right," Cherry said. "I'm worried, no call, text, nothing. This isn't like Rhythm."

"I know. I'm worried, too. But worrying doesn't get us anything but a migraine," Assata said.

"I take it you have a plan?" Cherry asked.

She smiled. "Girl, you know I do. Go grab your coat and meet me out front. I'll pull Moses's Dodge out of the garage. I'll explain everything while we're driving."

"Do I need to change clothes?"

"Nah, just freshen up a little if you want."

Assata walked though the huge spotless kitchen to get to the three-car garage door. Once inside, she hit the unlock button, opened the door and climbed up into the big four-door silver, Dodge Ram pickup. She just remembered something. She took out the small flip phone and dialed Cherry's number.

"I'm comin'."

"Bring your tools," Assata said, referring to Cherry's scalpel kit.

"I never leave home without them," Cherry said before disconnecting the call.

After opening the garage, Assata pulled around the horseshoe driveway to the front door, and slid over to the passenger's seat.

"I don't know why you moved," Cherry said. "If we get pulled over, it's a wrap. Or have you forgotten, like you, I'm on the FBI's most wanted list?"

"No, I haven't forgotten, but this is your city. You know your way around," Assata remarked.

"Oh, well, you do have a point there."

"I know," she said, while putting in some coordinates on the truck's navigation system.

"So, what's the plan?" Cherry asked.

"First, we find a 24 hour Kinkos."

"Kinkos?"

"Yep. And from there we go see this Bishop Wiley."

"They won't let us see him. It's way after visiting hours," Cherry explained.

"When have *they* ever stopped us? Besides I'm not going in with you. I'm going to Bishop Wiley's home."

"I guess you have a way for me to get into his hospital room?"

"I sure do, Dr. Alethea Hardin." She handed her a New Jersey driver's license. "All we have to do is follow the directions to the 24 hour Kinkos I just keyed in so we can get your new license laminated."

"How did you get this?" Cherry said, looking at the license-sized piece of paper in amazement.

"Rhythm's computer has amazing graphics. You'd be surprised what you can copy, paste and print from the Internet. It took me a while to find a program that can convert a low resolution file into picture-perfect high resolution. I just hope Rhythm doesn't mind that I used one of the credit cards on top of her dresser to purchase the program."

Cherry continued staring at the license. "What about the picture?"

"Girl, you got more pictures circulating on the net than Paris Hilton."

"Well, I was known as the black Lorena Bobbit, snip, snip," she said, making a scissor-cutting motion with two fingers.

"Don't sell yourself short. You had, and still have, all-female Wild Cherry fan clubs all across the country. I don't think I've ever heard of another woman going after pimps, woman beaters, and other deeply sadistic men like you did. Jihad needs to write a book about you."

"A book, girl my story would be the first R-rated Lifetime movie." Both shared a laugh as they followed the navigation system's directions to the closest 24 hour Kinkos.

"Nah, Jihad need to ride a book about TJ Money," Cherry said.

"Who would believe it? I still can't believe he's running for president. No way that fool gets in the White House," Assata said.

"Bush Junior got in twice and now the other brother is running this year," Cherry said.

"TJ makes baby Bush and any other Bush look like the Pope."

"He gon' need the Pope, God, and the twelve apostles if I get my hands on him," Cherry said.

"Not if. When."

After leaving Kinkos, the two decided to go to an all-night Target and purchase a name tag kit, and another pay-as-you-go cell phone. A couple hours had passed since they had left the house. It was almost one-thirty when Cherry pulled the huge pick-up into a parking space at the hospital's entrance.

"You ready, Dr. Hardin?" Assata asked.

"As ever." She slipped a black pouch full of scalpels into her white lab coat pocket. "I'm even prepared to cut on our patient if necessary," she said, getting out of the truck.

"According to the navigation system," Assata looked at the dash, "Bishop Wiley's house is only twelve minutes from here."

"Girl, you like that navigation system, huh?"

"Yes, I do. I never actually used one," she said, sliding over to the driver's seat. "Call me in an hour. Or if you run into any trouble. I'll see you in a few," Assata said, taking off in the truck.

A minute later, Cherry walked with confidence through the sliding glass doors at Hillandale Hospital.

"Hi, my name is Dr. Hardin. Can you direct me to the elevator that will take me to the fourth floor?" Cherry asked the security officer standing at the reception desk near the entrance she'd just come through.

"You must be new here?" the security guard said, looking to Cherry's left while adjusting his coke bottle bi-focals and exposing a mouth full of teeth a dentist would run from.

"Yes, as a matter of fact I am," Cherry said, about to faint.

The thirty-something guard leaned against the granite desk top and stuck out a rusty crusty hand, that looked like it hadn't been washed this decade. "Name is Leroy Brown, you know, like the song. Baddest man in the whole damn town."

Stankinest breath in the whole damn town.

He pulled his hand back and started making all types of gestures to emphasize whatever point he was trying to make. He was talking to her, but his hands and cross-eyes were in no man's land. "On the really-real, for-real-for-real li'l momma, I kinda run things on the night shift. I do so much more than secure the building and the grounds. I make peoples feel good about bein' here. It may not seem like I'm doin' much, but, uh, I'm always on the job. See, li'l momma, I got ears and eyes in the back of my head and up there," a few feet away from where he was pointing there was a small rotating camera in the corner between the ceiling and the bone colored hospital wall.

She made sure not to look directly at it. She nodded wondering, *how many ten-day-old wolf ass sandwiches has this man eaten?*

Cherry almost went for her black pouch as the guard found his mark, putting his dusty crusty hand on the back of hers. "Li'l momma, I see you ain't married. Me neither. My momma been sayin' I needs to find mes a good woman, but nigga like me gotta be careful. You know what I'm sayin'?"

Hell, nah, and I wish you'd stop saying anything until you go and drink a gallon of Listerine, she wanted to say, but instead she just nodded.

"I gotta job. I'm a straight brotha. Got my own car, paid fo'. I work out. A brotha got stayin' power if you know what I mean. Nigga like me a rarity in today's society." He looked her up and down. "I don't usually squat were I eat, but you fine as wet silk, li'l momma." He winked at her. "Play your cards right, and a nigga just might take you to Red Lobster on my off day. It gotta be day, 'cause my momma know my schedule, and she want me home with her on my off nights. You know how mommas get when they get up in age."

It was one thing to be thirty-something and still at home with momma, but this fool had to be retarded to offer up that info while trying to impress a sista'. "I'm flattered," she said, her hand still over her mouth and nose. "I have to check on a patient. Can you please just point me in the direction of the fourth floor elevator?"

He pulled his pants up. "I can walk you."

"No. No. No. No. Please, I just wanna remember our first meeting just like this. I wanna keep the visual in my mind of you standing there, arm on the counter with that tooth pick in your mouth, one leg over the other. You too cool, Leroy Brown."

"You know. That-that's what uh, the ladies say. I'm like Bill Gates in 1991. Nobody knew him until the next year, when he introduced Windows to the world. I'm in the gym real hard. Thirty minutes a day every weekend. I'm three months from being LL's twin."

LL, fool you a Twinkie away from being able to land a starring role as the earth in the next documentary, she wanted to say, but instead she went with, "LL, please just tell me where the elevator is."

"Right down yonder." He pointed at a plant next to the men's and women's restroom. "I'm gon' get at you now. Best believe, bad, bad, Leroy Brown gon' holla."

She began walking.

"Sho' is pig is pork, I'm gon' get them digits when you come back down. So don't fret or frown, Big Daddy jook'em good gon' lay it down. Just anoth' reason they call me bad, bad, Leroy Brown," he said talking to himself and doin' a little dance. His eyes were one with Cherry's behind, jumping from left to right with every sway of her lab coat as she walked down the corridor toward the elevators. "Woof. Woof," he barked as she disappeared onto the elevator hall.

Minutes later, she was at the door. The tag on the left read Maurice Gant. But the number on the door was 416. She was about to open the door when she heard what sounded like two people talking. She couldn't make out the words, but one of the voices sounded very familiar, and it wasn't the high-pitched voice of C. Wendell's.

Chapter 26

"*I*'m not even off the plane good when I get the report." Bishop Money threw his hands up. "I will not let you embarrass me. Do you hear me, Bishop?"

It was hard to take his mentor seriously. Bishop Wiley didn't know if it was the pain medicine or just the ridiculous-looking wig, makeup, red dress and high heels Bishop Money had on. "No, you don't understand."

"What is there not to understand?"

"They had guns."

Bishop Money reached down and slapped Bishop Wiley. *Pop!* "Don't you lie to me?"

The Bishop was stunned into silence. He lay on the hospital bed with his hand on his cheek.

"You take me for an idiot. I saw the video feed. How could you be so stupid? So weak? You let a woman whip your ass. You're a man, at least I thought you were," he shook his head in disgust, " until I saw a hundred-forty-pound woman whip your two-hundred-twenty-pound behind."

"You saw the video feed?" Bishop Wiley asked.

Bishop Money just stood there with a look of contempt on his face.

"You broke into my home?"

"And no, *I* didn't break into your home. A professional broke in. What was I supposed to do? I had to get to the truth. And lately, I haven't been able to depend on you tell me the truth."

"I can't believe you had someone break into my home." Bishop Wiley's voice was filled with hurt. "You invaded my privacy."

"Get over it. Hell, I can't believe you let a woman," he held a hand out toward the beaten and battered bishop, "do this to you. About the smartest thing you did was tell the police those other two were responsible for your injuries. I can't imagine the embarrassment the church would be subjected to if they found out the same woman that tried to kill me, tried to beat you to death in your own home. You should have called your blow-up girlfriend down to help you."

The bishop wanted to crawl up under the covers and disappear. He hadn't been this embarrassed, this vulnerable, his entire life. "I'm sorry," he muttered.

"You what?" Bishop Money asked.

"I-I'm sorry." Tears of embarrassment welled up in his eyes.

"I don't need a character reference. I need results. Sorry is the reason I'm dressed in this get-up. Sorry is the reason I had to sneak out of my own home, catch a cab two blocks from my house, to elude anyone that might've followed me. Sorry is the reason I had Sinclair pay off a security guard and a head nurse to get in here. Sorry is the reason that bottom-feeding witch is still out there. Sorry is the reason her little girl ain't on the back of a milk carton. Sorry is the reason Sam Turner is still breathing my air. Sorry has got on my last nerve." He reached inside his purse and wrapped his hand around the Walther P 380. It was Sinclair's idea. Her first good idea she'd had since the two were forced together.

"What about the kids I had our people snatch up off the streets today?" Bishop Wiley asked.

"What about them?" Bishop Money took his hand out of the red purse and put his hands on his hips.

"Well, did they—"

"You wanna ask them yourself? I can arrange it." Bishop Money smiled thinking that was exactly what he planned to do before he walked out of the room. Sinclair was right. Bishop Wiley was too close. He knew too much, and was entirely too weak and too stupid. He'd outlived his usefulness she'd said. "They should be getting thrown out of a van in their mother's front yard anytime now."

"I'm being released in the morning. You want me to go over to their mother's house—"

"Idiot, I was being facetious. The two are dead. Fifty thousand dollars for their heads and we still got nothing."

"I'm getting the child, Tuesday. I already have everything arranged," Bishop Wiley said.

"Unarrange it. We don't know what Sam Turner and the One-Frees know, but we do know they know that we're watching, so the game has changed."

"What do you want me to do?" Bishop Wiley asked, eager to make up for the mess he'd made while TJ had been away.

"We need to raise money. I have a couple hundred thousand of the church's money vested in the demise of that witch, her daughter, and Turner. Get back to the church, fix the accounting records. Time is of the essence. I have to destroy my enemies now. I have less than a year before the Secret Service will be guarding me day and night."

"Secret Service?"

"Oh, that's right. You were so busy dating a blow-up doll and getting beat half to death by a woman half your size, that you hadn't heard about the press conference where I announced my candidacy for president."

Bishop Wiley broke out in laughter. "President? Lawd, lawd, lawd. I can see the headlines now." He waved a hand in front of him. "President Bishop Money prays the troops out of Afghanistan. No. No. How bout this one? President Bishop Money makes Haiti the fifty-second state, and the first official church state." Bishop Wiley noticed that he was laughing by himself. He wiped the tears of laughter from his eyes.

Bishop Money stood next to C. Wendells hospital bed, tapping a red stiletto heel on the floor with his arms crossed, thinking how right Sinclair was having C. Wendell admitted under an alias. It would be that much easier to get to him and it would give them time to make it look as if the One-Free's, or the witch was responsible for his murder.

"You're serious," Bishop Wiley said as more of a statement than a question.

"Is pig, pork?"

"But how will you finance a campaign?"

He smiled. "The Lord is my banker. He's my strength. Look at the world. It's in need of a savior, a messiah."

"Bishop, this is me you're speaking to. Don't run the God game on me. I'm not as good at it as you are, but you can't deny that I am good, and me being a master bullshitter, I know bullshit before it starts stinking."

"Well, I guess I can show you better than I can tell you. But as of now, you are to leave the dirty work to me. If Fannie Mae Money didn't do anything else, she didn't raise a fool and she taught me that if I wanted something done right, do it myself." He reached in his purse for the gun.

"So, you really don't want me to get the child?"

The long black hair in the wig didn't move as he shook his head. "Nope. I have a surefire way of drawing the witch out of her hole."

Bishop Wiley looked up as the door opened.

Thinking it was a nurse, Bishop Money turned to the door relaxing his grip on the gun in his purse.

Cherry had a scalpel in each hand as the door closed.

Bishop Money smiled as he pulled the gun out of his purse.

Chapter 27

*T*he early morning winter night was like a huge dark room with the air conditioner blowing on high. The blue-black night was quiet, with the exception of the crunching sound of Rhythm's red and white Delta Sigma Theta running shoes that Assata wore while walking on the thin layer of ice and snow that blanketed the tennis court in the fenced-in back yard of the Wiley estate. The house was dark with the exception of a room to the far left. From where Assata stood, the room seemed to be lit up by a blue light.

The rear of the house seemed to have a million windows. A burglar's dream, or a burglar's worst nightmare. It was easy to see inside, but it was also easy for someone to see outside.

After reaching the back wall of the house, Assata took out a diamond blade scalpel-like object and cut a circle right above a lock on one of the many French double doors. Next, she took out a gray suction cup, which she attached to the inside of the circle. With just a little pressure, the glass came out, quiet and quick. She reached inside and unlatched the three dead bolts and the lock on the L shaped stainless steel handle.

She opened the door and took a cautious step inside the dark dwelling. The alarm hadn't been set as she had suspected. The owner of the home couldn't have set it in the condition that Rhythm had explained that he was in. Without turning on any lights, just using the light from her pay-as-you-go cell phone, Assata navigated her way toward the blue-lit room on the first level.

As she got closer, she heard the plickety-plack of keys being depressed on a computer keyboard. Whoever was typing obviously wasn't supposed to be in the house, or they wouldn't be in the dark. Assata moved through the house with the quiet calm of a corpse, armed only with a diamond blade and the deadly element of surprise.

"Exhale slowly," Assata whispered in the person's ear as she pressed the blade to their throat. "If not, you will never inhale again."

The person sitting in the high back chair facing a wall full of monitors and a twenty-six inch computer flat screen did as they were told.

"Now, I am going to move the blade three millimeters from your throat." Assata spoke slow and soft. "Just enough room for your Adam's apple to bob up and down as you slowly and quietly tell me who you are, who you work for, and why you are here."

Recognizing the scratchy melodic voice, the person in the chair said, "You're right. If I'm to have any chance at taking down TJ, then I have to get my anger under control. And after reading this," she depressed a key on the huge computer screen, bringing a document up, "there is no way that I will be able to do that."

Assata moved the blade and continued reading the document. "They did what?" Assata put a hand over her mouth.

"Keep reading," Cheyenne said.

"I can not believe that this man is the head of a church." Assata pointed to the screen.

142

"Shabazz must feel terrible about Pop Tart and his fourteen-year-old brother," Cheyenne said.

"I doubt he even knows. He's been in jail since early this afternoon, or better yet yesterday afternoon." Assata had just remembered that it was almost three a.m. "I'll explain it all later." She paused, reading more of the document that Cheyenne had pulled up onto the screen.

"How could they take two-hundred thousand dollars from the church account without anyone knowing? That doesn't make sense," Assata said after reading the invoice transfer. "So, Monae Loray really does exist." She turned to Cheyenne. "This is bigger than getting to you and Samuel."

"I don't see how. TJ is scared of Samuel because of Samuel's background and what he did to Samuel's father. He's scared of me because of what I almost did to him. You see how his evil mind works? It didn't cost him a dime. He used church member's tithes to hire Monae Loray, the mercenary outfit, to go after me, Samuel and now, my daughter."

"Monae Loray, technically, doesn't exist. The first documentation of its existence turned up in a 1959 F.B.I. log. It is said to have been involved with several high-profile killings from JFK to Cochran. Not even presidents or kings can get to them, only the king makers have access. And as powerful as TJ is, he's not even a bleep on the radar screen when it comes to the power that men able to hire Monae Loray have."

"So what are you saying?" Cheyenne asked.

She shook her head. "I don't know what I'm saying, but I do know that there's more pieces to this puzzle of murder and corruption than we know," Assata said, taking out a handful of black CDs. "As many locks and cameras he has in and around this place, I can't believe he would leave his computer—"

"He didn't. I know a good hacker. I had him on the line for a couple of hours as we tried to break in through something called a backdoor, with no success. My friend was just about to tell me how to remove the hard drive so I could bring it to him, when I heard footsteps on the marble floor up front. I hid in that closet," she pointed to a custom made white closet door, "while a plain looking white man came in and sat down and stuck some machine in a USB port, and in seconds he was in. Next I saw him copy C. Wendell's hard drive and in less than fifteen minutes he was gone."

"Were you here when they locked Shabazz up for beating the bishop?"

"Shabazz didn't have anything to do with what I did," Cheyenne said.

"What you did?"

"It's all on this." She held an external hard drive in the air. "And every document and homemade video, including the one used to make Jordan jump from that window."

"Good, you saved me the trouble," Assata said, putting the CDs back into her pocket.

"After I saw that man copying everything, before I read anything, I knew I had to do the same, so luckily I found a brand new external hard drive in the top drawer." She pointed.

"Come on. Let's get outta here," Assata said.

"First thing in the mornin' I'm going to have Rhythm bring me in and I'll give the police this hard drive," Cheyenne said.

"Like hell you will."

"What do you mean? We got C. Wendell on enough to send him away for life," Cheyenne said.

"We've got the devil's dog, but not it's master," Assata said.

"They can put two and two together."

"Two plus two equals four, not a conviction.' Assata said. "Besides, TJ is entirely too popular and he has an unseen hand behind him that we know very little about. Either we get more concrete evidence on him, or we find a way to take him out. And like researchers use cancer cells to kill cancer, and the flu virus to kill the flu, we need to use seeds of evil to kill evil, and the information on that hard drive are the seeds we need. Now hurry up, let's go."

Minutes later they were in Moses's truck heading toward the hospital.

"They are not going to touch my baby?" Cheyenne said. "I'll be waiting for them."

Assata put a hand on top of Cheyenne's. "We'll all be waiting." She drew her hand back and looked at her watch. "I can't believe she hasn't called."

"Who?" Cheyenne asked.

"Cherry."

Chapter 28

"*C*herry, Cherry, quite contrary," Bishop Money turned. The round black silencer was larger than the nickel plated .380 hand gun pointed at her forehead. "Cut off anyone's balls lately?"

"No, I'm still looking for yours, but since you have the same thing as I do, I guess I'm S-O-L." She smiled, not even fazed by the bishop dressed in drag. "I wonder if you can drop me before I can send one or both of these flying though your neck," she said, referring to the scalpels she carried in both hands.

Not taking his eyes off her, he said, "See you have your operating tools with you. Surely you weren't going to castrate my right-hand man?"

He could have easily killed me if he wanted, but I was still breathing. Why? "I don't carry unless I plan to use," she said.

She's a fugitive. If I let her take out Wiley, then it will only make my popularity grow. I bet killing a bishop will shut all her Facebook fans and them One-Free, Black Panther wanna-be's up. And then, I think I will tap that tail one more time while I'm cutting her open with her own scalpel. That is after I capture her. "I guess we have a Mexican standoff." He began walking toward the door.

146

Cherry began backing toward Bishop Wiley's bed.

"I know you're not going to do anything to Bishop Wiley because I've seen you."

Bishop Wiley's eyes became cartoon-like. "Don't leave me with her?"

"Shhhh." She held a scalpel to her lips. "You'll be dead before that scream gets out your throat," she said as Bishop Money disappeared through the door.

"Please! Please!" Bishop Wiley held his hands out.

"With friends like that, I'd start hanging out with my enemies." She bent down close to his face. She gently ran the scalpel from the corner of his eye down to his lips. "If I wanted you dead, you'd be a memory. TJ knows that as well as you do. Anytime I choose, I can put my blade on you. I'm giving you a chance to do the right thing. I'm also giving you the chance to die doing the wrong thing. I'll be in touch," she said hurrying out of the room and toward the elevator.

Bishop Money had been off the elevator for a few minutes talking to the head of hospital security.

"I ain't gon' lie. I ain't even gon' try. Gull, you is sweet as a sugar cube, dipped in honey," Leroy Brown said looking at a wall but speaking to Bishop Money. "What color dat is?" he said, touching the air, instead of Bishop Money's dress. "That's, that , uh" the cross-eyed, bat-blind man, snapped his fingers, "what you gull's call it?"

"Red," Bishop Money said. "Look, Leroy, we have a situation. There's a woman disguised as a doctor on the fourth floor. She's armed and dangerous."

Leroy put his hands to his sides and spread his legs. He wiggled his fingers and cracked his neck.

"This is serious. You have to stop her before she hurts one of the patients."

"What her name is?" Leroy asked with a serious look on his face.

"Cheryl Sharell, but she has a name tag on that reads Dr. Hardin. Dr. Alethea Hardin." The longer he stood talking to the half blind, half retarded security officer, the more he was convinced that he was wasting his time.

Without warning, Leroy drew two cans of mace from the left and right holsters on his belt. "I call this crouching rat." He held both cans of mace in each hand above his head while going into a deep knee bend.

Bishop was too exhausted to entertain this fool. He now understood the saying, reality is stranger than fiction. No one would believe him if he told somebody about the fool he was walking away from.

"Shaw-tayyyyy," the guard called out. "Gull, don't walk away from me. No one walks away from bad, bad, Leroy Brown."

"Leroy?" A nurse walked up to where Leroy was performing. "Don't make me call your momma."

"No, please. I'm sorry, Ms. Ella."

"I can't let you come up here and play security guard overnight when I'm working if you're going to bother people. You'll get me in trouble."

"Yes ma'am. No ma'am. I'll be good. Watch me. I'm just gon' go back to the door and look for s'picious characters."

"Suspicious," she corrected as Cherry walked out of the same hospital double doors that she had walked in.

Bishop Money watched from his cab as Cherry got into the passenger's side of a black Dodge Ram pick up. He tried taking pictures from his phone, but he was too far away and it was too dark. The tint on the windows prevented him from seeing inside, but he did get the tag number.

Chapter 29

"*G*od done brought me a present." The linebacker-built prison guard stood inside the county jail pod where thirty-seven ladies awaited court. "Ain't no sunshine when Goon Calhoun enters a room." Remnants of the ass whipping Rhythm gave her last week covered Officer Calhoun's huge bandaged nose as she stood in Rhythm's face.

"Good morning, Officer Calhoun." Rhythm smiled despite her frustrations of not being able to reach anyone with a land line that could take collect calls since being locked up yesterday afternoon. "How are you, Queen?"

"So, I'm a queen now? I've come a long way. I was road kill last week when you and your boys jumped me from behind."

"I'm sorry, Queen. You must've suffered brain damage," Rhythm looked around the hulking woman that stood in front of the two female smaller guards that stood a step behind Officer Calhoun. "I was alone in your townhouse. I couldn't help but notice the cheap 1980's flea market black lacquer décor while stomping a mudhole in your behind. You should seriously consider hiring someone to help you decorate your place."

"You should seriously consider marrying my stick." She pointed the wooden black nightstick in Rhythm's face. "I'm going to enjoy shoving all eighteen inches up your nasty twat."

Rhythm was scared, but she refused to give Officer Calhoun the satisfaction of seeing or hearing her fears.

Rhythm stood her ground as Calhoun whispered in her ear. "You don't have to like me. You just have to make love to my stick." She wiggled her tongue in Rhythm's ear.

Rhythm cringed, before wiping her ear with her hand. This was the first and last time a woman would touch her in any sexual way and walk away, Rhythm vowed.

Calhoun depressed the Talk button on the receiver clipped to her guard uniform. "Lock down on two."

"Lock down on two. All inmates to your cells. Lock down on two. All inmates to your cells," the deep voice boomed over the two-tier pod's intercom system.

Minutes later, Rhythm sat on her bottom bunk, writing phone numbers down. She addressed the malnourished, freckle-faced female that sat on the bunk above her. "Queen, you don't know me, and I understand if you don't wanna help me, but that guard who was in my face will be up in here any minute now. She's corrupt and very ang—"

"Whachu need me to do?" the stringy haired white drug addicted former prostitute asked.

Rhythm handed her a piece of paper. "Have your people call my husband's cell, tell him where I am, and the other number is my brother-in-law's cell. Just have them call him, too and tell him the same."

Rhythm grabbed the hand that the white girl extended over the side of the top bunk. "I don't know what you did to Goon Calhoun, but whatever it was, you have got major problems now. But I got you, girl. I just got here this morning, but I ain't nowhere near new to jailin'. Us sisters have to stick together. In this jungle, we all niggas to them and they all crackas to us."

"Open up fourteen." The electronic door slid to the right. "Strip search. Jumpsuit, panties, bra, socks," Calhoun looked up at Rhythm's cell mate. "You! Out!"

"Girl, the meds in here are not like the cocktails we get down at Grady. They'll make you sick at first but you'll get over it. Hell, your T-Cell count is lower than mine, you might get lucky and be sent to the hospital."

The three officers gave the white girl a wide berth as she took her time getting off the top bunk.

"What the hell are you talking about, Christine?" One of the female prison guards asked.

"Nothin'." She waved. "Goes to show how small the world really is. Who woulda' thought."

"Who woulda' thought what?" Officer Calhoun asked, visibly getting more frustrated.

"You'd put me in the cell with Shooter," she said walking out of the cell.

"Christine! Get yo' half dead ass back in here," Officer Calhoun ordered. "My patience is runnin' thin now. You better talk before I have you put in the hole."

"I came out of a hole. My whole life I been in a hole, and as soon as this AIDS claims me, I'll be going back into a hole. So, threaten me with somethin' else, okay?" She smiled.

Under normal circumstances Christine would be bruised black and blue by now, but Calhoun was scared to touch the woman. It was as if you could catch the HIV virus by touch. And having dealt with the sadistic guard on more than one occasion, Christine knew the power that she had over Goon Calhoun. She was HIV-positive, a meth, crack, heroine, glue, any drug she could shoot, ingest, smoke or snort addict, but she wasn't completely a fool.

Officer Calhoun took a small plastic baggie out of her shirt pocket. She put her hand inside and came out with a small white pebble. Christine's eyes sparkled as Officer Calhoun turned the small white rock around in her fingers. "Talk and you smoke."

Christine held the left breast pocket of her prison issue orange jumpsuit open. "Put it in here and the record'll play."

After Calhoun dropped the crack rock in her pocket, she began. "We call her Shooter because back in the day, I guess I was around sixteen, eleven years ago, ol' Shooter was known as the vein finder. She would shoot up and stick anyone that had trouble finding a vein. That was before she went and caught that package. She was HIV-positive way before me. But when she found out she had it, she got clean." Christine pointed to Rhythm. "Look at all the good it did her. She's in here with me and she's got full blown AIDS."

"You better get on yo' knees, bitch," Officer Calhoun said taking a step back from Rhythm. "And pray you ain't scratched me. 'Cause if I got it, you gon' get the stick." She tapped the black night stick against the metal bed frame. "And a whole lot more than just a drug charge." She held the crack-filled baggie in the air.

Rhythm's husband, Moses, his brother Solomon, not even Shabazz could help her if no one knew where she was. Her only hope was the two notes. One, she gave to the woman that had just saved her and the one she hoped got to Shabazz on the men's side of the jail.

*****

"I'm just gon' preach it real with ya." The chaplain said, trying to be hip during Sunday service at the county jail. "Finally, the good Lord has sent us a savior. A lion amongst men that will slay the evils of corruption in government. A man that will not let man's law supersede God's law. I've been on this earth for fifty-nine years. I marched in Selma. I was in DC in '63. Heard Martin King give his 'I have a dream' speech. Watched a man walk on the moon. Voted for the first black president. Shed many a tear when he passed. But nothing, you hear me," the chaplain banged his hand on the podium in the room that served as a church in the county jail, "nothing prepared me for the miracle of seeing one man bring church and state together like Bishop TJ Money has done virtually overnight."

Shabazz got up. "Excuse me, King," he quietly said as he made his way past the other inmates.

"Son, you need to hear this. I'm talking about your savior," the gray haired chaplain said.

"No disrespect, but the only thing TJ Money can save me from is getting to the Kingdom. When I was a child, I used to say this prayer every night before I went to sleep. Now I lay me down to sleep I pray the lord my soul to keep. If I should die before I wake, I pray the lord my soul to take." Shabazz put his hand over his heart. "This is my soul, and I ain't trying to give it to no man, only God. How you gon' tell these kings in here," he waved a hand around the twenty-four inmates in the room, "that a man more flashy than a drug king pin and more flamboyant than the pimp of the year at a player's ball is they savior? I don't care if Bishop Money bags' church is givin' more to the community than any church in the state. Look how he livin' off the money of the poor. They call it love offerrin's. Half the people that go to his church and give to his TV ministries would love a decent job. Some decent shoes for their children—"

"Son, you're out of line." The chaplain pointed a finger.

"No, sir. I'm in line. You're out of line calling Satan a savior. We didn't choose Bishop Money, the media chose him. Just like they've chosen all of our leaders since Dr. King. Only mountaintop he'll be leading anyone to is the one overlooking hell. I know Bishop Money because I know God. And the way he livin' and breathin' ain't got nothing to do with my spiritual upliftment," he said, looking directly into the white chaplain's eyes.

For the next couple of days, Shabazz did a lot of soul searching. Since speaking out during Sunday service, everyone seemed to want to know why he thought as he did. The guards and the inmates. He was careful not to say anything concerning the private war between the Bishop and his people. Shabazz wanted the people to exercise their minds instead of their ears. Although he considered himself Muslim, he used biblical scripture to help the brothers that came to him understand God's purpose for man. It scared him when he would finish speaking and he would notice a light coming on inside of those he spoke to. He was a former criminal. A hustler. A wordsmith. And suddenly, he became afraid. Just like that, he turned inmates away and quit giving up the God game as he called it, because he was afraid that if he kept goin' he'd enjoy it more and would possibly end up being like the man he hated, Bishop TJ Money.

Money was a mother, and in the past, when Shabazz had lots of it, he shot it up in his arm. He played women, and was deep into the world of sin. He didn't want the temptation of money sending him back to the hell he fought so hard to get out of. God knows he wasn't a saint, far from one, but he was proud of knowing his past. Proud of the men that came before him. Proud to have God ordering his every step.

"Shabazz. Yo, Shabazz," a voice called out from behind the door.

"Come on in," he said.

"I know this may sound strange coming from the mouth of one of your captors."

"King, my mind is my captor, not you. We all in the belly of the beast. You just getting paid to be here."

"I wish the other inmates felt the way you do," Officer Hunter said.

"Every man's feelings are based on what he sees and hears. Talk to the brothas."

"I do, but they don't hear me."

"I said talk *to* them. Not *at* them. They are men, however misguided and misled, but at the beginning of the day, they put on their pants like every other man," Shabazz explained.

The guard nodded. "I'll work on that, but I came here for two things. I was wondering if I could reach out to you? Call you from time to time? Just listening to you these past couple days has made me want to reevaluate so many things that I had been taught."

Shabazz got up and hugged the guard. "King, you my people. I would never turn my back on a hungry man. Lodge this number in your brain. 770-473-9614."

The guard broke their embrace and wiped the tears from his eyes with the back of his hand. "Your charges have been dropped."

Chapter 30

*I*t had been less than a week since Bishop Wiley had been attacked. But since then, he'd dropped a few pounds, had most of his hair cut off, and beside the track like scars on his face and the bandage on his ear, he almost looked normal. But, C. Wendell Wiley was far from normal as he stood in front of Bishop Money's desk.

"You did what?" Bishop Money had been casually laid back in his custom-made throne-like office chair until Bishop Wiley dropped this latest revelation on him.

He flinched at the tone in his mentor's voice. Sinclair smiled while sitting cross-legged on the beige leather couch, pretending to read the Washington Post in the library part of Bishop Money's church office inside of the six-thousand square foot church administration building. She hated weak people.

"I... I dropped the charges." He shrugged his shoulders. "I had to."

"Only thing you have to do is die. " He paused, staring daggers into Bishop Wiley's eyes. "You don't even have to stay black these days, but die you must. And it seems that some are knocking down the hardware store doors to buy a shovel to start digging their own grave."

"What are you saying?" Bishop Wiley asked.

"I'm saying what I said. Don't read into it." He shook his head, crossed his arms and leaned back in his chair. "I'm merely stating facts."

"The fact is that if I didn't drop the charges, a trial would ensue. The fact is, the pictures and the medical records would show that someone with long fingernails put these scratches on me. The fact is, Dr. Jamison-Hayes could be in custody by then and she could testify. The church would be embarrassed. I'd be the brunt of everyone's jokes. I'd look like a fool."

Sinclair used her long hands to smooth her dress out before standing and stretching.

"It's one thing to look like a fool, but what you have done by your actions is remove all doubt, at least in my mind." Bishop Money closed his eyes and took a deep breath. "I'm running for the highest office in the country. And with the backing I have, I've got a damn good chance at winning, but not with these idiots out there trying to scandalize my good name and worse, trying to kill me." His eyes popped open. "How in the hell do you think you were taken to the hospital and admitted under another name?" Bishop Money was on his feet. "If it wasn't for me, you'd be all over the news and in the papers. I can see the headlines" He waved an arm in front of him. "Hundred-forty-pound psychiatrist-soccer mom whips Bishop's big ass. I'm the Moses of the 21st century. The miracles I've performed over the last couple months. How could you not think?"

Bishop Wiley stood there, fuming at the way his friend spoke to him. And what made him wanna explode even more was that he was being berated in front of a woman. But the rage in Bishop Money's eyes and the fear in his own heart caused Bishop Wiley to stand there with his chin on his chest like a grammar school kid being disciplined by the school principal.

Bishop Money banged a fist on his desk. "How? If I can travel seven-thousand miles across land and sea to a foreign country and negotiate the release of fourteen hostages, you didn't think I could make this disappear? You didn't even think to call me before you did something so irresponsible and so detrimental to my campaign." He walked around his desk and stood in front of Bishop Wiley.

"I, I didn't—"

"Think." Bishop Money tapped a finger repeatedly on the side of Bishop Wiley's head. "That's your problem. You don't think. How do you expect me to turn over the reins to the main church to you, when you continue to disappoint me?" He looked Bishop Wiley up and down. "How can you represent me and my vision when you are blinded by ignorance and incompetence?"

This was an all-time low. He couldn't believe after all he'd done. Embezzlement, entrapment, the video recordings. For what? Six years. Six years of doing his dirty work.

Bishop Money adjusted his pants and sat on a corner of his desk. "Bishop, I made you my second in command because I believed in you. Still do." He exhaled with a humph. "Am I disappointed? Yes, I am, but you've proven yourself in the past to be loyal. I don't know what has happened to you as of late, but for us to get through this, you are not to do anything unless it goes through me or Sinclair."

"Sinclair? That...that. She's not even a member of the church and you haven't even known her but for what, two, three months. She's..."

Bishop Wiley hadn't even noticed that Sinclair had moved from the couch to his far right. He didn't see or feel her arm wrap around his neck until her thumb and index finger were clamped to his Adams apple. Her lips tickling the hair in his ears, she softly said, "She's the future wife of Bishop Money and your wettest dream or your worst nightmare." She kissed him on the cheek before letting go of his neck.

Bishop Money shrugged his shoulders. "You asked," he said while Bishop Wiley was doubled over in pain trying to control his breathing.

By the time Bishop Wiley rose to his upright position, Sinclair was standing by Bishop Money's side, holding onto one of her fiancé's manicured hands.

"For now, go home, and concentrate on your congregation and think of ways that you can prove your worthiness to me and my kingdom."

What happened to our kingdom?

"You can start by setting up membership drives. Have the junior pastors set up revival tents across the city. More members mean more money. More money buys more votes."

"What about our little problem?"

"Little problem? Was Jesus hanging from the cross a little problem? Was Dr. King lying on the ground outside the Lorraine Motel taking his last breath, a little problem?"

I am not a child, he wanted to say, but ninety percent fear and ten percent common sense caused him to just stand there until Bishop Money was finished putting on a show for his alleged fiancé.

"Were they?" Bishop Money asked.

"Were they what?"

"That's the very reason it's no longer *our* problem. You can't even focus for five minutes. I asked if..." He shook his head in disgust. "Never mind."

Sinclair squeezed TJ's hand. "I told you."

Bishop Wiley crossed his arms. "You told him what?"

She took a step forward. "I told him that you were weak."

Bishop Wiley took a step back.

"That you had the backbone of a worm. I told him that savages eat worms."

"She was right," Bishop Money interrupted. "When you referred to the problem as being little, I knew that you had underestimated the savage. There is nothing little about anyone attempting to assassinate God's chosen child."

Was he putting on a show for this over-the-hill she-man? Or was he really beginning to believe the garbage we fed the church every Sunday?

"When backed into a corner, a savage is the most viciously violent beast in the animal kingdom. There's no taming them. You just have to find them and cut out the heart and the head. Although Dr. Jamison-Hayes is not the head , she is their heart. Don't worry, I got something very special planned for Sam Turner, the One-Frees, and that witch, Cheyenne." Bishop Money nodded with a devious look on his face.

Chapter 31

"**I** got it," Assata said in Spanish before disconnecting the call.

Assata didn't hear Cherry's footsteps as she walked onto the hardwood kitchen floor. "What do you have?" Cherry asked, using the Spanish that she had learned from being in Cuba the last year.

Assata put a hand over her heart. "Nothing, but I almost had a heart attack, you sneakin' up on me like that. I thought you were still asleep."

"I was, until Shabazz called." She sniffed the air. "Damn, Girl what are you cooking?"

"Frituras de maiz tiernos."

Cherry walked over to the stainless steel grill, encased in granite on the island adjacent to the closet-sized sub zero refrigerator. "Wish we had time to enjoy them. We have to meet Shabazz in East Atlanta."

"Where has he been?"

"All I know is that he just got out of the county jail."

"What?"

"I don't know why. I didn't ask any questions. I just took an address down and told him we were on our way."

"What about Cheyenne?" Assata asked.

"Let her sleep. She needs it worse than we do. We'll come see about her later. I left a letter by the sink in the bathroom."

She took the vegetables and the diced chicken off the grill. "Let me get my coat, and I better get an umbrella," she said, leaving Cherry in the kitchen while she pulled out her phone and headed to the hall closet. The open closet door prevented Cherry from seeing her redial the number she just disconnected from. She texted the word "now" to the invisible party waiting at the other end before retrieving the hooded black nylon and cotton North Face bomber she wore a few nights ago.

It wasn't as nearly as cold as it had been over the last couple of weeks. The snow had melted and the day was overcast with rain clouds, but there was very little early afternoon wind as the girls pulled up to a small fifty-year-old wood and cinderblock box-like shotgun house in desperate need of repair. The house was in the heart of the hood, Kirkwood.

Kirkwood was once a middle class city inside the city of Atlanta, with burgeoning black businesses and the home of prosperous African-Americans, such as the famous civil rights leader, Reverend Hosea Williams. But now it was a den for drug dealers, addicts, and thieves. Even gentrification had been paralyzed by the wave of crime that had builders crying to their insurance companies.

Before a house could be renovated, addicts and thieves stole everything from front doors to furnaces. It had become so bad that builders would often buy their materials from the thieves who stole them, of course at fifty to sometimes, eighty percent less than Lowes and Home Depot prices.

"What's up, Bazz," Cherry asked as she approached the screened-in porch that looked as if it would collapse any minute.

"I can't even call it." He rocked back and forth on the bench suspended in the air by two rusty chains. "I swear I can't."

Cherry and Assata walked through the broken screen door that did little to keep anything out, including the winter wind.

"They were just kids." He shook his head. "Fourteen and twenty. I'm the one that convinced Pop Tart to get out the life and give self-love a chance. I told him if he followed me I'd give him and his set a new life where they could get money and not have to look over their shoulders. And look what happened."

Assata sat next to Shabazz on the bench. He hadn't looked up once since they came through the broken screen door. Assata already knew what he was referring to. She'd read the document on Bishop Wiley's computer.

"Two days ago, Ms. Barnes, Anwar and Pop Tart's mother walked outta her door, headed to church to celebrate Dr. King's dream, when she walked into her worst nightmare. Her boys' heads were displayed like trophies impaled on top of," he pointed, "the left and right front gate posts."

"Where is Ms. Barnes?" Assata asked rubbing Shabazz's back.

"I don't know. She had a nervous breakdown and an ambulance took her away Sunday morning. The lady next door told me the whole story. It's only been two days and the police have already chalked the king's murders up to drugs."

"How could they—"

"Its poor black people in the hood," Assata said. "They don't care about us. And I'm not talking about white folks. Our own people hate each other more than any white man ever has."

"I might as well've had cut their heads off," Shabazz said.

"That's insane and you know it," Assata said. "I know you're hurt, mad, upset, and angry. But you had nothing to do with what happened. Now, if you don't do anything about their murders, then yes, you might as well have chopped their heads off."

Cherry interrupted. "Show their friends and family that they died for something noble. Show their people, our people, that they were heroes that died in the service of truth and justice."

Assata interjected. "Before you were a thought in your mother's mind, I was only fifteen when I sat down with Malcolm at Small's in Harlem one evening and I asked him why was he on a suicide mission. He cocked his head to the left and displayed his ever-popular disarming smile before telling me that a man only has one life to live. And it was better for a man to have died at seventeen for something, than to have died at one hundred and seventeen and had lived their entire life for nothing."

"What's that noise?" Cherry asked, interrupting Assata's soothing voice.

"Just my phone," Shabazz said. "It's been buzzing non-stop for a while now."

"Aren't you gon' answer it?" Cherry asked.

"They can wait. I'm all messed up in the head right now."

"What if it's Rhythm?" Assata asked.

"I doubt that, unless she got a bond."

By the way the two women looked at each other and then back at him, he knew that they didn't know.

"Rhythm's locked up," Shabazz said.

"What?" they both said in unison.

"They came and got her while she was visiting me on Saturday. They got her on camera in Cheyenne's room."

"Then, they must have the man on tape that came to kill Cheyenne also," Cherry said.

"What man?" Shabazz asked.

"Never mind. Why you didn't tell me when you called?" Cherry asked.

"I don't know. I was in a daze. I just wanna... Just put my hands around his neck. If a man don't believe in the devil, just introduce him to Bishop Money."

"So, who else knows about Rhythm?" Cherry asked.

"In the taxi, on my way to pick up my ride, I called and left Moses and Solomon a message. Both of their cells went straight to voicemail. I haven't called Sam yet."

"Will you please at least see who that is?" Cherry asked, referring to Shabazz's buzzing phone. "It might be Moses or Solomon."

Shabazz pulled his phone out of his jeans pocket and flipped it open. "Talk to me."

"I've been trying to reach you and Rhythm since early this morning. Moses and Solomon should be here any minute. Although they came from two different directions, they were able to catch flights that landed twenty minutes apart." Samuel was talking a million miles an hour.

"Sam, calm down. I've been locked up in the county for the past three days. What's wrong?"

"They took Ariel."

Chapter 32

"*A*riel was right here." Samuel pointed to the unmade futon bed in the spare bedroom of the former crack house he had purchased and renovated. "I got up to pee, I don't know what time it was, but I looked in on her. Her Princess and the Frog nightlight was still on and she was sound asleep with," Samuel got down on his knees and looked under the bed, "Groggy Froggy's gone. too."

"Huh?" Moses and Solomon said in unison.

"Her favorite stuffed animal."

"Are you positive you set the alarm?" Solomon asked.

"Yes, I'm positive. Every night, even when Shabazz stays over to help me with..." He banged his fists against his head. "I can't believe this is..." Samuel turned over the futon, before he picked up the nightlight and slammed it on the carpeted floor.

Moses wrapped his arms around Solomon. "Calm down. A tirade won't get us one step closer to finding Ariel."

Samuel broke the stronghold. "She's just seven. She's a..." He closed his eyes tight. "Fuck!"

"Where is the main phone box?" Solomon asked.

"I don't know. I don't even know what that is," Samuel said.

"The phone box, where all the circuitry coming from the outside lines feeds into. It's usually near the circuit breaker box," Solomon explained.

"It's in the basement."

"I'll be right back," Solomon said.

"It never fails." Samuel shook his head as the tears began to flow. "My dad. My auntie. Now Ariel." He slid to the floor with his back to the ground. His hands covered his face.

"It's not your fault, Son," Moses said.

Memories of how the happiest day of his life became the worst day of his life, flooded back into his mind. Him and his father had looked and were dressed like first and second generation twins. It had taken eighteen years and both of them ending up in the same prison for them to meet. And almost a year to the day they had met, his father had been gunned down at church, minutes before he was to be married to Samuel's mother.

"Don't say that. Please do not tell me that, when I know it's a lie. I watched this man singlehandedly destroy my family. TJ raped my teenaged cousin, before I was even born. They were supposed to be friends. Best friends, before TJ stole my father's church, turned the congregation against him, and there's no doubt in my mind that he was behind my dad's shooting. And my mom died of grief less than a year after my dad was gunned down. And look at what happened to my cousin, Shemika."

"The home invasion," Moses said remembering the story that put a damper over what should have been one of the most joyous times in every black man and woman's lives.

Samuel violently shook his head. "You know damn well what that was. Shemika had spent years planning how to take TJ down for raping her sister. She tricked him into marriage and the night of the election she told me that in two days the world would know what TJ was. She wouldn't even tell me what she had on him. But it was big enough for TJ to stage a home invasion, the day before he was to be exposed."

"They both were shot," Moses said.

"My cousin was shot in the heart and the neck. TJ was shot in the leg. And don't no burglar use a .22. Only a professional uses that small of a caliber pistol. All of this and the man is still walking and chewing his own food. When I was a child, I killed for less. Now that I'm a man, I haven't done anything. You hear me?" Samuel lifted his head. "Nothing to the man that's taken everyone I loved."

Moses took a seat on the floor next to Samuel. "You call all the work you've done in the juvenile detention centers, the boys and girls clubs, the church youth ministries, and the other youth organizations you've worked and work with to teach our youth their history, nothing?"

"None of that has anything to with TJ."

"Really? So you arming the future generation with knowledge of themselves so they can be victors instead of victims of the TJ Moneys of the world is nothing?"

"Come on, Moses, you know what I'm sayin'."

"Yeah, I know exactly what you're saying, but do you?"

Solomon was about to enter the room, but decided to wait and see how his younger brother handled Samuel.

Moses put a consoling arm around the young man's shoulder. "I was you almost forty years ago. It was the most conscious period for black America. The late sixties and early seventies. I was only thirteen when I watched a carload of Chicago police beat Cornbread Jones half to death. Every day like clockwork, rain, snow or shine, Cornbread sold fruit from his makeshift wooden cart on wheels. The police knew Cornbread had nothing to do with whatever had happened to make them have ten brothers hemmed in, hands up on the front wall next to J.J's pool hall. But yet, they still harassed him. First, one cop addressed him as boy before barking orders at him. In his slow soft manner, Cornbread said, *name's Cornbread, sir,* before going back to spraying water on his fruit. The officer became frustrated when Cornbread didn't do what he was told. The cop swung his nightstick at Cornbread's head. And would have bashed his head open if Cornbread wouldn't have grabbed it. And in seconds, four patrol and two beat cops were flailing away at Cornbread. The Southside streets of Chicago just watched. No one came to his rescue. No one told the cops that Cornbread was retarded, although two beat cops knew. And no one raised a fuss afterward. That day, I watched a man deemed insane by the state, stand up to injustice while the sane did nothing.

"Sounds like Cornbread was the only sane person that day," Samuel said.

"Exactly. But watching him get beat. No, watching as others did nothing gave me the idea to start the Disciples. I started the gang to fight against cops and anyone that came onto the Southside looking to harm our people. Over the next few years, the gang grew and evolved into a conscious reading revolutionary movement. By the time I was eighteen, we were successfully hijacking eighteen wheelers. We didn't harm the drivers. We even gave them cab fare sometimes before we took off with their rigs and sold everything from cigarettes, to floor model televisions. Everything we sold. We used the monies for books, clothes, and food for the poor."

"So, that's the real reason you became a target of the police?" Samuel said.

"You got it. Framing me for Congressman Perry and Fiona Holmes's murders got rid of me and the popular black congressman. I spent ten years in the penitentiary for nothing. Richard James, the police commissioner, spearheaded my down fall. He had my mother, Rhythm's brother and a host of others killed. Like you could have, I could have easily prevented so many deaths, if I had had him killed. It would have only taken a one minute phone call from prison and Richard James would have been a memory, and believe me I wanted to, but I had to expose him first. I couldn't let him die a martyr. I had to prove to the world that he was evil and corrupt, and even when I'd accomplished this, he was exonerated of all charges. But the world knew. And that's when Rhythm made him beg for death, for days until she finally gave him his wish. So trust me, Son. We're going to expose him, and we'll get justice one way or the other."

The footsteps were fast and loud as someone came through the kitchen back door.

Moses pulled his pants leg up and took the mini sawed-off shotgun from the sheath attached to his leg. The Reverend already held a pistol in each hand, Clint Eastwood style, when Moses entered the hallway.

Chapter 33

*T*he long reddish brown dreads and the Black Power aura that followed Rhythm didn't reflect the nearly all Jewish sixties and early seventies middle class suburb of Springfield Gardens, in Queens, New York, that she grew up in. She was a law student at Howard University when her brother Pablo "Picasso" Nkrumah, emphatically and intelligently argued how Moses had been framed and sentenced to natural life for rape and double murder.

She decided to argue his case in a mock trial as a school assignment, but the more she studied the case, the more holes she found in the A.D.A.'s case. By the time Rhythm got through the three hundred and ten page trial transcript, she was dumbfounded. She could not believe that one juror, let alone twelve, found him guilty. And for ten years, she had dedicated her life to overturning his case. During that time, she fell deeply in love with this passionate, well-read, freedom fighter.

During the time of Moses King's incarceration, Rhythm watched the Disciples grow and evolve into something he never intended. She also watched her brother split from the Disciples and start his own drug-running gang, the Gangsta Gods. The two gangs went to war over drugs and turf. It was a war created by the unseen hand of a government-funded counter intelligence splinter cell.

After three tours in Vietnam and graduating an honor student with a master's degree from Loyola University's School of Divinity, Solomon went on to start New Dimensions First Church of God, on the South side of Chicago in the middle of the two gang war zones. He was known as the Soul King, having put cool and rhythm into his God-ordered steps.

His popularity increased as he began ministering to gang members in back alleys, bars, pool halls, street corners, and anywhere he found them congregating. Slowly, members of his brother's gang started attending Sunday service in the old abandoned warehouse that Solomon used for church. When Reverend Ike was preaching the message of financial prosperity, Reverend King was preaching the message of unity and cultural awareness, and how that led to community prosperity.

Rhythm's half-brother, Pablo Picasso's untimely death by the hands of the former police commissioner and Chicago mayor, Richard James, brought both of the warring gangs together, with Reverend King leading the newly-united two groups to fight against the system. As a show of unity, they decided to all change their last names to One-Free, symbolizing their togetherness and their fight for individual and group freedom, justice, and equality. The One-Free movement grew like weeds in an unattended fertile garden.

First, Chicago, Milwaukee, Indianapolis, and then Detroit. Gang members, college students, young men and women all over the Midwest and later, the nation, began legally changing their names as New Dimensions spread to other cities. But the movement had subsided and lost its romantic pull as prosperity preachers began to emerge and build convention center-like churches in the nineties.

Preaching the money game began to really grow during the Reagan era, and by the time baby Bush stole office, it seemed like every crook, con man, and preacher was selling the prosperity dream to those who had never known what it was to be prosperous. The only thing was that they couldn't see that the only person prospering was the man spreading the message and pocketing their money.

This and so much more crossed Rhythm's mind as she sat in the six-by-nine cold concrete and metal cell, isolated from everyone else. She'd been locked up for three days and in the hole for one. And to her surprise, she had never thought as clear as she was thinking now. The way the community and the One-Free family came together to take Richard James and Part Two, the FBI-like government faction, down gave her the idea for a plan to take down Bishop Money.

*****

The taxi dropped Bishop Money off at a Shell gas station. It was two in the morning on a Thursday. The Stone Mountain, Georgia streets were sleeping, but the lights on the gated Comfort Garden retirement community across the street were wide awake. It was a small setback, but not anything to deter the bishop from the task at hand. He wasn't too worried about anyone being able to identify him because he was more covered up than a Muslim woman on Friday. He stuck his hands in the pocket of his black hooded coat and walked across the street.

Comfort Gardens was one of the nation's largest luxury nursing homes and assisted living retirement communities. It was more like a small city for the elderly. Grocery stores, a movie theatre, a mini-mall, two rec centers, an eighteen-hole golf course, you name it, Comfort Gardens had all the simple things and all the luxuries of life.

Novovae Jamison packed up and had left the Cheyenne reservation in Pacqua, Missouri five years ago. For sixty years she served as the after-life seer for Native Americans on the reservation. She prepared the dying and their loved ones for the transition from this life to the next. It wasn't a job you applied for, it was one that you wore born to do. At eight years old, her parents had discovered her gift, and at fourteen, she went before the tribal elders and drunk from the cup of life.

The cup was filled with blood from the elders. It was said to enhance her gift of seeing. Her gift had proved to be more of a curse, at least as far as her personal life was concerned.

Fifty-two years ago, she took a shotgun and blasted holes in all the tires of her stubborn husband's truck after he refused to stay home from his job at the lumber plant alongside the Red River, not too far from the reservation. That day all twelve men on her husband's team were crushed to death in a freak accident.

A year had passed without any visions. It was a relief not to see death in her day and night dreams. She had just wished her husband could get over the guilt of not being there to try and save his men. A guilt that led him to the bottle to drown out his shame. Then one day, she dropped the two bags of groceries she carried and fell to the dirt ground outside of the market screaming the words "my baby."

On the other side of town, her drunken husband had just plowed his truck into a gas pump, instantly causing an explosion, killing him and their two-year-old son.

Years later, Navovae remarried, this time to a well-to-do black attorney and Native American rights activist. It had been twenty years since she'd been pregnant. Navovae thought God's punishment was for her to remain barren until, at forty, she became pregnant with her second child. Nine months later, she gave birth to Cheyenne Navovae Jamison on May 19, 1975.

Mother and daughter had been the best of friends until Cheyenne's father passed away nine years ago. Since then, their relationship had been almost non-existent. So, five years ago in 2007, Navovae packed up and left Pacqua, Missouri and moved to Atlanta in hopes of repairing their relationship. She'd had a little success but not much. But she did get the chance to meet and fall in love with her granddaughter, Ariel.

Although she hated her gift, she enjoyed consoling and preparing others for life in the hereafter. Christianity was not very different from her religion, so it was easy for her to continue doing what she loved in a Christian environment. At first, she began as a volunteer at Comfort Gardens, but a month later, she decided to move in. She made friends easily, and she was used to being in a close-knit community, just not one with so many luxuries. Being a full-blooded Native American, Medicaid paid forty percent of the annual quarter million dollar living expenses instead of the twenty-five percent everyone else that received Medicaid was entitled to. But money wasn't a problem, her husband had a ten million dollar life insurance policy, which Navovae collected on after he had passed away.

Finally, the day she had dreamed about years ago was here. The dream, that when fulfilled, would give her daughter peace and hopefully earn her forgiveness.

Novovae Jamison sat in an antique rocking chair in the front room of her apartment. The deadbolt wasn't even in its locking position, which made breaking into the apartment much easier. In no time the intruder navigated his way down the dark entry way.

"I've been expecting you," Novovae said, her back to him as she slowly rocked in her chair.

He stopped a few feet from her. His heart began to race. No one, not even Sinclair knew were he was or what he had planned. And why wasn't this old woman in bed? It was two-fifteen in the morning.

"Don't worry, no one knows you're here but me, you and God. So, if you will get on with what you came to do, I'd appreciate it," she said.

"If you know why I'm here, why are you here?" he asked.

"Destiny. I tried to alter it twice before, and both times I lost twice as much as I would have if I just would've let God's will play out as it was written before the first man walked this earth."

Bishop Money didn't believe in anything he couldn't see, but this woman made the hair stand up on the back of his neck. Navovae didn't turn around. She was calm. She was like a still wind right before a tornado.

"I will not resist until the end. And then, my struggle will only be out of reflex and instinct," the woman said, slowly rocking back and forth in the dark.

Bishop Money put the plastic bag and the shoe string that he planned to suffocate her with back into his coat pocket and ran up out of that small apartment, leaving Navovae as he had found her.

Chapter 34

*M*oses and Rhythm had just gotten into the back of the black Lincoln Navigator that Solomon had rented two days ago after he and Moses had flown into town.

Rhythm reached forward and put a hand on Solomon's arm. "Thank you so much—

"Woman, if you don't quit with the thank yous. We're family. I only did what you would have done for me."

"I've known Judge Gonzalez for years. I can't believe she denied my bond." She looked over at Solomon. "I don't know how you did it, but I'm just glad you did whatever you did to get me out of there."

"I didn't just promise I'd treat Bill to a game, but I had to promise I'd let him win at golf. All of that for him to just talk to his wife."

"You'll have to introduce me to Hillary so I can thank her myself." She sat back on the gray leather seat, and grabbed her husband's hand, while silently thanking God for him and his brother. "I know this sounds crazy, but over the last few days, staring at the four dull gray metal walls of my six-by-nine cell in solitary confinement, I was able to relax. I mean fully relax."

"What were you in the hole for?" Moses asked.

She squeezed her husband's strong, calloused hand. "Nothing. Just a miscommunication. But it all worked out for the best. I came up with a plan to take Terrell down. How soon can we get everyone together?"

"Everyone's already together. They're up at the cabin waiting for us." Moses bit his bottom lip.

"Baby, what's wrong? You're biting your bottom lip," Rhythm said.

"Ariel was taken from Samuel's home day before yesterday in the middle of the night."

She leaned forward. "What do you mean taken?"

"Samuel was sleep when someone cut the power and disconnected the houses' back-up alarm battery in the basement."

Solomon interrupted. "Actually someone had gotten into the house when Samuel or Shabazz was there, went down into the basement and disconnected the back-up battery. This could have been two days or two weeks ago. But the main power was disconnected and reconnected sometime between midnight and four Wednesday morning when she was kidnapped."

"Two days ago, Wednesday?" Rhythm asked.

Moses nodded.

"Why would they reconnect the power? And how could someone have gotten in while Samuel or Shabazz was there? As overprotective and paranoid as those two are."

"That's what everybody's asking themselves," Solomon said while getting onto the expressway.

"Any word from Cheyenne?"

"Yes and no," Moses said.

"What does that mean?"

"Assata found her at C. Wendell's house," Moses said.

"Huh?" Rhythm said.

"Long story. I'll explain in a few, but she was taken from our house between the time Assata and Cherry were with Shabazz or with us the afternoon after Ariel was kidnapped."

The hour and a half drive up to the North Georgia Mountains was just enough time for Rhythm to be filled in on everything she'd missed over the last five days she'd been in jail.

*****

It was six in the evening, but by the way it looked outside you would have thought it was much later. Assata, Cherry, Babygirl, Shabazz, Samuel, Solomon and Moses had been there for two hours, playing catch up and asking the same two questions. Why and how? Why was Bishop Money doing this and how was he doing it?

"Look, we've been feeling sorry for ourselves and for those we've lost since knowing Terrell. We've reacted instead of acted."

"What do you mean?" Samuel asked his sister-in-law.

"All of our responses have been to what Terrell has done to us directly or indirectly," Rhythm said. "We've been trying to figure out why he has done what he has, and how he's been able to not only get away with it, but become more loved by the communities he morally tears down."

"What's wrong with us analyzing everything?" Solomon asked.

"Nothing, but you can't analyze the illogical. Bishop Money is insane," Rhythm said.

"Or he's a genius at deception," Cherry said.

"He's both. An insane master of deception. We've always thought money was why he did what he did, right?"

A couple heads nodded.

"We were wrong. It's never been about money. It's always been about the power that money brings. The man has

179

a short man complex bigger than life." She looked over at Samuel. "Doing what he did to your teenage cousin was about control, power. And helping your father build One World Faith, and becoming one of the most respected men in the city, and then tearing him down to nothing and taking his place on the pulpit was about control. Power. Marrying your cousin, the sister of the girl he raped all those years ago was about control and power. And then years later, having her killed was about—"

"Power," Samuel said.

"Yes. So you see, this man likes to watch and help build people up before slowly tearing them down and taking everything from them. Exactly what we are going to do to him."

Everyone nodded as if a light had just popped on in their heads.

"We are going to wait, hope and do everything we can to help him win the Democratic nomination."

Cherry looked at Rhythm as if she had lost her mind. "Girl, I don't know what they did to you in the County. Them five days you spent in jail was way too much."

"Not too much. Just enough for me to see what none of us saw. This man's blood-thirsty lust for power. I say we give it to him and when he wins the nomination, we start to do what the government did to every great black leader before they destroyed him."

"Assassinate their character." Assata spoke up. "Play him against the people he's closest to."

"What about my peoples? Pop Tart, his brother, Anwar, Extra and the others." Shabazz stood up. "I love all y'all more than a rat loves cheese, but the streets want blood and I do, too."

"And they'll get it little brother." Moses squeezed Shabazz's shoulder. "The nomination is four months away. You just need to mobilize the youngsters, you and Samuel, groom them, both of you, I'm sure my Queen has a position for them to play." He winked at his wife.

"In the meantime and in-between time, what we gon' do about Ariel and Cheyenne?" Shabazz asked.

"First," Rhythm looked over at Samuel, "you have Ms. Jamison's phone number with you?"

He nodded.

"Good. Tell her that Ariel has been kidnapped and that you need for her to meet you down at the police station to report it."

Cell phone service was up and down in the mountains, so he went into the master bedroom and made the call while everyone stood and sat in the kitchen, verbally redefining their roles in the plot to expose and destroy Bishop Money.

Ten minutes later, Samuel walked back into the kitchen.

"What did she say?" Babygirl asked.

He shook his head. "Nothing."

"Samuel?" Moses said, looking at the young brother.

"Ms. McMichael, the lady who cooked and cleaned for Novovae answered her cell phone. She had been hoping Cheyenne, a family member, or someone from her tribe back home would call since all the numbers in Novovae's phones address book had been deleted."

"What happened?" Cherry nervously asked.

"She's dead. Asphyxiation," Samuel said.

"Cheyenne's mother was smothered?" Babygirl asked.

"When? How?" Rhythm asked.

"Duct tape, a plastic bag and some shoestring. Ms. McMichael found her this morning in her rocking chair, wearing a wedding dress."

Chapter 35

" *L*isten to me, TJ. The people I work for are killers. The absolute best. They invented killing. They are *the* apex of master manipulators. They had to manipulate, kill, and even eat their own offspring to survive in the caves of Europe ten thousand years ago. They have more money than God, and they will kill you, forget the money they lost, and forget that you ever existed."

He grabbed her by the shoulders. "Sinclair, I swear to you I did not touch that woman."

"Bullshit. You crept out last night and lost the tail we, they had on you. The woman who shot you escaped from prison and two months later, her mother was smothered to death. How do you think that looks?"

"Looks like a damn good day to me."

"Do you think this is a joke, Terrell? Did you forget that these men killed President Obama, and convinced the world that he died of natural causes? And did you forget that these men spent a lot of money turning you into a microwave Messiah? And now you're jeopardizing everything, your life, my life, and the future of America with your vengeful ways."

"Look, Sinclair. I'm going to level with you. I broke into that crazy Indian woman's apartment around two this morning. The old bat was waiting for me."

"What do you mean waiting?"

"What parts of waiting don't you under damn stand? The wait or the ing? This old hag was sittin' in her rocking chair, in the dark, talking to me as if I were her long-lost child."

"What was she saying?"

"She was telling me how she was…" He threw his hands in the air. "Hell, I don't know. The witch wanted to die. She knew that I was there to kill her. And she just sat there rocking in the dark and talking to me like we were old friends. I didn't know what to think, so I just got the hell out of there. And she was alive when I left. I don't care if you believe me or not. I know what the hell I did and did not do."

She crossed her arms. "Who killed her then? The boogie man?"

"Are you retarded, deaf, dumb, or all three. Didn't I just tell you what happened?"

"You told me your side. Now, tell me the truth."

"The truth is that you were a waste of your daddy's sperm. The truth is that you are old, ugly, and you're probably half man, being that you never had kids."

The hurt that crossed her face gave Bishop Money joy. When he berated her for never having kids, her iron demeanor seemed to melt. "I'll tell Frank, but if they find out that you—"

"They aren't going to do shit, but try and scare me like you're trying to do. Like you said, I'm the microwave Messiah. I'm quickly catching up to Hillary in the gallop polls. Everywhere I speak, the people go wild. So I am saying all of this to say, they need me. They have too much invested in me."

"They also need you not to be self-destructive. And before they let you self-destruct, they will bury you. Damage control 101."

Maybe she was right. After that old woman last night, maybe I should devote a hundred percent of my focus on the campaign. But then again, it would be a shame to squander such a prime opportunity to burn a witch at the stake.

*****

The steak and eggs on Shabazz's plate were untouched.

"I know you're upset, baby, but you have to eat," Nakea, Shabazz's girlfriend said as she sat across from him, eating everything in front of her.

"I appreciate you flying down from Philly to be here for me, but you should've called. My peoples are being killed around me. I done already halfway lost it. If something happened to you... I don't even wanna think about what I'd do to that fool."

"Now, you know." She took off her Jackie Collins big lens sunglasses. "Bishop Money bags would rather fight a hungry bear over a steak than to mess with me."

He smiled. "Baby, that fool done fought the bear and won. You crazy, I ain't gon' take that from you, but that walnut adds a whole new meaning to the word." Shabazz got up from the table. "Baby, I know you gon' trip." He pulled out a wad of cash. "But I need you to take this, catch the next flight back out to Philly, and wait for my call."

"What? Are you—"

"Yes." He grabbed her hand. "I'm madly in love with you, and I'll do anything to protect my baby boo. Trust me like I trust you. And know that I'll make it do what ever it need do, to be with you."

She grabbed his other hand. "Daddy, you just know that I'm the Bonnie to your Clyde, I'll never leave your side unless you see fit for me to. Although I don't agree, you are my king and I will do what you tell me to." The lone tear that ran down her cheek eclipsed everything she had said and felt.

Shabazz turned and left the airport IHOP, vowing to marry this queen after all was said and done. But right now he had a homegoing service to attend.

*****

The Donald Tremble Funeral Home was a historical landmark in the East Atlanta community. The family-owned business had started in an old house and was now housed in a huge state-of-the-art facility, with more limos and hearses than a new car lot. The funeral business, at least Donald Tremble's, was a multimillion dollar annual business. One of the few recession-proof businesses in America. As a matter of fact, funeral homes in or near the hood were more busy than ever since the recession, and as the poor got poorer, the crime rate rose as did the murder rate.

This day was one of the rarest of times. Shabazz wore a suit. Not just any suit. He was modeling a black and white pinstripe Armani replica, straight from Taiwan. Shabazz was sharper than the two boys that rested on either side of the podium up front in their brown wood caskets.

Slowly, Shabazz walked past rows of current and former gang members, drug dealers, family, and friends. Shabazz knew Pop Tart was loved, but not by so many.

After climbing the three stairs that elevated him to the platform stage, he walked to the middle of the room and grabbed the microphone.

He squeezed his eyes shut and put a hand over his face.

"Take your time, baby. It's okay," a grandmotherly figure said from the front row.

"Eric 'Pop Tart' Barnes was a soldier, a warrior," Shabazz began. "He lived the life of the young urban male. Now, I'm not a preacher, or a deeply religious man, and although I don't look it, I was born from a black woman's womb and raised by the ghetto streets, from which most of us are entombed. It took me learning about yesterday to understand today. It took learning *me*, for *me* to understand *me*," he patted his chest, "in order to free *me* from my self-destructive lifestyle in society. And with what little I know, I gave bits and pieces to Eric. He didn't know me, but he knew my heart, as it beat like his. That's why toward the end of his life, it wasn't hard for him to give up the fast money and hood fame, that came from being king of the drug game. The bullets I gave him, he loaded into his mind. The light that came on, he took as a sign, and soon he began to realize that his crime wasn't his nor mines, but were the crimes of the state that don't care about a black man's fate. So, on a quest for redemption and our souls we fought against a perpetuator of ignorance and injustice." His head dropped. "We might've won if it wasn't just us. But what I ask of you today is to honor his memory by joining me and taking up this fight. I can't pay you or promise you victory, but I can promise you that you will sleep at night knowing that you are doing and have done something right."

Shabazz continued captivating his young audience and at the end of the service, even the mothers and grandmothers were urging their sons and grandsons to help in the fight.

He felt bad for the boys and the boys's family, but at least their family was able to say their last goodbyes, unlike Cheyenne's poor mother. The only family that would be at her funeral would be the One-Free family that she never knew.

Chapter 36

Service room one was located on the first floor, directly under Service room two where Shabazz had eulogized the two young kings earlier that day.

It was a few minutes before midnight when money exchanged hands before the caretaker got onto the funeral home elevator.

One of the two armed hispanic men standing outside of Service room one, extended an arm. "You may go in."

She looked back at the person the voice belonged to. "How long do I have?"

"The rest of the night if needed."

Cheyenne opened the door and stepped into the well-lit room. Up until now, she didn't feel. The hate in her heart and soul for the man that had stolen her compassion and her power to reason had numbed her from feeling anything about her mother and her death until the door closed and it was just her and Navovae.

Her sense of time and place disappeared with each step. Time was invisible. Not even the air breathed. As she got closer to the open casket, her hands began to shake. Her mother was only a few feet away when Cheyenne's body began to convulse. She took another step before dropping to

187

her knees. She reached out, arms extended toward the casket. "Mommy?" she cried. The room began to spin slowly at first, then faster. The chairs started moving in a counter clockwise circle while the room spun clockwise. She squeezed her eyes shut and put her head in her hands.

"Don't cry, my beloved," a voice in her mind said.

She opened her eyes and looked up at her mother's casket. The room was suddenly still, back to normal. Nothing was out of place. Not one chair was turned on its side or back. Not trusting herself to stand, she crawled on her black-stockinged knees, the few feet to the shiny black open casket. She used the casket's stainless steel rails to pull herself up. Standing on rubbery legs, looking into her mother's cerebral face, she said, "Make me understand."

"I did it to save his soul. It was never about the insurance policy." Navovae lips didn't move. She was dead, but her voice was as clear as if she were sitting up speaking to Cheyenne like they used to before Navovae's husband and Cheyenne's father passed away.

"Why couldn't you just let nature take its course? I thought you loved him. You could have been wrong this time. He was my father. You didn't even consult with me."

"My child, your father was the greatest man that I'd ever known. I don't think a person could love another person more and harder than I loved your father."

"How could you, after what you did," she said, squeezing the casket rails and looking down at her mother's peaceful face.

"In over seventy years of seeing death before it came knocking, my visions had never been wrong. As I'd already told you, your father was going to hang himself."

"Daddy had nothing to be depressed about. You two were doing well. My career was flourishing."

"You are looking from the outside in. You're a psychiatrist. You should know that the human mind is a logical and most times, illogical, computer. I couldn't understand why he'd do that to us, to himself. I didn't see any signs of depression."

"So why'd you do it?"

"Beloved, you know that suicide is the only sin that you can not ask forgiveness for. If he was mentally ill, then okay, but I could not and would not take that chance. This life is but a second compared to eternity's endless hour. And I could not fathom spending that hour without him.

"But even that didn't stop me from being angry with myself after I poisoned your father. I had uncontrollable crying fits almost a year after he'd passed. I was angry at God for letting me see tomorrow, today. It took time for me to understand that I wasn't meant to understand everything. I had to stop being angry before I was able to understand and love again. And when I stopped being angry, God's purpose for me became so very clear. What I viewed as a curse my whole life was a tool to help others deal with a tomorrow when someone they loved would be gone to live in the real world of eternity. Once I found comfort in knowing, I was able to forgive myself and have peace within myself. So, Beloved, to answer your question, I did it out of love. I couldn't bear to live today, not knowing if I would spend eternity without your father tomorrow."

"But what if this time, just this once, you were wrong?" Cheyenne asked.

"I questioned that also. But when I started digging, I found that your father had amended our life insurance policy two-years prior."

"What do you mean amended?"

"He doubled it from five to ten million."

"And what's wrong with that? Insurance companies don't pay off on suicides," Cheyenne said.

"Some insurance companies do not, but ours did if the victim took their lives twenty-four months after the policy was started or amended."

"Mom, why didn't you tell me?" Cheyenne cried.

"I don't see where I had to, and even if I wanted to, you wouldn't sit down long enough for me to explain."

"Momma." She reached down and hugged her mother's corpse. "I'm so sorry. I'm so very sorry. I let nine years go by, holding a grudge, being angry. I never stopped loving you, mom. I just couldn't face you, knowing that you had taken daddy away from me. I don't know. I just didn't... I just..."

Her mother's voice interrupted her. "Beloved, use love. It is the greatest power. It will help you control your anger. Love will conquer the greatest hate. And just to let you know, I am with your father."

Cheyenne smiled.

"Right now, I know how you feel. Alone. Like you have no one. The weight of the world is on your shoulders. But, Beloved, remember this. God, will put no more on you than you can handle. Sometimes you have to go through hell to get to heaven. Just be strong my child, and know that I will always be with you. You may not hear or see me, but just know that I will never leave your side. And remember, love is the key to freedom. And when you learn to love your enemies, you will be truly free."

Cheyenne let her mother go for the last time and stood up. "I love you, mom."

"I love you, too, Beloved. More than you will ever know."

Chapter 37

"More than you will ever know," Samuel answered. "I love that little girl as if she were my own. If he hurts her or Cheyenne, the Army, Airforce, Navy and Marines won't be able to save him."

Assata and Samuel had been sitting inside the borrowed Custom Care Cleaning van for an hour and a half watching the front of the funeral home with binoculars.

"It don't make sense for TJ to have killed Nova. The clown is too busy with his campaign. He got Cheyenne and Ariel."

"Think about it, Samuel. He doesn't have you," Assata paused, wondering if she was doing the right thing letting everyone think that Bishop Money was behind the disappearance of mother and daughter. She continued, "Terrell knows that you know that he has Cheyenne and Ariel. He knows how close you are to them, and he knows that you will be at the funeral."

"What if he has people inside and they tell him that I'm not there? Nah, I can't take that chance. You wanna draw a rat out, you have to put out some cheese." He stepped out of the van. "I'm going inside. If I'm the bait, then I gotta be visible."

"No, get back in Samuel. I see something," Assata said, looking out the tinted rear van window.

"What? Whachu see?" he said, getting back inside and climbing over the front seat.

"King one, to King two, over?" Samuel said into one of the all-black radio shack walkie talkies they'd purchased a couple days ago.

"King two, here, over?" Shabazz said from behind the dumpster at the back of the funeral home.

"Queen one has something, over," Samuel put his walkie-talkie to her ear so Assata wouldn't have to put the binoculars down.

"A homeless looking white man is wrapping a chain around the funeral home front doors," Assata said, dropping the binoculars, stepping out of the van and putting the black sweat suit's hood over her head.

This morning, Rhythm had gone through a lot of trouble to have Navovae's body transferred to Donald Tremble's midtown, much smaller funeral home for the day's services. She'd changed funeral homes specifically because it was located in the heart of Yuppieville, near downtown Atlanta, across the street from Piedmont Park, one of the most popular places for joggers and bikers in the city. So it wouldn't be unusual for two people to be jogging in the cold at one o'clock on a Friday afternoon on either side of the street, like Assata and Samuel where, each on opposite sides of the street. Assata raced toward the man that had just chained and locked the funeral home double front doors.

"Move it and lose it," Assata said, standing at the man's back with her arm wrapped around his waist, her gun's barrel touching his zipper.

"Drop it or die, sweetheart." The man wearing the dirty, torn and ragged long black coat said. "There's a gun across the street pointing at your head."

"Got mine, Queen one. I'm walking the dog back to base, King one, over." Samuel's voice came through the walkie talkie that Assata had in her sweat pants pocket.

"Looks like the only dying around here will be you if you don't do exactly as I say." She quickly patted the man down from behind. "A browning .380 double action Cooper special. Nice," she said putting the man's gun in the stomach pocket of her dark sweat shirt. "I know you probably have another gun that I didn't feel, but my orders are to only kill you if three things happen. One, you turn. Two, you question my orders. And three, if anything happens to that funeral home, or the people inside."

"Sweetheart, I'm going to give you one chance and one only to run as fast as you can. Keep the gun. Consider it a parting gift. But run, if you want your family to see another sunrise."

"Pow!"

"Friggin' fuck!" He grabbed his hand. "You shot me."

"King one, to Queen one. King one to Queen one," Samuel said trying to reach Assata.

The barrel of her palm sized Sig Sauer .25 grazed the middle of the clean shaven man's forehead. "What did I tell you about turning around?" She pressed the Talk button. "Everything's fine. Just a little misunderstanding. Hold your positions. I repeat hold your positions everyone. I have to cut off radio contact for a few minutes, Queen one, over," Assata said, turning off the radio before anyone could protest.

The man squeezed his bleeding and burning hand as he faced the large old building that now served as a funeral home.

"Go take the lock and chains off that damn door."

"I can't."

"Let's see how long you can live with out any testicles," she said, poking his groin with the gun. "Go for it," she said as his hands instinctively moved toward the gun.

His arms and hands froze. His alto voice suddenly became a high pitched soprano whine. "No. No. No. Don't shoot. There's a bomb inside."

"Oh, well," she said, about to fire.

"Okay. Okay. Reach into my right coat pocket. There's a cell phone inside."

Somebody had to hear the gunshot a minute ago, but Assata could care less. She quickly scanned the area and the park across the street. Nothing but a middle-aged homeless woman pushing a half-full junk-filled grocery cart, making her way up the sidewalk on the other side of the street. "Now what?" Assata asked.

"Press star, then pound and then the number seven."

"Done."

"*We* have about seven to eight minutes to get the bomb and fully deactivate it."

"*We* hell. *You* will get the bomb and deactivate it. I'll be close enough to shoot you, but far enough to feel safe," she said, nudging him with the gun.

Seven minutes later Assata turned her radio back on and headed to the van with the would-be killer leading the way.

Samuel sat in the back of the van with his target taped and twist-tied up, watching Assata lead a bleeding duck strutting white man toward him with his pants down on his knees. A pants-on-the-ground white killer. Samuel would have laughed if the situation hadn't been so serious. The first time the man stopped to pull his worn and torn jeans up, Assata opened up a cut on the guy's ear with the butt of her gun.

A minute later, Samuel shot Assata a what-the-hell-are-you-doing look as she pushed her target into the side door of the white van.

"Be careful tying this one up. He has enough C-4 taped around his little man," she pointed to his groin area, "to send us to the moon."

Samuel's target shook his head at his partner's bloody and embarrassing sight before turning his attention to Samuel as he worked on the bleeding man. "Surely you two don't think you're going to get away with this. I mean, really?"

Samuel shook his head. "How many times you gon' ask the same question?" Samuel finished tightening the twist ties on the bleeding man's wrist before climbing into the driver's seat.

Assata had her gun trained on the two would-be bombers, as Samuel put the white cleaning van into gear. "Queen one to Queen two, over?"

"Queen two, over," Rhythm replied.

"You really think you're going to get away with this, don't you?" The same would-be bomber asked again.

"We have two dogs and we're on our way, over," Assata said.

"I can guarantee you that you won't get away with *this*."

"Queen, please put tape over his mouth. Do whatever, just please shut him up," Samuel pleaded as he got onto the I-75 interstate.

POW!

"Ahhhhh!" the man screamed.

"Assata!" Samuel hollered, forgetting that they were using code names.

"You shot me?"

"I didn't say shoot him."

"You said shut him up," Assata replied before turning her head back toward the you-won't-get-away-with-this guy. "We've already gotten away with *this*. Ask *that* question or any question," she pointed the gun at his left eye, "and the next time it won't be a toe."

Close to an hour later, Samuel got out of the van and opened the rusty four-foot farm gate. It took longer than it should have because he had to pick up the metal no trespassing sign and secure it back to the gate. Moments later, they were driving down a long gravel and dirt road. The sun had melted the snow, leaving so many puddles of mud on the road that they had to take to the wet, high dead grass and weeds. They passed what was left of an older burnt-up decaying farmhouse to get to the two-story wooden barn, fifty yards behind the old house. The two-story barn wasn't in much better shape than the old house. It looked as if it would fall in at the slightest wind.

"Damn, Sam," Shabazz said, watching the two bloody prisoners limp and waddle into the barn with their hands tied behind their backs with clear plastic twist ties.

"I can't take the credit on either," Samuel said while looking Assata's way as he led his two bleeding prisoners past Shabazz.

Assata shrugged her shoulders. "Some people just need a little extra motivation to follow orders."

"Whatever works," Rhythm said, leaving Shabazz and Samuel looking at the two women in a whole new violent light.

They all turned their heads at the sudden crashing sound that came from the back of the barn.

"King!" Rhythm shouted running toward her fallen husband.

"I'm okay." Moses began to rise from the muddy barn floor. "Ahh." He grimaced before falling back to the floor and grabbing his left ankle. "I knew them stairs were dryrotted when I took the other two up," he said, looking at what was left of the wooden ladder that he just fell through.

"Yo, you all right?" Shabazz shouted from the front of the old barn.

"I am, but my ankle isn't," Moses said, sitting on the dirt barn floor holding his left ankle. "It's sprained pretty bad, but I'll live."

"I'll kill you if you don't." Rhythm winked. "Baby, just rest right where you're at. I'll take over."

He smiled. "I love you, Queen."

"And I love you, King," she said, kissing him on the forehead before going back to the others.

"What was he doing up there?" Samuel pointed to the second-floor loft.

"Although our excursion wasn't nearly as eventful as yours and Assatas," Rhythm answered as she approached the others. "Shabazz and I caught two men trying to put chains on the rear doors of the funeral home. They're up there." She pointed to the loft just as the rest of it began to cave in. The two men hollered as they fell to the muddy floor.

Assata kept her gun trained on the two white men in front of her as the others ran to the rear of the barn, where rotted wood, dirt, and hay blended with the mud and rocks on the barn floor.

"Help me out," Shabazz said looking at Samuel as he tried to free the wrists of one of the two wounded captives.

"He'll die unless you get him medical attention," the other man said as he crawled to his knees with his hands still secured behind his back.

"And you'll join him, if we don't get some answers," Rhythm said, gun drawn and aimed at the mans head. She stepped over wood and hay past the pleading man, to get to his badly bleeding and injured friend. There was no sympathy in her eyes. Only disgust shone through Rythm's orbs for both men, for all four that had attempted to kill every man, woman and child at Novovaes homegoing services. Shabazz and Samuel had the critically injured would-be-killer propped up against a pile of dirt and hay when Rhythm kneeled down and stared daggers into the man's starry eyes. "I can't promise you that you'll live, but I can promise that you will die right here, right now." She wrapped a gloved hand around the ten-inch splintery rust colored wooden plank that protruded from the man's stomach. "You have one chance to answer one question."

The man managed to nod while grimacing in immense pain.

"Where is Dr. Cheyenne Jamison-Hayes?"

Chapter 38

"*D*r. Cheyenne Jamison-Hayes." Bill crossed his legs and shook his head. "It's a shame. No, it's a tragedy what happened to Senator Hayes, and now his wife and daughter.

"It is, but I'm a praying man, and every day since the three months that they've been missing, I've prayed for their safe return," Solomon said as he and the former president had lunch at a private resort on Martha's Vineyard.

"Spring is my favorite time of year. Not too warm, not too cold. Look out at the flowers and see how green the grass is," the former president said, looking out on the well-manicured golf course.

"Bill, we've known each other for what, twenty years?"

"Twenty-five, old man," Bill said.

"Do you trust me, Bill?"

"Of course I trust you. What kind of question is that?"

Solomon leaned forward. "You have to get Hillary to denounce me and the One-Free movement in the media."

"What?"

"Bill, lately I and the One-Free's have been bombarded with all types of negative press. The primaries are a month away and if Hill doesn't get ahead of this now, it will hurt her campaign, maybe even kill her chances at winning the nomination."

"Sol, you are one of my closest and dearest friends. Who cares what's said, I know you and I know the child molestation allegations aren't true."

Solomon shook his head. "No, they're not, but it isn't about what's true and what's not. Public perception is all that matters. And the worst thing that can happen to a man of the cloth is to be accused of child molestation."

"If Hillary denounces you and everything you are about, then what about the thousands of followers and potential followers you have and would have had?" Bill asked.

"Those who know me, know that I didn't do what the media alleges. I don't even know the teenage girl that is screaming foul. When my day in court comes, the nation will see, but that won't be until after the election."

"Hillary is my wife, and I love her dearly and want more than anything for her to win the nomination and the election, but not if it means helping to destroy the greatest man that I've ever met."

"Bill, no man can do what God doesn't allow him to. Trust me, I'll be okay. We have a plan to uncover who's behind these allegations."

"TJ Money?" Bill interrupted.

"That's what we think, but even if it's not him, we have a plan to expose him. My people think he'll win the nomination, regardless, but I don't. I think Hillary can win, and should win. After what happened to President Obama, the country," he looked out over the patio to the golf course, "the world needs strong uncompromising leadership. If Jeb Bush wins, I can almost guarantee within eight-years the economy will completely collapse. And if God forbid, TJ becomes president, Armageddon will soon follow."

"Now you sound like my grandmother," the former US president said. "She used to always say that we were living at the end of time, and for me to get right with the Lord because He will soon be here to collect the righteous and destroy the evil."

"Two different cultures, two different races, two different generations and your grandma sounds like mine," Solomon said.

"You mean one race, the human race, one culture with bits and piece of many cultures to make up the melting pot of America, and you and I are about the same age, so our grandmothers were of that same generation."

"Too bad America isn't color blind, and too bad America doesn't acknowledge African-American culture and what we've brought to the history table," Solomon said.

"I couldn't have said any words that had any more truth to the words you just spoke, my friend. And those words are why I won't do what you ask. I am your friend and my walk with God is way more important than my walk with man. I'm staying on the right side," Bill said, looking up at the cloudless sunny April sky. "Sounds like my ride is coming."

"Sounds like a helicopter to me."

"It is." He wiped his mouth and rose from his designer lawn chair. "I hate to cut our lunch short, but I'm speaking on behalf of Hillary at Harvard," he looked at his watch, "at four, in a couple hours. And don't worry yourself so, old friend." He smiled. "Terrell Money doesn't stand a chance against a Clinton."

*****

Bishop Money pulled the microphone from the stand attached to the podium. He looked out at the standing room only auditorium. "First, I'd like to thank the faculty, staff, and the board of director's for even considering bringing me in today on this wondrous occasion. It is an honor to be here this beautiful sunny afternoon of April 15, the day that the great

201

emancipator, our 16th president, Abraham Lincoln was shot one-hundred and forty seven years ago." The auditorium was standing-room only. For the last three months, Bishop Money had become use to all-white or almost all-white audiences. The camera loved him almost as much as he loved the cameras that seemed to be everywhere he went and definitely everywhere he spoke.

"The words freedom, justice, and equality for all espoused everything President Lincoln stood for. Mr. Lincoln believed that every man was born equal, and I agree," he pointed a finger to the dome ceiling, "but it is what every man does with his God-given talent that separates him or her from others." Microphone in hand, he walked across the stage. "America. Home of the brave, land of the free. I believe that the brave have to protect the free. The strong must lift up the weak. The intelligent must teach the ignorant. We are only as strong as our lowliest class. When I am president, I will provide jobs by renovating our dilapidated primary, middle, and high schools. I'll offer upgrade and rebuilding grants to our historical private and public institutions of higher learning. I'll build schools, no, I'm sorry, I meant," he extended an arm out to the audience, "together, *we* will build schools and together as a team a family, *we* will rebuild our older schools. It will be a new era of education and understanding. A new day where America's children will have endless opportunity for progress."

Applause rang out from the audience.

"I'm going to write a verbal check that you can take to the bank and cash on the spot. Not a check of hope. Not one of change, but one of action. One that will bring our sons and daughters home from the Middle East and other parts of the world, to rebuild and build up America's infrastructure. I'm not going to give you a four hundred dollar tax credit. I will teach you and provide you with the opportunity to make four-thousand, forty-thousand, four hundred thousand dollars. In the past, my predecessor gave you fish. That fish ran out. Now you're hungry. Your children are hungry. Your mothers and fathers are..." He turned the microphone out to the audience.

"Hungry," they shouted.

"I'm going to teach you how to fish. You and your families won't eat for just a day, you will all eat for life."

The place erupted with a standing ovation and fist-in-the-air chants of "President Money" could be heard throughout the large university campus.

Bill was awestruck. He couldn't believe his eyes and ears. He left the auditorium with his two Secret Service escorts and went to the car. He couldn't get Reverend One-Free on the line quick enough.

"Are you watching C-SPAN?" were the first words out of his mouth when Solomon came onto the line.

"What happened?"

"Hold on, Sol." Bill looked at the caller ID. "It's Hill."

"Okay, call me back," Solomon said.

"No, I'll call her back. She probably is responding to the text I sent her. Right about now, she's got to be seething," the former president said.

"I thought you were—"

"I did, too. But, when I arrived, I was told that my office sent a telegram and an e-mail stating that I had been called away on emergency business, and it just so happened that Terrell was in Boston and he agreed to replace me with only a three-hour notice."

"Unreal. This man is unreal," Solomon said.

"This is just... How does he do it Sol? How did he do it?"

"On the ground now," Bill heard someone bark on Solomon's end, before he heard a clanging noise, that sounded like Solomon's phone had dropped to the ground. "Solomon One-Free, you are under arrest," was the last thing the former president heard before the phone was disconnected.

Chapter 39

"*D*isconnected, how do you mean?" Bishop Wiley smiled at the middle aged, well-dressed woman that had been sitting up front and dropping sealed love envelopes with two-thousand dollars in cash into one of the six plates that were passed around during the two-hour Thursday evening revival services.

"I don't know." She shook her head. "Since my Harold passed away a year ago, New Dimensions hasn't done anything to help me feel," she paused, "whole. It's hard to explain. I just feel disconnected. Disconnected from the church. But since I've been coming to hear you the last three Thursdays, Bishop, I've felt closer to Harold. Closer to God."

"It's okay, Sister." Bishop Wiley pulled a white monogrammed handkerchief from his robe pocket.

After wiping her tears, she continued. "Hearing you preach about prosperity and how no one should be ashamed of being successful, hit home with me. My late husband amassed a small fortune in the eighties dot com era. We've given millions over the last twenty years to a variety of different organizations. But none of that seemed to matter to New Dimensions. The last straw was three months ago, back in January." She reached into her purse and pulled out her checkbook. "I tried to donate this." She showed him the check. His eyes lit up at all the zeros behind the number five. "Would you believe that they have a two-week thinking and counseling policy for any individual wanting to give over one-hundred thousand dollars?"

"Nooo. Really?"

She nodded. "Yes, I'm afraid it's true."

"Now, that doesn't make the least bit of sense. As a matter of fact, it's just downright disrespectful. As if someone wanting to give to God hadn't already consulted with God about the gift." He took her hand and put his arm around her. "Ms., I'm sorry, I am so terrible with names."

"Joanne. Joanne Chesimard," she said using her slave name, one that she hadn't used for decades.

"Ms. Chesimard."

There was a line of people waiting to have a word with the bishop, but he could care less.

"Call me Joanne."

"Joanne, we need more brothers and sisters like yourself. Brothers and sisters that understand that positive change only comes with Christ and a price. You can bash mega churches all you want, but you can't deny that mega churches have brought more lambs to the Lord in the last twenty years, than were brought by smaller church's over the last fifty years. You can get so much more out of a large community of believers than a small community. And unfortunately, it costs to run a mega church. The monthly costs for radio ads, billboards and our new television commercials cost. This is a business. God is the biggest and most important business, and no dollar should be coveted in the service of our Lord. Don't you agree?"

"I definitely do." She looked around Bishop Wiley's purple and gold robe at the long line of people that seemed to be growing more impatient. "I want to join One World Faith. I'm even willing to make a huge donation to Bishop Money's campaign and one to the church, but I really don't wanna go through the new member classes."

He patted her hand. "How is your schedule looking say, ten tomorrow morning?"

"I'm playing tennis at the club at twelve—"

"I'll have you out by eleven, and you'll be a new member when you hit that court."

"Sounds like a plan," she said.

"I need you to bring your last year's tax papers if you have them handy. If not, a copy of your bank statements from all of your accounts for the last six months and," he smiled, "don't forget that checkbook. We'll even waive the two-hundred dollar new member fee." He winked at her, before she turned and walked away.

*****

The next morning, Bishop Wiley and Joanne showed up at the church administration building near the same time.

"Joanne." He grabbed her hand. "How are you this fine, fine, sunny Friday morning?"

"Blessed and highly favored." She let the bishop lead her into the huge building and past Bishop Money's office.

"Bishop Wiley?" A young lady wearing a headset interrupted them as they waited for the elevator. "I need a signature on this." She thrust a plastic clipboard in his hand.

"Can this wait for about an hour?" he asked.

"Reverend Polk said to have you sign it immediately."

He closed his eyes, took a deep breath and exhaled. This is what his doctor had told him to do whenever he was in a stressful situation.

Pastor Polk came out of Bishop Money's office. "Janet, Bishop Wiley." He walked up and took Joanne's hand. "God morning, Sister. I'm Reverend Polk."

"Paul 'the slam dunk scientist' Polk?" Joanne asked.

He smiled. "My NBA playing days are over. Blowing out my knee might've been the best thing that ever happened to me, with the exception of Bishop Money bringing me into the One World Faith pastoral family."

"Pastor, Ms. Chismard's in a rush, we're going to my office to talk about her becoming a new member," Bishop Wiley said.

Pastor Polk turned his attention to the impeccably dressed, middle-aged salt and pepper shoulder length dread lock wearing vogue-like model. "Congratulations and welcome to the One World family." Pastor Polk looked up at the Bishop. "I'm sorry, Bishop, but your office is inaccessible."

"Excuse me?"

"We had to uhm, expand the campaign headquarters. I've had some volunteers rearrange your office and Jason from Kline Solutions is training the staff on using and syncing the new phone system with the computers we've set up in your office for the new volunteers."

"How did you get into my office? And who—"

The young pastor pulled out a set of keys. "Bishop Money overnighted his master key ring last week. I thought he told you."

"What about my office?" Bishop Wiley asked.

"Now that," he pointed out, "I take full responsibility. I am so very sorry. Bishop Money sent me an e-mail Monday evening, instructing me to expand our company headquarters. He asked me to turn your office into another media room. Of course, I forgot to tell you and I didn't get on the job until two days ago." The young pastor put a hand on Bishop Wiley's shoulder. "I—"

Bishop Wiley jerked the young pastor's hand off his shoulder. "I am the only other Bishop in this seven-church ministry. I am second in command. I don't understand why all this didn't come through me."

Pastor Polk shrugged his shoulders. "I don't know. I guess with everything going on, Bishop Money in a different city, sometimes two cities a day, he must've forgotten or he probably thought you had enough on your plate."

Bishop Wiley smiled. "So, you're thinking for Bishop Money now?"

"I—"

"Just joking, Paul." Bishop Wiley turned to Joanne. "I apologize for the inconvenience, maybe we can—"

"Use my office." Pastor Polk interrupted. "It's private. Here, let me give you my key."

"That won't be necessary. I have a key to all of the offices." Bishop Money reached out to press the down button on the elevator.

"I'm not next to you in the basement anymore. Bishop Money had me move the copy and record room to my former basement office that had been next to yours."

Bishop Wiley felt the pressure in his brain mounting up before he asked his next question. "Sooooo, where is your office now?"

"Where the copy and record room was. Please excuse the mess. I haven't had time to call the decorators."

"I'm used to messy, Mr. Polk. I've been apart of this church for a very long time now." He paused to let the message sink in. "I suppose you changed the locks on your new office."

"Hadn't had the time, but it's unlocked. But before you go, can you sign that document," the pastor pointed to the clipboard Bishop Wiley was holding.

"What is this?" he asked, as he began scanning the first page. "My brother's company has the cleaning contract for the three Atlanta churches," he said.

"Bishop Money hasn't been happy with Thomas Cleaning for a while now. So, I went out and found this company." The junior pastor said. "No one told me that Thomas Cleaning was your brother's business."

"Probably because you don't make any decisions as it pertains to church business."

"I apologize, Bishop, but what's done is done. I'm just following Bishop Money's orders."

"What about my brother's contract?"

"We've decided to pay him for the next three months. By then, our one-year cleaning contract will be up."

He handed the clipboard back to the young lady that gave it to him. "I'll look into it after I finish with Joanne," Bishop Wiley said.

"Bob Anderson." He pointed to a twenty-something looking white man sitting in the lobby reading a book. "He's the owner and he's been patiently waiting for an authorized signature for over an hour."

Bishop Wiley put his hand on the young pastor's shoulder, "Well *Bob Anderson* will just have to wait a while longer now, won't he?"

A minute later, Joanne and Bishop Wiley were sitting in Pastor Polk's new office.

"I am so sorry about the confusion," Bishop Wiley said as they took a seat next to each other in the large cluttered office.

"Not as sorry as you're about to be," she said.

"Excuse me?"

"There is no excuse for murder."

"What?"

"Murder, embezzlement, money laundering, I can go on, but I won't," the woman said.

Bishop Wiley stood up. "I think you should leave, Joanne."

"Joanne was my slave name. That name represents the white men and women that raped our people and stole our legacy. My real name is Assata Shakur. Does that name ring a bell?" she asked, still sitting comfortably in the black leather office chair.

"No it does not, and furthermore, I don't know who you are. I don't care who you are, anything about you, your slave name, nor do I care about your money. You have disrespected me and this church." He pointed at the door.

She reached into her bag and pulled out an eight-by-eleven manila envelope before standing and pushing it into his chest. "Open it."

He pulled out some stapled papers. "What is this?"

"Information we documented from the hard drive of your home office computer."

He smiled. "That's impossible." He found himself staring at a page of explicit Black Planet messages between a code name he used with two other gay men.

Assata reached into her bag. "I have pictures, also."

He vigorously shook his head no.

"I even have surveillance pictures from your home cameras showing Dr. Jamison-Hayes beating—"

"How much?"

"I don't want your money."

"Then, what do you want?" he asked.

She sat back down and crossed her legs. "I want Money. Terrell Joseph Money. And before you say anything, I think you should know that months ago, before the Secret Service detail was assigned to him we made a copy of everything on his hard drive as well," she lied.

"That's none of my concern. What he does is his business."

"You need to be concerned. Especially since part of his business is getting rid of you."

"You expect me to believe—"

"You're deaf and blind if you don't see what's happening. He's brought in some good-looking, young former pro basketball star to take your place."

211

"That's the least of my worries. That boy can't hold a candle to me in the pulpit. And besides," he smiled, "the board of deacons are the only ones that can fire me, and if you have what you say you do, than you know that will never happen."

"I never said anything about being fired. I know and you know what Bishop Money is. He's made it look as if you used church funds to hire Monae Loray. He won't go down for murder, you will."

"Murder? I haven't killed anyone."

"Monae Loray, the blackwater operation you hired, killed," she pulled a piece of paper from the second folder she'd taken out, "Eric 'Pop Tart' Barnes, and Anwar Barnes." Assata had the file turned so he couldn't see that she was reading from a blank sheet of paper. "Now what makes you think that Bishop Money won't hire someone to kill you?

Chapter 40

"**H**ire someone to kill you," Lester Dobbs sat shaking his head. "That's preposterous."

"Prep who?" the twenty-eight-year-old dark-skinned woman whispered as she and the older white haired attorney sat through part of the new ReShonda Tate Billingsley blockbuster movie, '*Let the Church Say Amen.*'"

"Preposterous, crazy," he whispered.

"I may be a lot of things but crazy damn sho' ain't one of 'em."

"Shhhhhhhh," someone sitting behind them shouted.

This was a completely different woman than the little sweet plump Courtyard by Marriott housckeeper that the married fifty-something attorney had been having for lunch three times a week for the last six months.

She took her voice down to a loud whisper. "A'ight, let me see that nigga lurkin' around my apartment again." She pointed a long glitter, glow-in-the-dark gold fingernail in the attorney's face. "And don't you say shit, Lester. You know damn well, whoever hired you to hire me and my child got a nigga watchin' us, like we gon' go back on our deal."

The middle aged white attorney frowned up. "You know how I hate that word—"

"Nigga! Nigga! Nigga! You think I give a flyin' pig's ass what you hate? Hell, y'all the ones gave us the damn word."

"Okay. Okay." The attorney looked around the close-to-empty theatre. "Keep your voice down. You want everybody to know our business?"

"If I'm dead, everybody gon' sho nuff know our business. And just so you know, I got cell phone pics of your old naked wrinkled behind barkin' on all fours in the middle of the hotel bed. And if I should so much as get hit by a city bus, one of my girl's gon' go straight to CNN and FOX and then to the po-lice." She batted her long blonde eyelashes before smiling. "But as long as them Ben Franklin's keep comin' and that nigga yo' people got sweatin' me and mines gets to steppin', my baby gon' stick wit' her story and you gon' keep getting' yo' lunchtime rocks off with momma." She ran a fingernail down his pink leathery face.

"You know what you're supposed to do, right?" the attorney asked.

"I don't know why you keep playin' me for Belinda Bologna. I'mma' handle mine. You just handle yours. Nine times outta ten, they gon' arrest me, and wit' tomorrow bein' Thursday, I'll go for a bond hearing on Friday. I hope I get Judge Dorsey, he soft on us cute girls. And if I get Judge 'hang man' Harris, yo' ass betta make sure I getta bond and yo' ass bet not let me sit in jail this weekend or it'll cost you another five thousand."

"How do you know so much about Dekalb County circuit court judges?" he asked.

She put his hand on her crotch. "Don't let the smooth taste," she moved his hand to her cheek, "or my cute face fool ya, Suga' bear. I done been locked up so much, the post office even know what it is when my mail start getting' backed up."

Lester was well off. Very well off. He was known as the attorney that could get anything done for a price. His wife had always said that greed would be his downfall. He knew he should've hired a professional, but a professional would have cost ten times what he was paying Luscious.

With his habit of young black girls and pills, he needed the extra forty grand he skimmed off of Bishop Money. After all, he knew Luscious, or he thought he knew her. This overdramatic hood cow was not even close to the young, chubby, sweet housekeeper that he had come to know on his Monday, Wednesday, and Friday lunch hours spent across the street from his firm at the Courtyard. And the more he listened to the woman he hired, the more he wished he hadn't taken the job.

He slid her an envelope. "I'll give you the rest after you take care of tomorrow."

"This don't feel like no five-grand," she said, taking the bills out of the envelope.

"It's fifteen-hundred, but—"

"But, hell." She stood up and put her hands on her waist. "I told you the last time, that that was the last time you was gon' try and play me."

"Sit down, Luscious Trenice," he said, calling her by her whole name, something he did to everyone that angered him.

"Until you have yo' name added to my birth certificate, you don't *tell* me to do nothin'," she said as her blonde microbraids moved with the sway of her neck. She held out her hand. "Either you unass another thirty-five hundred like we agreed or I get it from ol' boy." She snapped her fingers. "What his name?"

"Shhhhhh," someone behind her said.

She turned around. "Shhhh, ya' motha' fuckin' self. Yo' ass up here in the daytime on a weekday at the movies. You need to be on somebody's job, instead of shushing me, and if you ain't got no job, you need to be up front fillin' out an appli-damn-cation." She turned back around. "Coward-in-the-dark-shushin'-motha'-fucka's."

Lester got up and handed the woman thirty-five one hundred dollar bills.

"See how easy that was." She smiled. "I ain't askin' for nothin' I ain't got comin'. You just make sure you get me the other five after I put on an Oscar-worthy performance tomorrow. And remember, make this shit disappear. I done already tol' you, my baby ain't goin' to no trial, and she ain't testifyin' to shit."

"I already told you, by morning, everything will already have been taken care of. If not, we wouldn't be here finalizing tomorrows plans."

An usher walked up the stairs where Luscious was standing and grabbed her arm. "Ma'am, you will have to sit down or leave."

She looked at him and then at his hand on her arm. "You must don't want that hand."

He jerked his hand away.

"Solomon, yea. Reverend Solomon One-Free," She snapped her fingers, that's the nigga name. I bet he'd pay a grip if I made my baby tell the true truth," she said before walking out of the movie theatre.

*****

It was like a movie premiere. A hundred flashing cameras and microphones jockeying for position. All waiting for the star. At twelve-forty-seven sharp the spring sunshine was the first to attack the three people that came through the tinted courthouse double doors.

A microphone was thrust into his face before he could get to the courthouse steps. "Reverend One-Free, is it true that you were molested as a child?"

He looked at the reporter sideways.

"Hell no," Moses said, walking next to his brother. "What the hell kind of question is that?"

"No comment is all you need say," Attorney Colvin informed her client and his brother.

"Reverend One-Free, while en route back to Georgia. In those six days, were you molested or had anyone tried to molest you for what you did to that fourteen-year-old girl."

"No comment," Solomon said as he took a step down the top courthouse stair.

Moses exploded. "Either you all are insane or you're just plain stupid."

The long, thirty-something, slender, beautiful, burnt-brown attorney put a hand on Moses's arm, which he ignored.

"You idiots know the charges were dropped. My brother had never laid eyes on that little girl until—"

"You a lie. You a damn lie." The crowd of camera men, women and reporters spread apart like the Red Sea, just in time for a crazed-looking black woman to send the thick red liquid flying out of a gallon sized blue plastic bucket. "Pig blood for a pig. Wear that, you rapist."

In no time, two police officers had the lady facedown on the stairs. "Why y'all lockin' me up? I ain't raped nobody's kids."

Solomon, Moses and the attorney were covered with pig's blood. Moses wasn't mad because his suit was ruined, he was mad that black women across America would have to answer for this woman's ignorance. Solomon felt sorry for the young mother of the lying teenage girl, and although Attorney Colvin was embarrassed, she was from the streets of Chicago, and if this had happened anywhere other than the courthouse steps, she would've pulled every blonde microbraid out of the hoochie momma's head.

The cameras flashed and now all the attention was on the mother of Lovely Beautiful Trenice, the fourteen-year-old girl that had made the allegations.

217

The officers had the woman on her feet and were escorting her up the stairs with her hands cuffed behind her back.

"Yeah, y'all write this down. I dropped the charges, 'cause I ain't gon' let my baby be some sideshow."

The door opened and before the police got Luscious inside, she turned back to the reporters. My name is Luscious Trenice. Victoria, Dr. Phil, Jenny, Tyra, Ellen, David, Larry, my cell number is 770-912-8225, that is 770-912-8225, and if I don't answer, leave a message."

Chapter 41

*B*ishop Money stumbled and almost tripped as he took his place for the last Democratic debate. He didn't the least bit resemble the colorful flamboyant pastor of a year ago. The new Money wore an off-the-rack black Hugo Boss suit jacket, matching slacks, a Van Heusen white button-down shirt and a black and white pinstripe silk tie, held in place by a large American flag pin.

Over the past couple months, Bishop Money made Secretary of State, Hillary Clinton look like what the media had made President Obama look like when he was alive. Weak, indecisive, and too much of an everybody-hold-hands president.

Fifty-two minutes into the debate, CNN correspondent, Roland Martin begun to read the last question. "These past few months have been very reminiscent of the '08 primaries. In three minutes, can each of you tell our viewers how the next four years will be different than the last four?" He extended an arm to both podiums. "Either of you can go."

The Secretary of State began. "In the previous—"

"My entire life, I've been a man of action," Bishop Money interrupted Hillary. "If you want a go-along to get-along president, then I am not your candidate. It's great to be a passionate orator and wordsmith. Those," he turned to the Secretary of State, "kinds of individuals get the people riled up. But without action, those words are just empty promises. Really, America, ask yourself what campaign promise has the current administration kept? I voted for change, and all I got was more of the same. Do you know why our troops are still in the Middle East? Do you know why Americans still don't have and can't afford health care? Do you know why the unemployment rate is not much better than it was four years ago?" He banged a fist down on the black gun metal podium. "It's because the current and former president was so busy trying to please both political parties that nothing got accomplished. The Republicans are not casting my name on their ballot sheets come November. So why would I jump through hoops to try and please them? The Republicans are the reason the nation is in such a state of disrepair. Can you see the chicken going to the weasel and trying to repair their relationship? No! For far too long, we have been the chickens just waiting for the weasel to come gobble us up. For far too long, the Republican Party has been the party of the predator that feasted on us, the prey. America needs a lion to lead us into tomorrow, not a scared chicken that is more concerned about party relations than the American people's welfare." Again, he banged a fist on the metal podium.

"Dammit, I will bring the troops home. I will amend and make the health care bill clearer and more reflective of what the American people want and need, and most importantly, I will provide at least two-hundred and fifty thousand jobs in my first year as your president. America, you wanna see change? You wanna see action?" He reached into his suit jacket pocket and pulled out a rectangular piece of paper. "Back in November of last year, the day I was shot, before I knew I was going to run for office, I pledged to my congregation that we would not try, but we would raise five-hundred million dollars by November of this year, and no matter who won the election we would use this money to begin rebuilding this nation. I am so committed to America and its children that I sold over eighty percent of my worldly possessions and donated seventy million to the three hundred and twelve million that we have raised in six months."

The University of North Carolina auditorium was on its feet. The audience had either forgotten or didn't care that they were asked to hold all applause until the debate had ended.

Roland signaled that Bishop Money's three minutes were up, but the bishop unbuttoned his suit jacket grabbed the microphone from the podium and walked out to the middle of the University of North Carolina auditorium platform, where he spotted a reporter that didn't get out of her seat or applaud. Her name tag read Sylvia One-Free.

"And before I can clean up the nation, I have to clean up the administration. I will pass new laws. Tougher laws that will make governors, senators, congressman, and even pastors think twice before misappropriating government money, taking bribes, sexual misconduct, and even," he looked directly at the One-Free reporter, "molesting children."

*****

"No, he didn't." Rhythm said with her mouth wide open. "That big-mouth bastard is really going to do it."

"You might as well stick a fork in Hillary. She's done," Assata said.

"Well done. Damn near burnt," Cherry said as the three watched the debate on the forty-six-inch TV, suspended from Dr. Naison's sunken living room cabin ceiling.

"And so are we, if these next two weeks don't fly by," Rhythm said.

"We've stood idle for almost three months, waiting until after the primaries. Another two weeks won't kill us," Assata said.

"I don't know." Rhythm shook her head. "We lost over a thousand members shortly after the embezzlement and child molestation allegations surfaced. And we lost another four-thousand after that girl's mother threw pig blood all over Sol, Moses, and Sol's attorney a couple weeks ago."

"That's because every news station in the nation ran that clip every day for the better part of that week," Assata said.

"And what's her name? Luscious, that girl's mother is making her rounds on the talk show circuit," Cherry said.

"What's wrong with this country? You don't even have to hear that woman speak. You can just look at how she's dressed and you know she's an idiot," Rhythm said. "What are people thinking, listening to her?"

"As bad as I hate to admit it. It's partly the reverend's fault," Assata said. "The people are taking his refusal to speak out against the woman and her daughter as an admission of guilt."

"Well, I'm not going to sit back and just watch as we lose five, ten, maybe even fifteen thousand members over the next two weeks." Rhythm got up and grabbed her purse.

"Where're you goin'?" Cherry asked.

"Solomon's house. Me and the reverend are going to have a come-to-God talk whether he wants to or not," Rhythm said, walking out of the door.

Two hours and two Starbucks double Espresso's later, Rhythm was ringing Reverend One-Free's doorbell.

"Rhythm," he said, opening the doorbell wearing a white terry cloth robe.

"Where's Sunflower?" Rhythm stormed into the house past her brother-in-law. "It's a beautiful May spring day." She started opening blinds. "And why aren't you dressed?"

Answering her first question, he said, "Uh, she's still in New York with Dr. Naison."

"Don't tell me that they're still lobbying the U.N. to sanction the U.S. for African, Hispanic, and Native American human rights violations?" she asked, now opening some windows. "You need to let some fresh air in here."

He took off his house shoes and slipped back down into his favorite lounge chair.

"They're going to kill his old white butt," Rhythm said. "It's a wonder he hasn't changed his name to Dr. Mark X. He has to be the whitest black man in the history of the world."

"I wouldn't say the whitest black man, but maybe the rightest white man. And if forced to turn a blind eye to oppression or die, fighting oppression, he wouldn't think twice before choosing the latter. I've known Dr. Naison for twenty years and everyone thinks he's this white, black man that has a maniacal passion for African-American awareness. That's only part of it. Because of how he was awakened to the tyrannical system that perpetuates racism for personal capital gain, he knows that the easiest class to raise, is the class at the bottom. People that have a pocket full of nothing and a head filled with unrealized dreams. Black people. Now, after forty-years of being immersed in black culture, he's become an African-American, white Jew. He just better get my wife back here in one piece or I'll make him a martyr." Solomon looked up at his ball-of-energy sister-in-law. "How did we get on this subject anyway?"

"I don't know." She walked over to his chair. "But you have to get up and fight. You just went on about a sixty-three-year-old white African-American studies professor doing what you have to continue to do. He hasn't stopped fighting, and you can't either."

"I haven't stopped." He heaved. "I just took a break."

"A break? Reverend, you can't take a break in the middle of the movement." She grabbed his hands and pulled. "Stand up on your own two feet. Didn't Dr. King say to pull yourself up by your own bootstraps, even if you don't own a pair of boots?"

He looked like he'd fall right back down into his sunken old chair if she let go. "I never thought my people would turn against me. Rhythm, I've been me all my life. I never strayed from being a man of God. I didn't speak out after that woman threw blood on me, because I felt sorry for black women. Because of the way they've been treated by the slavemaster and over the last hundred and fifty-years by black men. I understand the desperation to lie on a man that represents black men and the way black men have abandoned the black woman and child." He shook his head. "I just can't go on the air and destroy that woman and her child."

She let go of him and put her hands on her hips. "So, you mean to tell me that it's okay for her to destroy you and what you've spent your life building?"

"No. Of course that's not okay. But my actions speak much louder than any words I can say."

"What action? You sitting in this house, closed up in the dark on a beautiful sunny day. That action." She finger-poked him in the chest. "Or are you referring to the action of doing nothing? Tell me something, Solomon," her hands returned to her hips, "because I'm confused. You know what? You a grown man and I love you, but I'll be damned if I stand by and let this woman destroy what you and Moses built, what I helped to build, what my brother died building," she said, pushing him back down in his chair before storming out of the house.

She sat in Reverend One-Free's driveway, crying mad and so full of energy she just wanted to get out and run a marathon. She picked up her cell phone and dialed Dr. Naison's number.

"Mark, I'm going to kill you."

"Hello?"

"Dr. Mark? Why didn't you tell me I'd be bouncing off the ceiling?"

"Huh?"

"The Double espresso's. You know, you told me when you needed a burst of energy you drank them. I had two."

"To whom am I speaking?"

She looked down at the phone to check the caller ID. "I'm sorry, I've got the wrong number," she said pressing the End button. Before she knew it she had pressed redial and the same voice picked up. "I'm sorry," she said before hanging up again.

"Damn, damn, damn, damn," she hollered while beating up her steering wheel. She started the SUV and threw it into drive. She hadn't made it a block before the radio advertised that Luscious would be on the "Victoria Christopher Murray Show" next Monday afternoon.

She pulled over to the side of the road. This time, she went through her phone address book. She dialed the number. His voicemail picked up. "Dr. Mark, I know I'm about out of favors, but I just need one more. Call me when you get this message, it's extremely important."

Next she dialed her police friend.

"What it do, boo?" William said.

"What kind of way is that to answer a phone?" Rhythm asked.

"I got it from my nephew. He's teaching me hood talk 101."

"I need your help."

"Figures."

"I need you to get me a last known address for Luscious Trenice. That's L-U-"

"I know how to spell it. The girl been all over the newspapers and the TV the last couple weeks. I done seen ghetto, but that child is back alley-hood fabulous. Does she have a different color wig for every day of the week or what? And why does she have to wear make-up that matches the color of her wig of the day. She looks like a clown trying to catch a trick."

Rhythm listened to William go on and on. She knew that he wouldn't get her the information until he got through talking. William was the biggest drama queen that she knew. Other people's drama was his hobby and talking about folks was his favorite pastime. And Luscious Trenice gave him plenty to talk about.

"Get outta here," he said reading the info he'd just pulled up on the police computer database.

"What?" Rhythm said.

"All that money she gettin' from TV and the newspapers and she live in Zombieland."

"Where is that?"

"Girl, you gotta get hip. That's what they call Vine City, in the West End. You know, Zombieland. Crackhead and heroine addict central. 1323 Elm Street, apartment 3."

Chapter 42

"*1*323 Elm Street, you have arrived at your destination," the computerized voice said.

Before she could throw her SUV into park, a forty-something, crayon-brown bald man with a red, backpack strapped to his back knocked on her window.

She waved for him to move out the way as she opened her door.

"Ms. Ma'am, I'm dead broke, hungry and I ain't gon' lie, I need whatever you can spare so I can get me a fix. I got hepatitis. I'm HIV positive and I'm a diabetic. Shooting up takes me away from my reality."

"How old are you?" she asked.

"Twenty-seven."

"Where do you live?"

"Wherever I fall."

She eyed his outfit.

"Oh, my clothes," he said, looking down at himself. "All street people ain't dirty."

"I didn't mean—"

"Nah, I understand." He pointed to his left. "Poppa doc, brings me leftovers and enough change to wash and dry my two outfits three times a week, in exchange for me sweeping up and wiping off the machines at the washhouse."

"That's slave wages," she said.

"No ma'am." He shook his head. "Poppa doc don't own the place or work there. He just come to watch people. He say you learn more by watching people than listening to the words that come outta they mouths."

She pulled a ten dollar bill out of her Coach bag. "This goes against everything I stand for." She placed the bill into his hand, before walking to the prison-like brick building that had bars on every window and door.

"Thank you, Ms. ma'am. I really appreciate this," the fiend said.

She sidestepped condom wrappers, empty milk cartons, and she even saw a needle in the dirt yard in front of the building. A school bus passed her as she walked to a rusty burglar-barred screen door.

"Kiss my ass, ho."

"Fuck you, nigga."

Rhythm let go of the burglar boor door and turned around. "Y'all two." She pointed to the little girl and boy she'd heard cursing.

The little girl looked at Rhythm before rolling her eight or nine-year-old eyes. "I 'on't know you."

The little boy around the same age didn't budge.

Rhythm walked up to the kids. "What would your parents say if they heard you two?"

"My momma don't care, she right dere'." The little boy pointed to a woman wearing pink house shoes, a skin-tight red mini and had a head full of rollers in her weave.

"Bring yo' ass in this house, little nappy head, bad ass nigga," the woman said as the little girl slapped the little boy in the back of the head before running past Rhythm.

"Oww!" the little boy said, rubbing the back of his head. "I'mmo' beat yo' ass tomorrow, bitch."

"Watch yo' nasty ass mouth boy," the boys mother shouted.

Rhythm just shook her head before following the little girl into the building. She put her hand over her nose as she followed the numbers to the rear two apartments on the first floor.

Someone had been using the hallway for a toilet, but there was no mess, just nasty indoor/outdoor carpet that was indistinguishable in color. She knocked on the door. She heard locks on the apartment across the hall turn. Seconds later, an old crispy-looking gray-haired man wearing long white tube socks, and blue and white boxers stood in the doorway, rubbing his huge belly while drinking from a Colt 45 bottle.

"Babygull, I ain't seent you around here." He took a sip from his bottle. "You mus' be new at da' club."

"What club?"

"You don't dance down at Drop It Like It's Hot?"

"Do I look like a stripper?" she asked.

"Hell, I don't look like *Daddy-do-da-damn-thang*, but every month on the first when my social security check drop, I have Luscious and one of the girls from the club hollerin' for more, talkin 'bout daddy-do-da-damn thang." He thrust his hips back and forth. "Pop. Pop. Pop."

Ignoring his lewd gestures, she asked. "Has she gone to work this early?"

"I ain't never said she was no stripper. Ain't nobody gon' pay to see her big belly on stage. She be at the club on a regular, catchin' tricks."

"She's a prostitute?"

"Hell, nah. She a ten dolla ho'. A prostitute is a step up from what she do."

"Where does she bring the men?"

"There you go assumin' again. She do men and women, and if they don't get it on in they car she bring um back here.

229

And if she do catch a trick durin' bankin' hours, she might take them to the Courtyard hotel, near downtown, where she work part-time."

"What about her daughter?" Rhythm asked.

"What's with the fifty, eleventy-million questions? Is you the police or one of them child welfare peoples?"

"No."

He smiled, exhibiting a mouth full of pink gums. "In that case, why don't you come on in and let me fix you a drink?"

"Negro, are you on crack?"

"Nah, but I got a crisp new twenty if you let me up in yo' crack." He smiled his winningest toothless smile.

She walked past him and out the door.

"Ms. Ma'am," the heroine addict she'd helped out a little while ago stood up.

"What are you doing sitting with your back up against my tire?"

"You ain't from around here, anybody could see that. So bein' that you helped me out, I decided I was gon' make sure no one was gon' mess wit' you or this nice ride."

She looked around. "There's no one around here but kids and it's broad daylight."

"Ms. Ma'am, you had a hundred eyes on you when you pulled up. You don't see 'em, 'cause you don't know how to look. And trust and believe, the wolves don't care if it's day or night, when they see opportunity, they gon' attack."

She clicked the unlock button on her key ring. "Thank you, uhm…"

"Lucious, but er'body call me L-dog."

"You wouldn't happen to know Luscious Trenice?"

"You seem like a nice lady. If you don't listen to nothin' else I done said, listen to me when I tell you to stay away from her. That girl ain't been right from birth. I know I ain't one to talk. I got my addictions and all type of messed up stuff goin on with me, but she don't care who you are, if she can get over or make a dolla' off you she will."

"How do you know so much about her?" Rhythm asked.

"She my sister."

"Lucious, I'm looking for your sister. I'm the sister-in-law of that pastor her daughter Lovely accused of—"

He pointed. "See that's exactly what I'm talkin' 'bout."

"You don't understand. Reverend One-Free didn't—"

"You ain't gotta tell me. I know that man ain't laid a finger on Lovely. I bet a dollar to a donut hole that Luscious made Lovely lie on that man."

"Why would any woman make their child lie, putting them through so much?" Rhythm asked.

"She'd sell her soul for a dolla', but look, I gotta get my medicine. Luscious been had a room for Lovely and one for herself at the Courtyard where she half-work, for a couple weeks."

*****

Twenty minutes later, Rhythm had paid the Courtyard shuttle bus driver twenty-dollars to find out the rooms that Luscious was renting. She didn't want to take a chance on the front desk alerting Luscious that someone was looking for her.

She looked down at the napkin, as she turned the corner. Room 115 and room 113. "I am so sorry," Rhythm said after bumping into the beautiful young girl, making her drop a handful of snacks. "Let me help you with that." Rhythm bent down, picking up the candy bars and bags of potato chips the girl had obviously just bought out of the vending machine to Rhythm's left.

"It's all right. Mistakes happen," the young girl said, before walking to one of the rooms that Rhythm was looking for.

"You must be Lovely?" Rhythm said, sticking her hand out.

The girl looked at Rhythm's face and then at her hand, like she was trying to decide if she was friend or foe. Rhythm's smile disarmed all doubt and the young girl took her hand.

"Is your mother around?"

"No ma'am, but she'll be here any minute now."

"You planning to eat all that junk?"

She smiled and nodded her head.

"You like pizza?" Rhythm asked.

"Yes, ma'am." The teen nodded.

"How about I order us a big ole cheese pizza while we wait on your mom?"

"With pepperoni, pineapples, mushrooms, onions, bell peppers, and hamburger?" the girl asked.

"Everything but pepperoni and hamburger."

"Okay," the girl said before handing the key card to Rhythm. "Can you open the door?" Lovely asked.

The two women had been sitting on the queen-sized hotel bed with their legs crossed talking for a couple hours about nothing and everything while eating pizza and waiting for Luscious. Lovely was nothing like her mother. She was bright, bubbly and very inquisitive.

"Lovely, I have not been completely honest with you. I'm Reverend One-Free's sister-in-law.

Lovely's hazel brown eyes got big.

"No, no. Don't worry, you aren't in any trouble. I just came to find out the truth. You see, Reverend One-Free grew up poor in Chicago. As a child, probably around your age, he decided that he wanted to help raise others from the slums and the ghettos through understanding God's purpose."

"He wanted to be a big-time preacher, back then?"

"No, Sweetie. He just wanted to help. And he has. He's saved hundreds, thousands of men, women, and children.

He's helped get them jobs, and in schools and most importantly, he helped them to feel good about themselves. Because of what he did to you a lot of those families, have turned against him."

The fourteen-year old dropped her head.

"Reverend One-Free is so sad. He says he didn't do anything to you, but he won't tell others."

"Why not?"

"He feels like he somehow deserves to lose his church and his following."

"Momma said he wasn't nothing but a people pimp, taking everybody's money and using it to live like a rap star. She said he wouldn't get into any real trouble."

"She was wrong. Reverend One-Free is far from being money rich. He drives an eight-year-old car and is married and lives in a normal house in a normal neighborhood. He uses the people's money to help other people that don't have any money."

They looked at the front door handle as it began to turn. A second later, Luscious was in the room. "Didn't I tell yo' ass not to let anyone in this damn room?"

"I'm sorry, momma." She looked at Rhythm. "But she said—"

"Bitch, I 'ont give a fuck what she said. What the hell did I say?" she asked with her hand on her hips.

Lovely dropped her head. "You said not to let anyone in the room."

"Now, who da' hell is you?" Luscious asked, slurring her words.

"I'm a friend of your brother's."

"What that gotta do with the price of tea in China?"

"Excuse me?"

"What my brother gotta do with you bein' here?"

Rhythm stood up from the bed and smoothed her dress out with her hands. "You know what? I'm just going to leave. I'm sorry I caused any trouble," Rhythm said.

Luscious almost fell, taking off a black stiletto heel and pointing it in Rhythm's direction. "Bitch, you ain't goin' no damn where until you tell me what you doin' up in here with my daughter."

"Momma, we wasn't doin' nothin'."

"Was I talking to you? Bitch, don't act like you deaf. I said, was I talking to you?"

"No, ma'am," Lovely said.

"Then shut the fuck—"

"Don't talk to her like that. Who do you think you are talking to a child like that?"

"I'm the bitch that changed her funky ass diapers when she was a baby. I'm the bitch that put food on the table and kept a roof over her ungrateful ass head. And I'm the bitch that gon' beat her ass and yours if I don't get some damn answers."

"Sweetheart," a middle aged, chubby white man walked up behind Luscious, "I only have about fifteen minutes," the man said, hugging Luscious from behind and kissing her neck.

"I'm sorry, Lester. I'll be right there. You just be ready for momma," she said, as he went back into the room next door. "You lucky I gotta go, but please believe, when I get back if yo' old ass still here, it's gon' be off and poppin'." She pointed to her daughter that had cowered into the corner and was sitting on top of the hotel room's heating and AC unit. "I'll deal with your stupid ass later," Luscious said, closing the door.

Rhythm looked at the girl, expecting tears, but instead the girl said, "Ms. Rhythm, I'm sorry. When my mother drinks, she acts crazy. You better go, before she gets back."

"What about you?"

"I'll be okay."

"You can come with me. I'll protect you."

"Thank you, Ms. Rhythm." The girl smiled. "But, if I go with you, who's gon' take care of momma?" The young woman shook her head. "Sorry, I can't."

Chapter 43

" **S**orry, I can't do that," Shabazz said to the forty-one young faces that gathered at the church. "I won't do that. I don't have to agree, but I respect the man's silence."

"Bazz, you my man and fifty grand, but you know Rev. is on some old SpongeBob Square pants-fifty-four fake out shit," Extra, the new unspoken leader of the group of ex-drug dealer and ex-gang members, said. "I ain't personally known Rev., but what, three, four months. But I ain't even had to know him that long to know that bumpin' a teenager wasn't in his M.O.   He done hipped us to Toussant L'Ouverture, Denmark Vessey, and the Reverend Nat Turner over the last few months during Sunday service, but here he is layin' down like a five dolla' crack ho'. No disrespect intended."

"Yeah, what up wit' that big homie?" another ex-gang member asked. "On the strength of the game you, Sam Turner, and OG Moses One-Free laid down, we put our beefs aside, put down that package and came on board. Everything was collard greens and gravy, learning about the past and seein' shit we never thought about, but I'm wit' Extra. Rev. droppin' mad science on Sundays, but he sleepin' Monday through Saturday."

"Yeah, what that be 'bout, big homie?" another asked.

"Everybody, peep game." Shabazz stood up front, staring at the concerned young faces that sat in the first two rows of the church this particular Friday evening. "Rev. reminds me of the late president, Barack Hussein Obama."

"Nah, Bazz, don't say that. Dude was cotton candy," a young brotha said.

"That's what the news wanted you to believe. He made a lot of promises. Planted a lot of seeds, but he didn't live long enough to chop down enough weeds. But the man fought the way he thought. Now, I don't agree with his tryin' to please the left and the right, he could never bring night to light. But you can't deny that the man had mad foresight, and the passion of a prophet for making America a better place. We expected him to part the Red Sea at record pace. We expected him to turn around a nation, ruled by a system designed for you to die before you were even a twinkle in your daddy's eye. A system that keep the poor ignorant and divided while the rich are informed and united. You've learned enough of your story these past few months to recognize the biggest game ever played on a people. A game that ain't changed and been the same throughout the shedding of a hundred billion tears, and at least a couple thousand years. President Obama mastered the game, 'cause he studied the past players and saw how they rose to fame. So he made himself seem lame, so the power structure wouldn't have any fear, he said all the right things the puppet masters of America wanted to hear."

"He ain't do jack for his own people. I ain't never seen him give a speech in the hood, but he went to off the map to redneckvilles, like Elkhart, Indiana," someone said.

"Come on, li'l homie," Shabazz put a finger to his forehead. "Think. There's 310 million in this country. About 40 million are black. And over one-third of the black men that is of voting age can't vote because of their records, and another third are too busy getting high and tryin' to get by. President Obama knew that the socio-consciousness of white

America is still either racist, or scared of what they don't understand. And that's the puppet master's plan. Keep the people ignorant about the intelligence of the black man. The only black man that most whites see are the athletes, criminals and entertainers that are put on TV. So, you see the president had to go to America's redneckvilles to let the hicks see who we really be."

"Too bad he didn't envision his death," another said.

"That's where you're wrong, soldier. President Obama knew that the puppet masters would save face by doing a Sadaam Hussein on him as soon as he stepped out of his place. He just hoped that he could implement enough change before they peeped his game. Like I said, I didn't agree with his soft approach, but I always loved the passion for which he spoke. He was a little naïve up until the end. But the end came before he had a chance to push a bill through that would come to our rescue. One that would give blacks free health care and free college education anywhere in the nation, and by the bill's end at the beginning of twenty-second century, I can't even imagine who we would be. And just think, Rev. was the president's right hand man. He influenced President Obama and laid out the reparations plan."

"That's straight up gangsta," Extra interrupted. "I thought Obama was a powder-puff president like everybody else. I can't believe I didn't see the play he was making."

"You didn't see it because the puppet masters were puttin' what they wanted us to see out in the media. Just like they still do. Just like they giving voice to a black mis-educated woman that dresses like a stripper and wears make-up and wigs that make her look like a clown, and worse, sound like an idiot."

"That's why Rev. need to go on one of them shows and set that trick straight," a female in the front row, said.

"And make the black woman look more stupid than this woman is making black women all over America look? I think a little of President Obama's naïveté rubbed of on Rev.

He thought that his past actions, the One-Free movement, and everything he stands for would outweigh the negative image that this woman and the media are portraying him to be. He didn't think our people would turn on him like they have, and are doing. I guess he forgot about how the media had assassinated the character of Marcus, Malcolm, Martin, the Panthers, SLAVE, and every person or movement that had the potential to wake America up."

"All right, so what's the plan?" Extra asked.

"The plan is for you all to continue running the landscape business, and the mobile car washes we started. Keep gettin' this money and continue to show by example how you can get paid legally."

"That's all good and gravy, big homie, but we came together for game and guidance on how to get at the suits that took Anwar and Pop Tart out. Don't think we ain't grateful for the game and the grip we getting, but you, Sam, and OG Moses said we was gon' be able to put some work in on the suits that killed our peeps," another brother said.

"You already puttin' in work. The suits who took out the young kings brought us together. You ain't out in the streets sellin' poison and killin' your people. You givin' them life when they see young soldiers sticking together, providing a service for the community and making paper while they at it. Now I know that ain't what y'all wanna hear right now, but that's real talk. And I ain't gon' give it to you any other way. And trust, everything is in motion to get at the fools that took out Anwar and Pop Tart. In just a few days, after the primaries Operation Get-back goes into full effect, and I'm gon' put everybody up on game then. But in the meantime and in between time, y'all keep doin' what you do and I'll see you right here seven-thirty Sunday morning," Shabazz said as the young kings and queens filed out of the church.

Reverend Solomon One-Free, sat in his back office with tears of joy in his eyes. When he first laid eyes on the forty-eight young men and women Shabazz and Samuel brought to the church back in January, he didn't think half of them would still be coming to church, and he really didn't think they would stick with the landscaping and mobile car wash businesses that the church had funded. Although he was saddened by the thousands that had left the church and the movement over the last six weeks since he was arrested, he was invigorated, and charged up about the future of the movement, and the future was only days away. He just had to continue fighting the urge to step up and speak out to clear his name. He was surprised that Shabazz understood him so well. He just wished everyone else, including Rhythm and his wife, understood his reasons for not speaking out.

"My wife," he said aloud. He jumped up. He'd forgotten to pick up Sunflower from the airport. It was half past nine, and her flight had landed at eight-thirty. He picked up the office phone and dialed her cell. Her battery must be dead, he figured after it went straight to voicemail. He hung up without leaving a message. Next, he dialed Dr. Naison's cell number. No answer. After three rings, Dr. Naison's wife picked up the home phone.

"Hello, this is Solomon—"

"Please tell me you've spoken to Mark?" Dr. Naison's wife asked.

"No, I haven't. What's wrong, Liz?"

"I don't know. After he dropped Sunflower off at JFK, he was supposed to come back and get me so we could attend his annual Malcolm X birthday all-night, read-in celebration at the Theresa Hotel ballroom in Harlem. His phone is off or the batteries dead. I've called around, no one's heard from or seen him. Has Sunflower heard from him?"

"I, I don't know. I forgot to … I haven't spoken to Sunflower. Her phone is going straight to voicemail."

"I know. I tried calling her, too."

He grabbed his keys of the desk. "I'm on my way to the airport. I'll call you once I have Sunflower, but if you hear something before I call…"

"I'll call you," she said before hanging up.

Solomon had a bad feeling. He paused to say a prayer for Doc.

Chapter 44

"**D**oc, all you have to do is give us something, anything or anyone of your One-Free friends and we'll let you go," one of the interrogators said.

Every room that they drug him into to be tortured or interrogated had blinding bright lights. And everyone wore military fatigues and their faces were covered with President Obama masks.

For two days, the sixty-three-year-old professor had been tortured so much that he was more upset that he was still breathing than he was at the torture that had been and was being inflicted.

Every time he thought he was about to die, the torture stopped and a medical professional tended to him. And when they gave the okay, the torture started up all over again. The worst had to be the peeling off of his finger and toenails with a pair of pliers, although it wasn't until his naked body was lowered into a pit of venomless snakes that caused the mild heart attack.

So now, blood and drool dripped from his mouth as he barely kept himself up in the chair.

"Doctor, do something," the interrogator of the moment said.

"I can't. If I give him another shot of Demerol, with his blood pressure and age he'll more than likely go into cardiac arrest and this time we won't be able to revive him."

"Shit!" The interrogator ran his hands through his hair, before taking a seat next to the professor. "Look, Naison, we hoped you would talk, but that's not why we brought you up here." The man slapped Dr. Naison in the face.

Dr. Naison turned his head toward the man. His eyes were empty windows staring at nothing and everything.

"If you understand me blink twice. If not, blink once."

Dr. Naison just sat there, staring, looking like one of Jerry's kids.

"I know you hear me. I wish I could just shoot you, get it over with," the interrogator said. "But unfortunately, I have to let you live to tell the story. Thanks to your cell phone records, we got a lock on a couple Georgia landlines. I'm telling you this, asshole, so when we get to your friends, especially the ones in your cabin, we won't be as accommodating as we are to you." The man stood up and walked around to the back of the chair that Dr. Naison half laid, half sat in. "Just think, if we will do what we did to a geriatric white man, imagine what we will do to," the man bent down and whispered in Dr. Naison's ear, "to some black bitches. I bet they'll tell us what happened to our men. First, I'll let all my men have a go with them, and if they don't talk then, or if they do, we'll still bring the horses in."

Dr. Naison's mouth and body remained faithful but his eyes betrayed him.

"Oh, you like horses, huh? Dumb question. All your friends are horses. What you teach should be renamed horse history, instead of African-American studies. They run like horses. Most of their women look like horses. They are definitely built like horses, which you can clearly see when a black bitch is on all fours. But do you think," he put a finger

243

to his chin, "say for example, Rhythm One-Free. You think she can handle a horse?"

*****

"My baby's built like a horse. I mean, Kameeka's a stallion. If it wasn't for all that horse hair sewn into her head, she'd be a ten," a client of Rhythm's said into the phone.

"Mr. Christian," Rhythm rubbed her temples. The stress was getting to her. She was tired of fighting the bar association, who'd taken steps to have her disbarred because of her pending case. She was tired of fighting Bishop Money and his minions. *When will it all end?* she wondered. "You've been ordered to stay away from your son's mother. If you violate that order, you will go back to jail—"

"But I love that ho.' I just wanna work it out."

"Mr. Christian," she closed her eyes and took a deep breath, "I doubt if any woman would want to even attempt to work anything out with a man that refers to her as an animal or a garden tool. Now, please don't call me on my cell phone unless it is an absolute emergency. And you getting arrested for violating a court order that I told you not to violate will not constitute as an emergency."

"But—"

"Good day, Mr. Christian." Rhythm pressed the End button on her cell phone before pouring herself a drink. She couldn't stop thinking and praying that Dr. Naison was okay. No one had heard from him since five o'clock Friday afternoon. Reverend One-Free and Sunflower had caught a flight the very next morning on Saturday to help the hood search for the doc. Liz was a mess and no help at all. Dr. Naison's daughter stayed with her mother while her son, Sunflower, Solomon, his students, faculty, and blacks from the Bronx and Brooklyn searched.

Rhythm had been so worried about Dr. Naison that she had completely forgotten about Luscious's appearance on the "Victoria Christopher Murray Show" until an hour before the show was to be aired live. This was her chance and she had failed herself and the most righteous man that she had ever known. Although she had an hour, there was no way she could get downtown to the TNT studios where the show was being recorded live.

The author and visionary, Victoria Christopher Murray had taken over where Oprah had left off. Her following was just as big, if not bigger than Oprah's had been. Unlike Oprah, Victoria was mobile. Her show was recorded and aired in different places all around the globe. She did interviews in homes, at grave sites, hospitals. The world was her stage.

Moses was thankful for the May Spring showers that kept him in. For the last few months he'd worked himself like an Alabama slave, plowing a field without a mule trying to keep up with the young kings and queens working the landscaping details that he, Samuel, and Shabazz had started. Rhythm was on the couch, waiting on the show to begin. This would be the first time that Reverend One-Free's fourteen-year-old accuser spoke to America.

*****

"Oh, hell no. I ain't goin' out there lookin' regular. I'm a diva and you can take me as I am or I'm like last year, I'm outta here," Luscious ranted.

"Please, everyone out. I need everyone to leave. Just for a minute," Victoria said to her producer, hair stylist, wardrobe, and make-up artists.

"Okay, but we only have thirty-three minutes before we go live," her producer said.

"I understand." She turned her head back toward Luscious, who was sitting in a stylist chair with her arms crossed. "Ms. Trenice, would you mind if Lovely waited outside, just for a minute?"

"Go on, Girl." She shooed her daughter out of the small dressing room.

"So, what's it gon' be, Ms. Victoria?" Luscious asked after the door closed.

Victoria Christopher Murray was the sweetheart of daytime TV. She was the definition of dark and lovely. She was what men would call a ten. But as beautiful as she was, she was even more graceful and classy. Victoria stood up, took the necessary steps before standing in front of Luscious.

Victoria met the younger woman's hateful stare head on. "Let me tell you what we're not going to do."

Luscious struggled to get out of her seat.

Victoria pushed her back in it. "And that's make more of a scene. Now what you are going to do, is let my people come back in this room and outfit you to represent me and every black woman in America. I'm not going to let you go out and get on my show, looking like a whore. Now, if you still wanna leave," she pointed at the dressing room door, "than don't let the door hit you on your way out."

"I ain't no ho. And you ain't got no show without me. The people wanna hear what I gotsta say," Luscious said.

"Sweetheart, the people wanna laugh at you. I wanna make you look good, because when you look good, I look good. And I don't leave my house to check the mail, unless I represent the classy black queen that Edward Christopher raised me to be. And as for my show, it's not called the Luscious Trenice show. It's The Victoria Christopher Murray Show, and if you walk out that door, I will do the show without you, about you and if you don't like what I say, than I suggest you get an attorney and file a lawsuit. Now, I am leaving, because I have to get ready. Do we understand each other?"

Luscious nodded her head, yes.

*****

Women's rights groups dominated the studio audience
and they also led the standing ovation as the Victoria
Christopher Murray Band began playing a jazzy slower
rendition of the Chaka Khan classic, "I'm Every Woman."
The streaking spotlights became one as they lit the red carpet
that mother and daughter walked down hand in hand.

Gone were the glitter nails and the colorful wigs and
eyelashes. The red linen, French-cut Pierre Cardin suit jacket
and matching pants covered up Luscious's sixteen tattoos.
Lovely complimented her mother as she walked down the
carpeted runway wearing a red Donna Karan loose fitting
long, linen spring dress. Lovely had never felt so proud. All
these people were clapping for her and singing the chorus to
the song the Victoria Christopher Murray Band was playing.
So much love, Lovely thought as she looked at all the colorful
cheering women from so many different races and places.

For forty minutes, Luscious was in tears and had the
studio audience in tears as she described what they'd said
Lovely had gone through with Reverend One-Free. It became
more difficult to nod each time her mother looked over and
sought her validation by remarking, "didn't he, Lovely,"
"ain't that right, Lovely," and "don't you, Lovely?"

"No, I don't." Lovely was on her feet and had already
shouted the words before her mind caught up with her mouth.
For weeks, her mother had been putting words in her mind
that kept a strangle hold on her heart, until Rhythm's words
pried the arms of ignorance from her mind and heart. She
looked around at the silent audience, scared but knowing she
was doing the right thing.

Victoria sat in the middle cream-colored box-like leather
chair, while Luscious sat to her right and Lovely now stood
on the left. Victoria got up, took two steps to her left and took

the teary-eyed young teen's hand. "No, you don't what, Sweetie?"

"I don't wanna lie anymore."

"What lies?"

"All of it."

"Shut up. Shut the fuck up, you ungrateful little bitch," her mother spat before standing up.

Victoria waved security away, before addressing Luscious. "I'll be kicked off the air, but please believe, you try to lay a hand on this girl, I will beat you down on national TV in front of two-hundred million viewers, and if you speak to this princess like that again, I will beat you down on national TV in front of two-hundred million viewers.

*****

Moses walked into the den, guzzling down a Red Bull.

"I wish you would. Just act like you wanna swing at that child."

"Honey, please don't beat up the TV. I don't have health insurance on it," Moses said to his wife who was standing in front of the fifty-five-inch screen with her fists balled up.

She pointed to the set and looked back at Moses. "This negro."

"Hold on, baby," Moses said taking a seat. If Rhythm called somebody a negro, then it had to be bad, and when it was bad, Rhythm usually gave a history class.

"Harriet Tubman said that she could've freed a thousand more slaves if only they knew that they were slaves. Negroes like Luscious are giving all black women a bad name. We wonder why we can't find a good black man." She turned and shouted at the screen. "Negroes like you make it hard for a good black man to stay good. Go pick up a book. See how the black man and black woman struggled, fought, and died for your stupid behind."

Moses crossed his legs, sipped on his drink and nodded his head when necessary. This should be about the time that she disowns us, Moses thought while listening to his wife rave.

"Moses Toussant One-Free, what is wrong with your people? I mean, I love who we were, and I'm in love with who I know that we could be. HAAAAAAAAAAAAAAA!" she screamed.

Her back was to him, so Rhythm didn't see Moses put the can down and get up from his seat.

"I can't stand who your people are now. This, this woman," she extended an arm toward the LED screen, "makes me wanna go join the Klan. I don't even need a sheet or a hat. I'll lead them to the Luscious Trenice's, the Bishop Moneys, the—"

"Shhhhh." He hugged her from behind and planted little soft kisses on the teeny-tiny little hairs that stood up on the back of her neck. "Rhythm One-Free, now I'm craving your body, is this real." He sang and rocked Rhythm from side to side. "Temperatures rising, I don't wanna feel." He softly sang the classic Earth, Wind and Fire classic, "Reasons." He sounded just as sensual and melodic as he'd sounded singing the song on the happiest day of both of their lives, twenty-five years ago, their wedding day on Tenerife, the largest of the Canary Islands located off the coast of the Mediterranean. "I'm in the wrong place to be real."

She reached in back of her, putting a hand on the back of his neck. "No, baby, you are in the right place to be, and stay real."

They were one as they swayed together. No longer looking at the TV, both of them enjoyed the sweet, melodic sounds as they enjoyed each other's energy as their souls danced to a king serenading his queen. "I'm longing, to love you, just for a night."

"Just one night, my king?"

He squeezed her. "Kissing and hugging, holding you tight."

"Uhmmm." She let all her stress and frustrations fall away. "Don't ever let go."

"Please let me love you with all my might." He spun her around and began unbuttoning her blouse with his mouth.

"Don't ever stop," she said, letting her man gently lift and lay her down on the soft white Persian rug that lay in front of the white baby grand piano behind them in the den.

"Reasons, the reasons that we hear, the reasons that we fear."

Rhythm interrupted. "Our feelings won't disappear," she sang.

It was just the two of them and nothing else mattered. So, Rhythm didn't hear Lovely thanking her on national TV for helping to give her the strength and understanding to tell the truth. And she also didn't hear Luscious point the finger at the man behind all the lies.

Chapter 45

"*L*ies! I'm telling you." The fat under Lester Dobbs's chin moved with his head as the gray-haired overweight attorney defended himself in the downtown government office building.

An impeccably dressed, middle-aged white man sat behind the metal desk with his legs crossed, nodding from time to time as Lester Dobbs tried to explain himself.

"I don't know why she lied. I mean really." Lester smiled. "No rational thinking parent would accept five-thousand dollars in exchange for their child to lie about something as embarrassing and sensitive as rape. What sense does that make? I gave her forty-five thousand, and kept five for myself like I told you I would. I did this as a favor to you."

"Lester," the man sitting across from him, said. "Please don't insult my intelligence. We both know you did this for two things." He held a finger in the air. "One, you're greedy, and two," he held up two fingers, "you wanted me to make your drug arrest go away."

Lester nodded. "You're right. I made a mistake. I should have never tried to buy those pills to help out a sick friend. And now this. I can't believe Luscious lied on national TV. I mean it's just—"

"Lester, calm down before you have a heart attack." The man listening to Lester stood up and went to a small table near the door. "Let me pour you a drink."

"No, I'm fine. I don't smoke, don't drink. I'm clean as a whistle."

"Relax, Lester. It's only water." The man poured water into two cups. He walked back to the table and sat down, pushing one cup to Lester. "You look like you need a drink."

Lester nodded, before picking up the cup.

The man put his hands behind his head. "Lester, you are a liar, and a drug addict. And I knew this before I gave you this opportunity, so I blame myself just as much, if not more than I blame you."

"No! No!"

"Lester." He threw out his arm in a stopping gesture. "Do not interrupt me. That will anger me and the last thing you want to do at ten o'clock, the night before the primaries is make me angry. My therapist says speaking slow and precise helps me relax. After today, I need to continue speaking slow and precise. Do you understand Lester?"

"I—"

"Ah-ah, a simple nod will do. Don't talk. Please," the man said. Now, I am not asking you for an explanation. I'm just thinking out loud. Just trying to figure out why you would even enlist the services of a black woman with a name like Luscious."

"I had no idea..."

"Shhhhhhhh." The man leaned forward and banged his fist on the table. "Do not open your mouth." The man stood up. "You put this operation in jeopardy by hiring a common whore. The whore part, I get. She's young, nice figure, looks much better than the dried-up raisin you're married to and she probably does things to you that a decent white woman wouldn't do. I get that. But you're a Harvard man. Been practicing law for thirty years. You've seen some of every kind of criminal. And yet, you hired a woman that can't put together a simple sentence. And..." He took a deep breath, then slowly blew it out of his mouth. "I feel myself getting upset." He loosened his black tie. "I am not even going to entertain reasons behind the clothes and her hair. I had no idea that Wal-Mart had a stripper section. And I had no idea that Barnum & Bailey sold wigs. The time we needed her to be dressed in the attire she was so proud of, she dresses like a respectable woman, adding validity to the accusations she made against you." He walked to the door and opened it. "Steve, Mike, get this piece of shit out of here."

"What about the—"

The man turned around. "One more word. Just say one more fucking word," the man shouted before leaving the room.

Thirty-minutes later, Lester was behind the wheel of his Mercedes, driving on the interstate. He couldn't believe that the deputy director of the FBI had flown down from DC immediately following that damn talk show. And, he really couldn't believe the man hadn't had him beaten or killed. He wasn't a fool. Tomorrow morning, the Law offices of Dames, Dobbs, and Raymer would be overflowing with reporters, and there was no way the FBI would allow him to be there. And then it came to him. The only people that had a chance to protect him were the people that they were after. He scrolled through his cell phone address book. He'd met Rhythm One-Free a couple years ago at a Mothers Against Mandatory-Minimum sentencing rally.

"Yes." He breathed a sigh of relief after seeing the name Rhythm One-Free in his cell phone.

253

*****

Rhythm was wide awake, thinking about how good Moses felt earlier and how good he felt now, not even touching her as she laid next to his god-like sculptured, physically-fit body. She watched as the beige sheer curtains danced to the song of the whimpering wind as the breeze filtered through the open bedroom windows in front of her. She'd always wondered what it meant to be in love. She and Lisa Johnson, her college roommate at Howard, use to stay up until the wee hours of the morning debating what loving and being in love was. Rhythm had loved and had been loved, but with time, her love always came to a plateau.

But her and Moses had been together for over twenty-five years. Her heart still fluttered and she became short of breath every time she heard his baritone voice. And whenever the word *queen* traveled up from that special place in his soul and was released from his beautiful brown lips, she became weak at the knees. Her nerve endings still went crazy at his slightest touch. She couldn't explain it. It didn't make any sense but she no longer tried to make sense of what was ordained by God. Moses was walking crack, and she was just about to wake him to get another hit when her cell phone vibrated off the night stand. She had no concept of time and didn't care, as it had always been after making love to her king, but she knew it was late as she threw off the ocean blue, satin Egyptian sheet and leaned over the side of the California king sized bed, feeling around for her Blackberry. By the time she put her hand on it, the phone had stopped vibrating. After grabbing it, she rose up and scooted right into Moses.

"Uhmm." She rubbed her behind against her man. "Something tells me that your hose is ready to put the fire out that's burning between my thighs."

"Never that. The fire must always burn." He kissed her left earlobe. "I'm here to contain the blaze." He kissed the right. "Without a fire, I wouldn't have a job."

"Uhmmm. King," she turned to face him, "this is a lifetime and forever after appointment. You will never be out of work."

Again, Rhythm's Blackberry began to vibrate.

"At this time of night, must be important. You might wanna answer that baby," Moses said.

"Hello."

"They got Assata and Cherry."

Chapter 46

"*J*'m a little excited. Are you excited?" The man wearing the black bullet-proof vest turned to the cage that separated him from the two women, before turning back to his partner in the driver's seat. "Brad, I have no use for grandma, but I'm going first with the big mouth bitch."

"Your momma's a bitch, white boy. And if any turns will be taken, it'll be me and my girl taking turns whipping your ass."

Assata interrupted. "He's probably one of those that like to be beat."

"Yeah, you right, Girl."

"Brad, you hear this?"

The driver had been listening to the back and forth banter between Cherry and the rookie for the whole hour they'd been on the expressway. "John, why don't you just shut up until we get back to base," Brad said, as he exited the freeway.

"Yeah, John, why don't you just shut up before your mouth writes another check that your ass can't cash," Cherry said.

"Bitch, you're lucky this cage is separating us."

"I keep telling you that your momma ain't back here."

He nodded his head. "I can't wait. After everybody has a turn, I'm going to take a large hammer and knock every friggin' tooth outta your big mouth. And then," hesmiled, "I am going to stick my—"

"That's enough, John," his partner shouted as they and the government-issued Suburban behind them pulled up to a metal warehouse garage door.

Assata just shook her head.

"Uh hmm." Cherry nodded. "I'm gon' kill you real good, white boy."

It took a few minutes before the metal door began to open.

Assata looked out of the dark tinted window. "This is your base? An empty warehouse?" Assata asked.

"It's our interrogation base," Brad said while slowly driving to a stopping point inside of the warehouse. Brad turned in his seat. "Have you ever heard of Wayne Williams?"

"The Atlanta child murderer?" Assata asked.

"I'm impressed." Brad said coming to a stop near the middle of the warehouse. "This is where we beat a confession out of him. If America knew the real truth behind the child murders, a race war would've been inevitable. This is also where we planned the King assassination."

"Dr. King was killed in Memphis," Assata said.

"True, but that was a last minute change. The original plan called for his assassination to be carried out in Atlanta with several other civil rights leaders. We planned Reginald Lewis's, Ron Brown's, and Johnnie Cochran's demise here also. Back then, this warehouse was our strategy center. But enough about the distant and not so distant past."

Brad and John got out of the vehicle. Two other men opened the rear doors and roughly pulled Assata and Cherry out of the back.

"So, this is where you're going to kill us?" Assata asked.

Brad ran a finger down the side of Assata's face. "Come on, what do you think we are? Savages? We're the FBI." He smiled. "Just don't drink *the* water, like the attorney accused of setting your fearless leader up did. Drinking *the* water has already proven fatal to the last president."

All seven of the agents were white. And they all looked to be in the age range between thirty and forty.

"I paid for the mattress, so it's only fair that I get the young, big-mouth bitch first," John said.

"Shut up, John," Brad said. "I'm the ranking leader. I'll go first," he said, walking around the women, inspecting them like they were farm animals. "I think I'll have the famous Assata Shakur first."

This was the first time that she was addressed by name. He undid the cuffs on her wrists. She didn't have time to massage the circulation back into her hands before he roughly grabbed her arm and pulled, guiding her over to the gray mattress on the other side of the warehouse. "Surely you didn't think that we did not know who you were?" he said.

"For over thirty-years, the U.S. government has hired every paramilitary outfit, including the FBI and CIA to capture me. A king's ransom has been on my head for years. I haven't been captured by anyone at any time, so," Assata stopped and smiled, "surely you didn't think that we did not know that you were coming."

"Come on." He yanked her arm.

"You got three seconds to let go of my arm."

"And what if I—"

Brad hadn't finished his sentence before his head exploded, decorating the dull gray warehouse floor and Assata with blood and brain matter.

"I said three seconds." Assata turned to where the rest of the men stood in stunned silence. "Move and you'll meet the same fate." She walked toward the metal garage door where they had entered. "I'm sure you gentlemen either have military or paramilitary training." She spoke with her back to them. "You see the window that the bullet came through. And you can judge for yourself how easy it would be to pick off any of you," Assata said, grabbing the chain beside the metal garage door.

Cherry interceded. "I just want one of you to move. Try to grab me. Run and try to grab my friend. Use me or her as a shield. Feel free to test how accurate a Winchester seventy caliber, thirty odd six sniper rifle is."

Moments later, the door was up and Shabazz, Extra and fifteen heavily-armed young brothas rushed into the warehouse. Samuel stayed at his post across the street on the roof of the old grocery store building. He clearly saw everything through the high-powered night vision telescope attached to the Winchester.

"It's about damn time. I guess everything about the government is slow. Thought I was gon' have to give you fools an invitation to get your kidnap on." Shabazz said, standing in front of the proud looking men, while the brothas stripped of their clothes. "I know all y'all anxious to tell us your future plans, but don't everyone speak at once."

None of the FBI men spoke. None of them moved.

"Shabazz, I ain't got all night, here," she placed the tracking chip that she had under her tongue in his hand. "Don't go getting' brand new on me, Bazz, a little spit ain't gon' hurt you. May I?" Cherry asked taking the nine-millimeter pistol out of his hand. She looked John up and down, before smiling at him. "I need two sets of boot strings."

"What for?" Shabazz asked.

She smiled. "Trust me."

"Okay."

Extra got busy taking four strings out of the high top black boots the FBI men wore.

Minutes later, Rhythm had two brothas holding John while she tied the knotted strings around his neck.

"What, what are you doing?" John asked in a panic.

"Nothing I hadn't planned while you were calling us whores and bitches during our little ride."

"I didn't mean, anything. Your own people refer to you as bitches and whores, I just was, you know—"

"Your buddy told you to shut up." She looked over at his friend's corpse. "Bad example," she said, pulling his red and white polka dot boxers down and tying the end of the boot string to his testicles. She looked back at the others. "One of you will talk."

The man with the boot string neck tie on his neck and his balls blurted out. "What do you wanna know? I'll talk. I'll tell you anything. Just don't kill me. I have a wife and son."

Chapter 47

" *J*'ll tell you anything you wanna know. Just ask," Solomon said, wishing he'd flown up long ago and filled in the blanks. In a city with over eight-million people, Solomon didn't understand how no one saw Dr. Naison being thrown out of a car in front of the St. Vincent Medical Center emergency room. Dr. Naison knew very little of what was really going on, and here he was in a Manhattan hospital bed recovering from the three-day torture he'd endured at the hands of the murder-for-hire mercenary group, Monae Loray.

The two old friends had been catching up for hours, since they'd all arrived at the hospital. Liz and the reverend's wife, Sunflower, had gone out for food, while Dr. Naison was sitting up in bed, trashing and bashing his torturers for not killing him.

"For nearly forty-five years, I've been the adopted son in the American black family. In that time, I've been involved with marches, stand-ins, sit-ins, sleep-ins, protests, almost anything and everything to help uplift the socio-consciousness of America. Now I truly know what it feels like to beaten down by the system."

"Monae Loray isn't the system," Solomon said.

"No, but they represent everything that is corrupt about the system. They are one of who knows how many, backdoor mercenary outfits hired by the government, thanks to the passing of the Patriot Act, to do what the FBI, and CIA can no longer do to people and organizations that fight for freedom. I know this sounds crazy, but I'm not mad, angry or upset at you, the girls, or even my torturers. I'm angry at myself for not doing more. But that's okay." He nodded his head. "The government is going to feel this white boy, before it's all said and done." He looked the reverend in the eye. "Now, fill me in on what's going on."

"Rhythm had taken a page out the FBI's, counterintelligence tactical history. For the last four months, she and Assata have been giving on-the-job training to me, Moses, Cherry and over forty ex-drug dealers and gang members from the Atlanta streets."

"On-the-job training?"

Solomon nodded his head. "Four months ago, back in January around the time TJ formally announced his candidacy, Dr. Jamison-Hayes's mother was found dead in her home."

"I knew that."

"Yeah, but what you didn't know is that the morning after she was found dead, a certified letter arrived at Samuel's home in the dead woman's hand writing. In a nutshell, Dr. Jamison-Hayes's mother not only wrote in the letter that TJ had killed her, but she explained that he did it so he could draw her daughter and Samuel out."

"I understand Cheyenne, but why Samuel?" he asked.

"TJ was behind the murder of—"

"His father, Bishop Turner." Dr. Naison snapped his fingers.

"Right, but what scared TJ was Samuel's background. As a teen, Samuel was trained to be a hit man."

Dr. Naison gave the reverend an I-can't-wait-to-hear-this-story look, but was disappointed when Solomon said, "That's another story. But TJ has done so much dirt to Samuel's family, that he knows that if ever given the chance Samuel would kill him without so much as blinking an eye."

"So TJ is behind Monae Loray?"

"No, he isn't nearly that connected, but the same people responsible for his sudden rise to international fame is."

"I still don't understand why anyone, including the powers behind government would want someone like Bishop Money in power."

"I know, it doesn't make any sense, but anyway, we were waiting when they tried to blow up the funeral home while the funeral was going on."

"Are you serious?"

"Very," Solomon said. "We got to them before they had the chance. The men responsible were taken to an undisclosed location and before their timely demise, we got just enough information out of them to piece together what we had learned from the docs and e-mails we retrieved from C. Wendell Wiley's hard drive."

"How did you get Money's right hand man to give you a copy of his hard drive?"

"We didn't. Dr. Jamison-Hayes and Assata broke into his house and copied the files on his master computer's hard drive."

"Hold on." Dr. Naison shook his head. "I thought Dr. Jamison-Hayes had been kidnapped."

"Not then. And this is where the story gets interesting," Solomon said, "Assata used information copied from Wiley's hard drive to convince Wiley that TJ was preparing to oust him from his position at the church."

"Ingenious! Take two super egos and pit one against the other and use them to destroy each other," Dr. Naison commented. "So why isn't Money in a maximum security prison?"

Solomon smiled. "Timing. We're waiting to see what happens in the primaries. If Bishop Money wins the Democratic nomination, it'll be catastrophic to the powers behind him, when we use what we have on TJ and the little we have on them to destroy him and expose the unseen hand of government puppeteers. If he loses, we still destroy him, but it won't be nearly as impactful as it would if TJ wins. But at the same time, we're trying to expose one of the biggest conspiracies the nation has ever known. The only thing is, we still don't know why they'd go through all the trouble of killing the first black president to put another one in power."

Liz and Sunflower burst through the door. "Have you heard?"

Chapter 48

"*C*oming from the church, which I have served so long and a people I have loved so well, this nomination fills me with an emotion I cannot express in words." Bishop Money looked out at thousands of faces. "Duty, Honor, Country. Those three hallowed words reverently dictate what we ought to be, what we can be, what we will be."

Enthusiastic applause rang out, as white, black, Asian, Hispanic, and others, stood and applauded as Bishop Money accepted the democratic nomination from behind his throne-like pulpit at One World Faith Missionary Baptist Church.

Sinclair couldn't think of anyone she'd hated as much as the man she'd married and was ordered to stand by. She had no idea why the people she worked for were handing him the keys to the White House. But the soldier she was trained to be, never asked her superiors why, only when.

Once the crowd quieted, having committed the speech to memory, Bishop Money walked from behind the pulpit and stood almost in the same place where he'd been shot almost seven months ago, in November.

"I teach my congregation to be proud and unbending in honest failure, but humble and gentle in success. I teach them not to substitute words for actions, nor to seek the path of comfort, but to face the stress and spur of difficulty and challenge." He held a finger in the air. "To learn to stand up in the storm but to have compassion on those who fall; to master yourself before you seek to master others; to have a heart that is clean, a goal that is high; to learn to laugh, yet never forget how to cry." He extended his arm. "To reach into the future yet never neglect the past; to be serious yet never take yourself too seriously; to be modest so that you will remember the implicitly and simplicity of true greatness, the open mind of true wisdom, the meekness of true strength. And with your help, America, your strength, America, as your next president, America, I will fill the empty cups of change. I will fill them with jobs, affordable health care, a new infrastructure." He paused a moment, before asking everyone to stand and hold hands. With thousands on their feet and holding hands, he continued. "Together, you and me, *we* will make America new. Together, we will make America beautiful again."

Again the crowd roared, and Bishop Money beckoned for his wife to join him in the middle of the stage. Not because he loved, liked or even cared about her. It was all part of his acceptance speech.

For a while, he was afraid that the Lester Dobbs fiasco, was going to blow up in his face before the voters had a chance to cast their ballots.

The first time he had used the attorney was over twenty-five years ago, when he was about to be charged with molesting a teenage girl, his ex-wife's sister. Lester made sure the story never made the paper, and his former best friend Bishop Turner provided him with an alibi, so he was never even charged.

Lester had also handled other sensitive issues over the past, that's the only reason he hired the attorney this last time. But the imbecile had used his money and had hired a sewer rat whore to take down Solomon One-Free. And yesterday, the day before the election, the sewer rat had exposed Lester on national television. Before the show ended at five p.m., he was on a secure line speaking with Franklin and Theodore, his handlers. And before midnight, Lester Dobbs had crashed his car into the front of a moving eighteen wheeler. An aneurysm had killed him seconds before the impact. That's when TJ was sure of two things. One, he was going to be the next president, and two, if he wasn't careful, he, too, would die of an aneurysm.

After he became president, what the men behind the aneurysms didn't know was that after he took care of Samuel, Cheyenne, and the One-Free movement, they would be next on his personal, to-be-killed list.

*****

"The list just disappeared," Rhythm said.

Everyone had been listening to Bishop Money's speech before Rhythm burst into the den.

"What list?" Cherry asked.

"You know, the list-list." Rhythm was so upset, that she couldn't think straight.

Moses got up and went to the front of their basement door where Rhythm stood.

"The e-mail list?" Samuel asked.

Rhythm nodded as the tears welled up in her eyes. "Everything is gone."

"Baby." Moses took his wife in his arms. "Just relax."

"No Moses, not this time," she shouted.

"Let me take a look, Queen," Shabazz said as he got up from the couch.

An hour later, Assata, Rhythm, Moses, and Samuel stood over Shabazz as they awaited the verdict.

"I've tried everything. I even dialed into Samuel's computer. And now I see what's happened." Shabazz said, lying on the floor under Rhythm's basement office desk. Shabazz removed the hard drive and held it in the air.

"What's that?" Assata asked.

"It's a computer hard drive," Samuel said.

"But it ain't the one that came with this CPU," Shabazz said. "You ever change out your hard drive, Queen?"

Rhythm was so upset, that she just shook her head.

"No," Moses interpreted for his wife.

After sticking the hard drive back in the slot and closing the case on the CPU, Shabazz got up and sat back in the beige, leather office chair.

"Somehow, they knew," Samuel said. "If they got Rhythm's, you know they got mine. Fuck." Samuel clasped his hands together behind his head.

"President Obama's sixty million e-mail list, gone. TJ Money, everything we took from C. Wendell's hard drive, the pictures, gone," Cherry said, as if she were in a daze.

"I have the e-mails saved on Constant Contact's server," Shabazz said. "But that ain't gon' do us no good without the pictures and the files to send out to the American people."

Everyone turned to Rhythm, their unspoken leader, but she was a mess.

"We still have C. Wendell," Assata said.

*****

Bishop C. Wendell Wiley turned onto his dark street. So much had happened today. It was three in the morning and he still couldn't stop trembling. His pride, his ego, and his pockets would never be the same, but he took the best deal, maybe the only deal that would keep him alive and out of prison. He still couldn't believe Bishop Money had done it, he thought as he pulled through the gates of his estate, and a minute later, one of his four garage doors began to open.

He didn't have time to react as a hammer crashed through the driver's side window, spraying glass all over the bishop's face and body. An arm reached through the window and Bishop Wiley hit the gas and crashed his 745 BMW into the garage wall.

Shabazz held his stinging arm. "I'll get CW." Shabazz ran into the garage, while Moses went looking for a water hose to put out the blaze.

"I need some help," Shabazz hollered out, as he tried to wedge Bishop Wiley's body from between the airbag and the seat.

A few minutes later, Moses and Shabazz knelt beside C. Wendell, who was lying in the cobblestone driveway away from the blaze in the garage.

Blood trickled out of his mouth. "The FBI gave me full immunity and assured me," he tried to cough, "that no evidence of anything I'd done would ever surface. They showed me four computer hard drives."

Sirens could be heard in the distance.

"They said the information from these hard drives were the only thing that could send me to prison." He coughed up a glob of blood.

"Why are you telling us this?" Moses asked.

"In exchange for my freedom, the FBI told me that all I would have to do is step down, from the pulpit and One World, and never mention TJ in a..."

"Clarence?" Moses lightly slapped his face. "Clarence?"

"We have to go, man. Come on," Shabazz said, pulling Moses to his feet.

Twenty-minutes later, Shabazz and Moses were parking the Camaro in the same strip club parking lot they had stolen it from.

"Go head, I'll catch up," Moses said pulling out two, one hundred dollar bills and putting them on the driver's seat before getting out and walking to where Shabazz had parked his Denali.

"What was that all about?" Shabazz asked.

"I left a couple hundred on the driver's seat. I figured, it would handle the damage you did to the ignition."

"Nah, I'm talking about C. Wendell. I was too busy watching out for nosy neighbors, I didn't hear everything," Shabazz said as he drove out of the parking lot.

"Did you hear the part about the FBI?"

"Yeah, most of it," Shabazz said.

"If they were FBI then I'm the director of the CIA," Moses said."

"Sounds more like the TJBI," Shabazz said.

"Exactly," Moses said.

Chapter 49

*F*ive months had passed since Bishop Terrell Joseph Money had won the Democratic nomination. Now, days before the election, it seemed as if he was a shoo-in to win. Jeb Bush fared well, but he hadn't raised half the money that TJ had. For every television ad Jeb Bush ran, TJ ran three or four. For every billboard Jeb had, TJ had five.

Assata and Cherry had returned to Cuba back in June. The bodies of Cheyenne and her daughter Ariel hadn't been found. Shabazz, and Moses were at the helm of two huge landscaping and mobile car wash and pressure washing businesses that employed fifty-two young men and women.

Bishop Money seemed untouchable. Everyone involved in the plan to expose TJ was saddened, and given the opportunity, any one of them would have given their life to take his. But TJ was impossible to get close to with all the Secret Service agents constantly around him. Rhythm was downstairs in her home, cooking breakfast when her cell phone almost vibrated off the kitchen counter.

On weekends, she had her calls from her office forwarded to her cell phone, so seeing the 'Private' on the display didn't catch her by surprise. Maybe the call was coming from a client or potential client calling from some jail.

"Hello?" Rhythm answered.

"Take the turkey bacon off of the stove."

She dropped her Blackberry and ran to the window. She peeked out the blinds. She didn't see anything but a million colorful autumn leaves in her front yard. She bent down and picked up her Blackberry from the hardwood kitchen floor and put the battery and the case back on and ran upstairs, wondering who was watching her cook breakfast, and how where they watching, how long had they been watching, and what did they want?

"Ow!" She bumped her leg running into the bed. "Baby, wake up." She shook her husband.

"In a minute," he grumbled, pulling the covers up to his chin.

"Baby!" She shook him some more.

"Huh, what time is it?" Moses asked without opening his eyes.

"Seven."

He turned over on his stomach. "Twelve more hours." He covered his head with the goose-feather pillow. "If I blow another leaf. If I see another leaf."

"Moses, wake up," she said, pulling the pillow away. "Someone is watching us."

He turned over and sprang up like a vampire in the night. "Who did, who?"

She couldn't help but laugh. "I'm serious, Moses."

Her phone rang again. She stared at it.

"Aren't you going to answer it?" he asked, wiping sleep from his naked eyes.

"Hello."

"Please put me on speaker," the voice said.

She did.

"Am I on speaker now?"

"Who is this," Moses asked, walking across the hardwood floor to their wall of windows.

"Who I am does not matter. What you now have, does."

"Baby, hand me that phone," Moses said extending an arm toward her.

She did. He took the phone off speaker and put it to his ear, thinking that it was the same people that had stolen all the evidence to expose TJ. "You won. You got what you wanted."

"No, on the contraire. You win. We all win. And you will see that once you check your wife's computer."

"What? Who is this?" He pulled the phone away from his ear and looked at the empty screen. He sniffed the air. "Baby, you smell that?"

"The bacon," she said, running out of the bedroom and down the hardwood stairs.

While she was scraping the burnt bacon off the island grill, Moses came up behind her. "Just the way I like my turkey bacon, crispy black."

"You think this is funny?" she asked, almost forgetting about the strange calls minutes ago.

"No." He hugged her from behind. "But I need to laugh to keep from screaming. And," he whispered in her ear, "these walls have ears, so be careful what you say. The man on the phone said to check your computer."

Minutes later, they were in Rhythm's basement home office. Moses sat on the corner of the pool table while Rhythm checked her e-mail. And there it was. She made a mental note to change her cell phone service over to Verizon. This wasn't the first time an e-mail message wasn't forwarded over to her Blackberry. The message in her inbox read. LOG INTO YAHOO MAIL. UNDER THE USERS NAME TYPE OPERATION _123MONEY AND THE PASSWORD IS GAMEOVER_123.

Once she did as the message instructed, six zip drive attachments popped up. "Moses?" she said, staring at the thirty-two-inch computer screen.

He nodded.

She opened the first attachment. The file was huge. It took two minutes to download.

His jaw dropped as soon as he saw what she was seeing.

Two hours later, they had scanned through pictures, church documents, the late president's sixty million member e-mail list, everything they'd had on TJ and more. Both of them were dumbfounded. They didn't spend much time wondering who, how, or why someone had sent the information nor why they had sent it.

Rhythm was the first one on the phone. Moses couldn't understand a word she was saying. He'd never learned to speak Spanish. And he didn't want to, because his wife spoke it so well.

He ran upstairs, got his phone, and called everyone else. Before Saturday turned into Sunday, everyone had booked their flights. And before Sunday turned into Monday, almost everyone was gathered inside the old crackhouse where Pop Tart and Shabazz had first met.

While everyone was reading over their part of the new plan that Moses and Rhythm had devised overnight, someone knocked on the door.

"That must be Assata and Cherry," Shabazz said, getting up from the metal folding chair that he'd borrowed from the church.

It had been almost five months - days after the nomination - since the S.W.A.T. team had busted into the house next door to Samuel's, looking for Assata and Cherry. Whoever had tipped them off gave the wrong address, even if they'd given the correct one, neither woman had been there at the time. And by the time the cops found out that they were at the wrong address, Samuel had called Cherry, and neither she nor Assata had been seen since.

"Am I always gon' get this type of reaction when you see me after a long absence?" Cherry said, hugging a shocked Shabazz.

"Ahhhhhhhh," Rhythm let out a high pitched scream and charged forward.

"Cheyenne," Babygirl hollered.

Everyone took turns hugging Cheyenne. Even Dr. Naison hugged the previously missing- in-action psychiatrist, and he had never even met her.

"I'm so glad you're back," Moses said with his arms out.

"Back from what?" Shabazz looked over at Moses. "Whachu you mean, back?" he asked Moses, before putting two fingers in his mouth and pushing out a loud, shrill whistle. "Everybody stop the celebratin'. I mean stop the party right damn now," Shabazz shouted. "TJ and that Monae Loray outfit kidnapped this," he extended his arm toward a healthy-looking Cheyenne, "woman and her seven-year-old child damn near a year ago. And here y'all carryin' on like this a family reunion."

Everyone looked at Assata.

"Oops," Assata put her hand over her mouth a second, before smiling and batting her eyes. "I love you, Shabazz."

"In the words of the Pretenders, what does love have to do with it?" Shabazz asked.

"Cheyenne was losing it. So I made it look like her and Ariel were kidnapped. I didn't know who to trust. I didn't know who was bugged and who was not. One by one, I told everyone as time went by what I had done and where she was at."

"Everyone except me."

"I'm so sorry, Shabazz," Assata said while walking over to him. She kissed him on the cheek. "Could you ever find it in your heart to forgive me?"

He shook his head. "I can't believe none of you told me."

"I swore them all to secrecy," Assata said. "I can't believe no one told you either."

He smiled. "Ah, ha. Gotcha. I been knew." He walked over to the stainless steel new stove. "Give me some love, King." He high-fived Samuel.

"Don't everybody look at me." Samuel looked around the newly-renovated older home that a couple of Pop Tart's young protégés purchased and fixed up. "What was I supposed to do? This fool practically lives with me. He was driving me crazy."

No one said anything. They just looked and listened.

"Okay, next time one of us gets kidnapped, I'm moving and I'm not leaving a forwarding address," Samuel said.

Everyone laughed.

"So, where's my baby?" Shabazz asked.

"She's in Cuba, taking care of her brand new baby brother."

Shock resonated on everyone, but the women's faces.

"I was pregnant when Jordan died." She smiled. "That's the real reason Assata wanted to get me outta here. Wait 'till you meet Jordan Shabazz One-Free Hayes. He is so precious."

Cheyenne got teary-eyed as she looked over at Assata. "If it weren't for Assata, my son would have never been born. If it weren't for the love you all have shown me I wouldn't have had the strength to step back. I'm just thankful that I'm here today, to step forward."

Everyone had so many questions and Cheyenne was happy to answer all of them.

After about thirty-minutes, Rhythm stood up on a five-gallon paint bucket and raised her hands in the air. "Okay, the reunion is over. We have two days before the election. The handouts Moses passed out when you got here are detailed instructions on how and when you are to do your part.

Chapter 50

"*My* part? What the hell are you saying?" Bishop Money paced back and forth on the white and black speckled linoleum campaign office floor. His office phone was on speaker.

"I'm saying that all you need to do is stay put. Don't leave the building. We are working on things from our end," Franklin said.

"Your *end*? My *end* is in the fire. Your *end* should never have let this happen. The election is less than twenty-four hours away and obscene pictures of me wearing lingerie, doing unspeakable things to the man that they're saying killed my former best friend, Bishop Turner, are floating around in Cyberspace."

Sinclair sat cross-legged in her favorite spot on the couch, facing the bookshelf in her husband's office. She had no idea what was going on, but she was enjoying watching TJ sweat. Her cell phone buzzed. She pulled it out to check the e-mail message that had just come through. It was a picture, followed by another, and then another. The three pictures said way more than any text message could have.

"It's not as bad as you think," Franklin said on the other end, talking to TJ. "You have an unprecedented thirty-point lead in the gallop polls, Terrell. You'll lose votes, a lot of votes, but you're so far ahead, there's no way you can lose this election. As long as you don't leave that office and don't take any calls from any reporters, you'll be fine."

"I don't know about that." Sinclair said aloud, before she uncrossed her legs and stood up.

TJ looked at her. "Woman, why don't you just kill yourself? Make the world a better damn place. For once in your miserable life, do something right. I mean just run and take a flying leap right out that damn window, you stupid waste of a man's sperm and a woman's egg. Always so damn negative."

"Maybe you'll consider taking your own advice after you see this." She held her cell phone out to him.

"I can't see what you're talking about," Franklin said. His voice was very clear considering the fact that it was being broadcast through an office phone mini-loudspeaker. "So, if you will, please share your information with me, Sinclair."

"I didn't touch that woman. I swear to God," TJ hollered as he scrolled through what had turned into seven picture mails.

"What woman?" Franklin asked.

"Navovae Jamison. Pictures of TJ breaking into Dr. Jamison-Haye's mother's home the night she was killed."

"She was alive when I left. I swear," he said watching himself carrying a plastic bag and a shoestring down the dark hallway of the old lady's apartment. "Someone is setting me up," the bishop remarked before turning his head to the church office door.

People shouting and heavy movement was coming from the lobby. "What in God's name?" The front-runner and Democratic nominee for president went and opened his office door to see what all the commotion was about.

"Terrell Joseph Money?" A man dressed in a gray suit extended a badge, while the other hand was on the gun that rested in his shoulder holster.

"Yes?"

"Sinclair Money?"

"Yes?"

The man moved to the side. "Cuff 'em," he said, as four plain-clothed FBI agents rushed in. "Terrell Joseph Money and Sinclair Charmaine Money, you are under arrest."

After hearing the words *you are under arrest*, Bishop Money fainted. And he didn't come to until the first of many cameras flashed in his face after being led out of his church administration building, which was doubling as his campaign headquarters. Immediately, his mind went to work. As he was led out of the church in handcuffs he smiled knowing that he knew and could prove not only that President Obama's death wasn't natural, but the whole conspiracy to make him the next president. His only question was would this be enough to get him into witness protection and would he live to tell the story.

Sinclair was mad. This was it. Her last mission. This was the last time her handlers would lead her down a dark road without a flashlight. Too many times, she had been sent on missions and was not fully debriefed. As soon as her people had her released, she was done.

*****

"Well done, people." George Bush, Senior popped the cork on the hundred-year old bottle of champagne, as six of the ten most powerful men in the world began the celebration.

Prince Nathan, England's next monarch handed the dollar over to Bush. "A wager is a wager. The plan was incredible and the way you and the others were able to execute it, was extraordinary," he said, taking a sip from his glass.

279

The 41st president put a hand on the future of England's shoulder. "Follow *a* people's steps and you learn where they're going. Study the way they step and you learn where they're trying to go. Once you learn these movements, then all you have to do is build a road to where you want them to end up, and put up appealing signs and they will go right to that road. And once enough people begin walking, then others will blindly follow."

"GB," Rupert, America's biggest media mogul interrupted, "don't confuse the boy," he said, while pouring himself another glass. "It's simple, Son." He looked at the prince. "Humans are creatures of habit. We move in circles. There's no such thing as a straight line. The earth. The world. Everything evolves and revolves. Everything repeats itself. I mean everything. So you study a people's past and you know the mistakes they are destined to repeat because they will never study their own history. They're too greedy trying to gobble up a today with no real plan for tomorrow."

"I'm sorry, I still don't quite understand," the prince said.

"Let me try," King Jaffi's son, the Middle Eastern oil billionaire interrupted. "When you know what people want, make them think you are giving it to them, and they'll be happy. When they figure out that they've been had, you give them something else they think they want, and so on. We knew that there was no way the American people would elect another Bush after the debacle Junior made. And because of the way the world came to view America, we had to give the world what they wanted." The billionaire stood up. "A peace keeper. A representative from the people that suffered the greatest horrors and atrocities in the history of the American government. A man linked by name to the culture that America is trying to destroy. Barack Hussein Obama. We used him to give us time. If China and France formed an alliance with the Middle East, we would potentially lose our political and financial stronghold over the Middle East.

Obama being elected gave us time to enhance the atmospheric pressure, technology that we've been testing that creates the conditions for tsunami's, earthquakes, hurricanes, and tornadoes."

The 41st president interrupted. "And unforeseen circumstances caused us to eliminate Obama. And Bishop Money was the perfect pawn to rally the people behind. We made them love and trust another Black man, this time a Christian, in a Christian country. You see, just like we choose Americas minority leaders by giving them a media voice, we gave voice to Terrell Money. We transformed a Satan into a God. We made him the people's champion. And after we built up this microwave Messiah, we gave his own people the tools to dismantle him.   So, what choice did the people have yesterday when they went to the polls? My son was their only choice. The only hope we created for the poor and middle class slaves. And before the next four years are up," he held his glass high in the air, "we will have worked out all the kinks in the technology to create natural disasters. And when we wipe out cities and entire states, we will force the world to bow at our feet, become our slaves."

A couple hundred yards away, Dr. Naison and Rhythm recorded and listened to the entire scandal from the hot dog stand in front of the White House.

Epilogue

$\mathcal{T}$wo seasons had passed but the atmosphere hadn't changed. Samuel put the hood over his head before kneeling down on the ground. The tornado-like winds had dust, trash, flowers and grass flying through the air. Forecasters were predicting more tornadoes, but that didn't stop Samuel from visiting his father on his father's soul day, the day he was born.

"Dad, I guess you heard. At first I was upset that I hadn't been the one that pulled the trigger. But now, I'm glad I hadn't. Isn't it strange how God works? I mean TJ was the personification of evil. He did so much wrong, but he was convicted of something he didn't do. Murdering Cheyenne's mom and kidnapping." He leaned in closer to the four-foot tombstone. "Assata Shakur is so amazing. I just pray that one day I find my Assata. It was all her idea. None of us even knew what she was doing. Well, we knew that she had staged Cheyenne and Ariel's kidnapping, but none of us knew that she had set it up to make it look like TJ had been behind it. You should have seen Cheyenne on the witness stand, Dad. She was Academy-Award winning awesome. I know it was wrong for her to lie, but I ain't mad at her one bit. And how about her and Rhythm's charges were dropped in lieu of their testimony. Thanks to Dr. Naison twisting the story of Navovaes death and he and his students and colleagues getting the information out to several Native-American tribes, the government had to put someone's head on the chopping block. So, with the evidence they already had but couldn't use they did the next best thing, use someone to say that TJ did what he didn't do. You know Rhythm, Dad, that was her and Dr. Naison's plan to get Cherry's pending charges dropped. It was the only way. Although they weren't dropped, I'm sure Cherry is glad that after she gets out of prison at the end of the year, her record will be expunged."

"I just hate that the reverend and Bill Clinton couldn't convince President Biden to pardon Assata before he left office."

"And, Dad you should see Ariel. That little girl is so intelligent, and very secretive. Now I know how Navovae was able to set everything into motion and I know why she killed herself. Ariel reads the little black history books I give her and when we discuss the books and the events of the past, she begins telling me what followed those events and she sometimes continues telling me what has yet to come. She doesn't want anyone to know what she can do and so far, I've respected her wishes. If it's terrifying to me, I can't imagine how a nine-year-old feels after looking into tomorrow. This is why we all have to continue the struggle. If the world knew what her and I knew, they'd all panic, but we have God on our side and as you always said, with God all things are possible. And that includes winning the war against the corporate puppeteers that are trying to destroy half the world before taking complete control of the half left standing. I just pray that Prince Nathan and Sinclair Charmaine don't slip and let them find out that they are on our side."

Samuel stood up and he had to hold onto his father's tombstone in order to stay on his feet. He had no idea that he was actually in the middle of a tornado created by the men him and the One-Free family were trying to destroy. He looked back down at his father's name on the tombstone. "Percival Cleotis Turner, I will never forget you and I won't let any that comes after me forget."

The lone tear that fell from Samuel's eyes melted into the rain. He spread his arms and threw them in the air. "I never got the chance to tell you, Dad, but, I never would have made it." He shook his head. "Never could have made it without you." He didn't even know that he knew the lyrics to the Marvin Sapp song. The words just came out and the son sang his soul out to his earthly and heavenly father. "I would have lost it all. But, now I see how you were there for me."

THE BEGINNING OF THE END

If you want to find out what happens next. If you want the story to continue show your support by purchasing my books from www.jihadwrites.com and e-mail me: at jihadwrites@bellsouth.net and let me know that you want more. Thank you, King. Thank you, Queen for your well-appreciated support.

And for all who have been waiting on the long awaited sequel to my blockbuster national bestseller **MVP** turn the page.

MVP

RELOADED

Karen Parker's Revenge

in stores

11/11/11

Read the beginning of **MVP RELOADED** on the next page.

STREET LIFE
by JIHAD

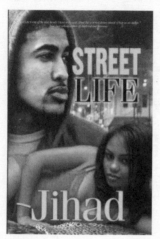

Street Life is a journey into the struggle of a young black male raised in America's inner city streets. Not since Donald Goines and Claude Brown has there been a comparable story written from the male perspective about the inner city streets. As the merry go round of life in the hood is relived; explanations will become evident for the events and circumstances that lead so many to the prison-gates. In this true to life story a vivid, colorful picture is painted of why growing up in an environment where happiness is sought in the bottom of liquor bottles, needles and dope sacks is just ordinary life in the hood. Whenever one tries to break the cycle, unseen hands pull at him to continue the course he was conditioned to complete. It takes a conviction and lengthy prison stay for Jihad to change his thinking and change the course of his life.

RIDING RYTHYM
By JIHAD

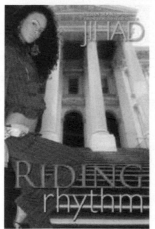

Riding Rhythm is a love story set in the early 1970's and 80's. Rhythm is a college student in D.C. who learns of Moses King, the man who started the Disciples, a street gang in Chicago. After reading his court case she writes him. The letters start to flow back and forth and Rhythm becomes an attorney to fight the system that has incarcerated the man she falls in love with. Moses' estranged brother, Bishop Solomon King, seems to have his own agenda as he becomes a controversial and popular Baptist minister. Lawrence One Free is Moses' friend and mentor in Atlanta Federal Pen whose guidance causes Moses to change the direction of the Disciples. Pablo "Picasso" Nkrumah was of the 12 kings in the Disciples. When Moses goes down he organizes the Gangsta Gods, a rival gang. The Chicago police and the F.B.I. stay one step ahead of Moses, Picasso, Law, and Solomon, until Rhythm brings them together and teaches what the power of love and unity can accomplish. When Rhythm touches the lives of these men, everything changes and all hell breaks loose. Rhythm's heavenly flow shows hell what love can do.

ENVISIONS PUBLISHING, LLC
P.O. Box 83008, Conyers, GA 30013

Enclosed: $_____ in check or money order form as payment in full for book(s) ordered. FREE shipping and handling. Allow 3-5 days for delivery.

ISBN 978-1893196483 RIDING RYTHYM $12.00
Name_____
Address_____
City_____State_____Zip_____

BABYGIRL
By JIHAD

This is a story of a girl born to L.A.'s rich and elite. She's known simply as Baby Girl. Circumstances force her and mother to end up living on the streets among Atlanta's homeless. Soon they befriend Shabazz, a white-heroin addicted scam artist who thinks he is black, and his best friend Ben, a scholarly alcoholic who analyzes everything. Baby Girl's mother is killed. She is now being raised by Shabazz and Ben, learning the intakes of hustling. She has it all until another tragic event causes her to take on a new fight. She is a female Robin Hood, robbin' the rich and givin' back to Atlanta's homeless and dejected. So, eventually she recruits and trains women like her, beautiful in appearance but poisonous to the touch.. Baby Girl will make every woman wonder, is it really a man's world or is it a woman's world where men only exist if women let them?

ENVISIONS PUBLISHING, LLC
P.O. Box 83008, Conyers, GA 30013

M V P
By JIHAD

*M*VP is the story of two best friends and business partners. Jonathon Parker and Coltrane Jones have a history. The best friends and business partners have been involved in everything from murder to blackmail, whatever it took to rise they did. Now they're sitting on top of the world, heading up the two most infamous strip clubs in the nation, the duo has the world at their feet. But now they both want out for different reasons. Coltrane is tired of the drug game, He's hoping to settle down with the new woman in his life. Jonathan, now a top sought after criminal attorney, is ready to get out of the game, that's because his eye is set on the Governor's Mansion. With the backing of major political players, he just might get it. There's only one catch. Jonathan has to make a major coup... bring down his best friend, the notorious MVP, Coltrane Jones. As two longtime friends go to war, parallel lives will collide, shocking family secrets will be unveiled and the game won't truly be over until one of them is dead.

ENVISIONS PUBLISHING, LLC
P.O. Box 83008, Conyers, GA 30013

Enclosed: $_____ in check or money order form as payment in full for book(s) ordered. FREE shipping and handling. Allow 3-5 days for delivery.

ISBN 978-0-9706102-1-8 MVP $12.00

Name_____

Address_____

City_____State_____Zip_____

PREACHERMAN BLUES
By JIHAD

WILD CHERRY
By JIHAD

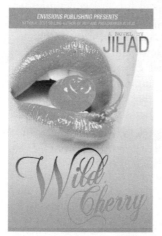

Cherry is one bad chick. That's no surprise since she's the granddaughter of one of the most thorough hitmen in history, Daddy Cool. An NFL Superstar and bad boy himself, Jordan Hayes is about to find that out the hard way when he decides to make Cherry a pawn in his game of lust, drugs and lies. After Jordan moves on, he forgets all about the girl he once called "Wild Cherry." But Cherry hasn't forgotten about him. In fact, he's all she can think about as she does her time in a state mental institution.

You play...you pay

Jordan's twin brother Jevon has been living in his twin brother's shadow for years. When an encounter with a beautiful young lady opens the door for him to not just follow in Jordan's footsteps, but assume his whole identity, Jevon jumps at the chance. But Jevon is in for a rude awakening when he discovers the real reason his new woman is called "Wild Cherry."

ENVISIONS PUBLISHING, LLC
P.O. Box 83008, Conyers, GA 30013

Enclosed: $_____ in check or money order form as payment in full for book(s) ordered. FREE shipping and handling. Allow 3-5 days for delivery.

ISBN 978-0-9706102-3-2 Wild Cherry $12.00
Name_____
Address_____
City_____State_____Zip_____

The Survival Bible
By JIHAD

Preacherman Blues II
By JIHAD

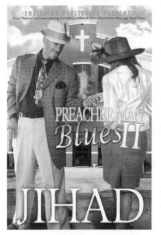

Bishop TJ Money has never made it a secret that he gets what he wants, when he wants, and by any means necessary. He has no problem robbing, stealing, and killing, to protect his holier-than-thou image. So the offer to succeed the first black US president is too tempting to resist. Who cares if the anonymous donors pushing his campaign were behind the mysterious death of the president? TJ is only focused on all the money and power the new position can bring.

But what Bishop Money and his new partners don't account for is the power of the black woman - four of them to be exact. All of whom TJ has wronged at one point or the other during his rise to mega stardom. And just as determined as Bishop TJ Money is to make his new home in the White House, these women will stop at nothing to keep that from happening.

In the riveting sequel to the best-selling Preacherman Blues, things aren't what they seem and one man's quest to get whatever he wants could cost him the ultimate price.

ENVISIONS PUBLISHING, LLC
P.O. Box 83008, Conyers, GA 30013